DENY

TRICIA MINGERINK

DENY

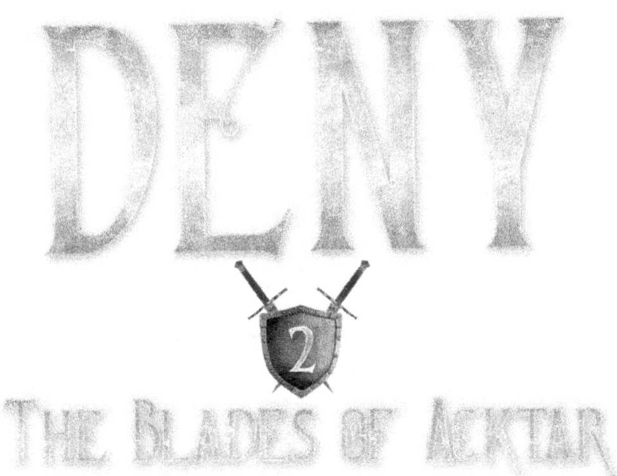

THE BLADES OF ACKTAR

DENY

The Blades of Acktar Book Two

Copyright © 2015 by Tricia Mingerink

Published by Sword & Cross Publishing

Grand Rapids, MI

Cover Art by Jesus Da Silva on Fiverr

Typography by Get Covers and Sword & Cross Publishing

Map by Md Shah Alam on Fiverr

Edited by Nadine Brandes

This book is a work of fiction. All characters, events, and settings are the product of the author's over active imagination. Any resemblance to any person, living or dead, events, or settings is purely coincidental or used fictitiously.

All Scripture quotes are taken from the King James Version of the Bible as found in the public domain. All song quotes taken from the 1912 Psalter as found in the public domain.

To God, my King and Father. Soli Deo Gloria

LCCN: 2015919002

ISBN: 978-1-943442-01-0

If it be so, our God whom we serve is able to deliver us
from the burning fiery furnace,
and he will deliver us out of thine hand, O king.
But if not, be it known unto thee,
O king, that we will not serve thy gods,
nor worship the golden image which thou hast set up.

- Daniel 3:17-18

If we suffer, we shall also reign with him:
if we deny him, he also will deny us:
If we believe not, yet he abideth faithful:
he cannot deny himself.

- II Timothy 2:12-13

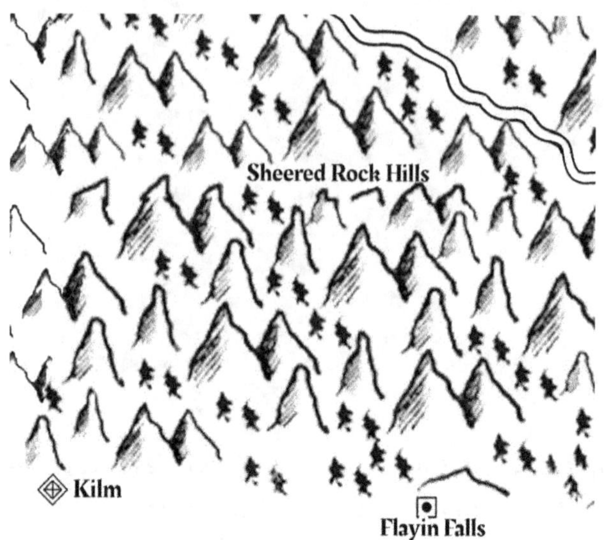

Sheered Rock Hills
Kilm
Flayin Falls
Surgis
Sierra
ACK
Calloday
Nalgar Castle
Aven
Dently
Blathe
Penning
Hakon
Mackton
Glarbon
Keestone
Arroway
Lanson
Dyman
Ably
VERDEN

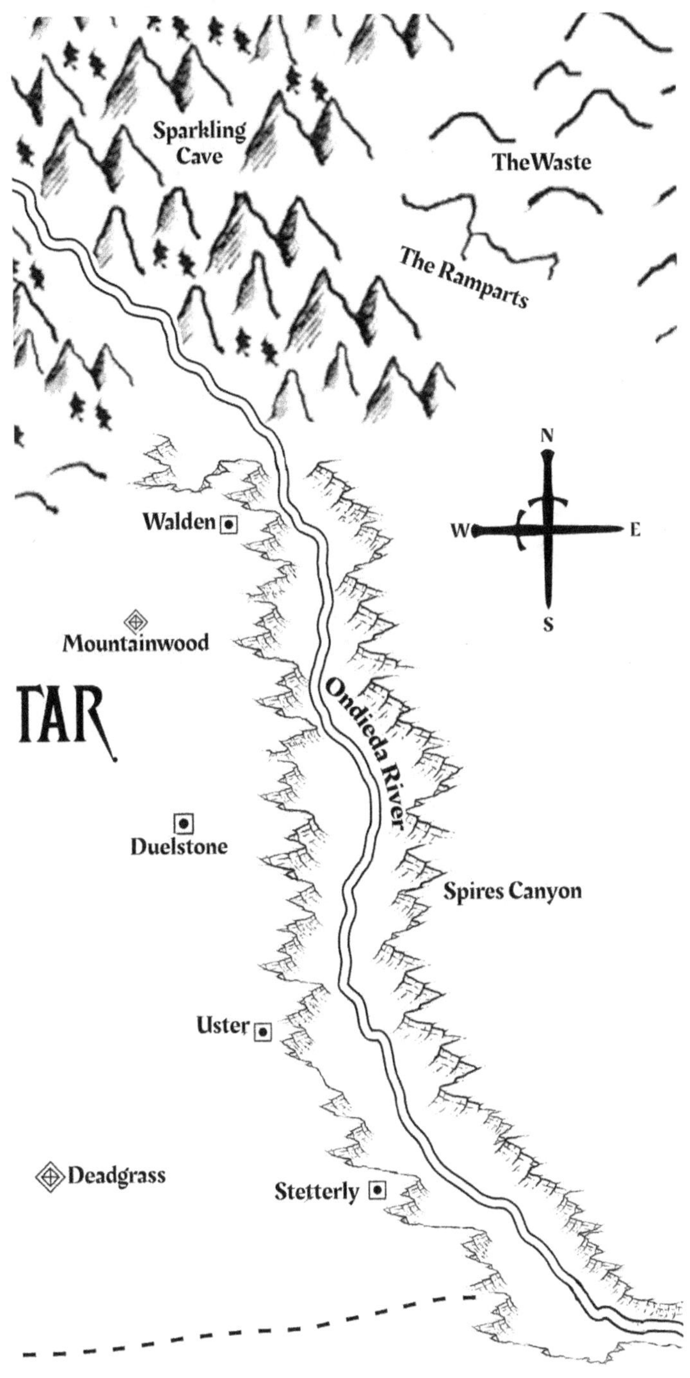

Resistance/Neutral

Towns who supported King Respen

1

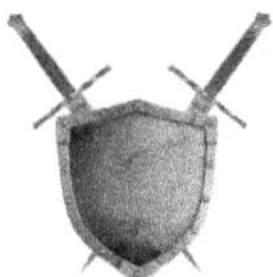

First Blade Leith Torren's mark of failure throbbed blood down his left arm. His knees ached against the cold, stone floor. How long would King Respen keep him kneeling after giving his report?

Respen leaned back in his throne, the candles' flames dancing in his eyes. "Claim your seat, First Blade."

"Yes, my king." Leith clenched his right fist and thumped it against his chest. Pain spasmed from the wound in his left shoulder, courtesy of former First Blade Vane's knife. Gritting his teeth, he eased to his feet and faced the table.

Shadows prowled the edge of the light cast from the two flickering candles. Eleven Blades hunched in chairs scattered around the long table, an empty seat for each of the Blades that had been killed three days ago.

A few of the younger Blades shifted. The Blades had never dealt with so many rapid promotions all at once, especially not promotions among the top Blades, and none of them had moved into the chairs for their corresponding rank yet.

Leith straightened his shoulders. He was the First Blade now and expected to take command of the Blades. He sharpened his voice and gaze into a dagger's edge. "Take your seats."

The other Blades scrambled to their feet. Their boots scuffed on the stone floor. Wooden chair legs grated. When the last Blade slid into his new seat, Leith claimed the chair to Respen's right.

Respen's jaw tightened his beard into a sharper point. "First Blade, you will remain here to recover from your wound. The Twelfth Blade will also remain here."

Leith tapped his fist over his heart again. "Yes, my king."

He bit the inside of his cheek, tasting blood and bile. What was Respen planning now? Leith had foiled Respen's plan to assassinate the Resistance leaders and supporters, but that failure wouldn't stop Respen long.

Respen swiveled his gaze to Martyn Hamish, now sitting on Leith's right. "Third Blade, you will take charge of the Blades searching for the traitor Vane. The Seventh and Eleventh Blades will go with you."

Martyn nodded, his curls flopping, and thumped his chest.

If only Leith had been given that mission. He could've slipped into Walden and talked to Renna. And Shad and Brandi too, of course.

Respen's fingers drummed a rhythm on his armrest. Leith's muscles tightened. The other Blades leaned forward. Only the hissing of the candles broke the hush. The darkness ringing the room closed around the table.

"Second Blade, you will ride to Blathe. There, you will meet with my army. Report to General Wentle. He will brief you on your mission from there."

Army? Leith fisted his hands below the table. He barely heard Respen send the rest of the Blades to other towns loyal to King Respen, some to send reinforcements to General Wentle and some to assist what Respen called the southern and western divisions of the army.

Had Vane known about this army? If so, then he supposedly would've told the Resistance. Unless this was something even Vane hadn't known?

This wasn't good. Leith's heart pounded in his ears. Not good at all. An army. Secret instructions. Leith needed to report to Lord Alistair at Walden. Now.

But he was stuck at Nalgar Castle.

Should he sneak out? If he did, Respen would know Leith was the real traitor. Was this important enough to break his cover? Or should he wait in case he learned more?

With a final salute, Respen swept from the meeting room. For a moment, none of the Blades moved. Eleven pairs of eyes swiveled toward Leith. No time to appear rattled.

He pressed the palm of his good hand on the table and shoved to his feet. He had to gather the cold detachment that had served him so well when he'd killed.

Leith's boots thumped on the stone floor as he strode across the room toward the line of iron pegs next to the door where his weapons hung. The other Blades' weapons dangled from the other pegs.

He drew one of his knives, whirled, and stabbed it as hard as he could into the tabletop. A sharp thunk speared the room. The tabletop vibrated.

Ranson Harding and Blane Altin, the youngest Blades, both cringed. A few of the others flinched.

Leith swept his gaze around the room. "I'm the First Blade now. Anyone have a problem with that?"

If only he didn't have to make them fear him. But Vane had kept them in line with fear. If Leith didn't do the same, the Blades wouldn't heed his orders. They'd question him, and questions could lead to answers that would endanger those he cared about at Walden.

"What about you, Second Blade Craven?" Leith planted his hands on the table and glared at the Second Blade.

Craven shifted his gaze to the candle a few feet away. "No. You'd thrash me soundly."

With Leith's injured shoulder, not likely. Craven had a good four inches on Leith, several years, and a stockier build. But Leith wasn't going to argue. If Craven wanted to continue to be the same obedient muscle he'd been with Vane, that was his problem.

"And what about you, Fourth Blade?" Leith switched his gaze to the thin Blade sitting next to Craven.

The Fourth Blade shook his head. The scruff below his nose, long and pointed like rat's whiskers, twitched.

Seventh Blade Quinten Daas crossed his arms, his fingers tapping on his elbows as if he itched to reach for a knife. When Leith met his gaze, Daas held it for several moments, a fire burning in their depths. When he finally glanced away, a chill crawled along Leith's arms. That one was going to be trouble.

Martyn scowled at the other Blades. Leith tipped his head towards him, a silent nod of thanks. Martyn had his back, honoring a promise they'd made years ago.

What would Martyn do once he learned Leith was spying for the Resistance? Would he side with Leith then? Or would he join the other Blades in trying to kill him?

"Good. Get out of here." Leith waved toward the door. "Move your things into your new rooms before you leave."

The Blades nodded, stood, and hurried towards their knives hanging from their pegs.

Martyn eased to his feet and sidled over to Leith. "So, First Blade, huh?"

Leith grimaced. Chief among King Respen's killers. "I'd rather be Third Blade, but that's your rank now."

They strolled to the door. Leith reached for his weapons and winced as he slung the leather straps over his shoulders. The knives settled against his chest. He swung his belt around his waist, ignoring the twinge in his wounded shoulder.

He faced Martyn as his friend finished buckling on the last of his knives. "You be careful. Vane will be dangerous." Not that a dead man could be dangerous, but Leith couldn't tell that truth to Martyn.

"If you could handle Vane, then so can I."

"I barely escaped." It was the truth. Mostly. "Steer clear of Walden. Lord Alistair will be doubly alert now."

Martyn leaned against the door. "I'll try, but if Vane is there, I'll have to track him there."

Leith nodded. What would happen if Martyn was caught snooping around Walden? Would he and Shad try to kill each other? Or would Martyn discover the unmarked grave and its secrets Leith had tried so hard to hide?

Leith pressed a hand to his shoulder. His wound throbbed again. Back at Walden, he'd thought he could handle returning to the Blades to continue spying. He'd thought it was where God wanted him to be. But how long would he last here when every word had to be a calculated lie?

Martyn threaded his fingers through his curls. "Are you all right with this? Being the First Blade and all?"

Leith leaned against the wall. The last time he'd tried to voice his doubts, it hadn't gone well. Leith met Martyn's gaze and put every bit of steel he could muster into his voice. "Yes. I know where my duty lies."

"Good. So do I." Martyn slapped Leith's good shoulder.

"I know." Leith did know. All too well. Before this was over, Leith might find himself on the wrong end of Martyn's knife.

2

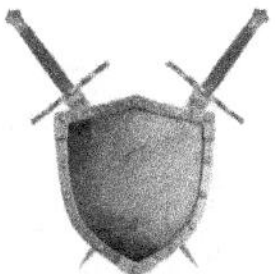

Leith leaned against the wall as Harding and Altin laid his straw tick and blanket on the cot in the First Blade's room. His extra set of clothes, one in all black and one in a prairie tan, hung from pegs on the opposite wall, along with a few extra knives.

Below them, a stand held his basin and pitcher of water, the only furniture in the room besides the cot and small table next to it.

Even the servant's room he'd been given at Walden had been cozier than this stone dungeon. Actually, Leith had seen the dungeons below Nalgar Castle's North Tower. They at least had a window.

"Anything else, First Blade?" Altin clasped his hands behind his back. Behind him, Harding rocked back and forth, as if all he wanted to do was bolt from his First Blade's presence. Did they think he'd turn into a monster because he was the First Blade?

Perhaps he'd have to.

"No, you're dismissed. Twelfth Blade, assemble the trainees in two hours."

The Blades saluted and slipped from the room. As soon as his door closed, Leith locked it and inspected the wall separating his room from the Second Blade's. He found a loose stone low in the wall. Apparently the rumors that the former First and Second Blades spied on each other were true.

At the base of the wall lay a stone wedge. Leith picked it up and jammed it between the loose stone and the rest of the wall. With the wedge in place, the loose stone couldn't move.

Once he'd searched the wall and found no more loose stones, he sank onto his cot. His shoulder had gone from aching to stabbing. He closed his eyes.

Had he done the right thing in returning to Nalgar Castle? Should he have taken up Lord Alistair on his offer to get him out of Acktar? Leith could've been far away from here. Free.

Then what? He would've been out of the fight. Craven would've been First Blade, Martyn Second Blade. And Leith wouldn't know about the army Respen was sending against the Resistance towns.

Should Leith slip out tonight to warn Walden? Lord Alistair needed to know about the army and the Blades sent to aid it.

But if he left, Leith wouldn't be able to gather any more intelligence for the Resistance. Should he risk discovery? Or wait?

Leith rolled his shoulder and sucked in a breath. He wasn't going to be climbing over the castle walls anytime soon. Could he bluff his way out the gates?

Perhaps he'd be better off waiting for his moment. Surely Respen would send him on some mission before the month was out. Vane had always been coming and going. Leith simply had to bide his time.

As long as he didn't slip up in the meantime. He leaned against the wall. The cold from the stones seeped through his shirt. A tingle swept down his spine. How long could he go on like this? Pretending his heart hadn't been touched by God and nothing about him had changed?

Best to be prepared. He unhooked one of his spare knives and sheathes from the wall. Biting his tongue to keep from crying out, he shimmied on his stomach through the dust under his cot and reached for the far corner. Moving by feel, he wedged the knife between the wall and the cot leg. He tightened the leather straps and wiggled from under the bed.

Hopefully he'd never need it, but just in case, he had it stashed away. If he were ever caught and locked in his room, perhaps the Blades searching for weapons might miss it.

Footsteps scuffed on the stone outside his door. He brushed at his shirt, but he couldn't get all the dust out. A knuckle rapped on the door once, twice, as if scared the door would bite.

"Come in." Leith leaned against the wall and buried his thoughts deep in his chest. As far as anyone could see, he was the First Blade.

Balancing a tray piled with bandages, salve, and a bowl of water, the oldest Blade trainee eased the door open and tiptoed inside. A foot shorter than Leith, the boy's arms looked barely bigger than Leith's knives. When the boy ducked his head, his mop of dark brown hair fell across his blue eyes. "Sixth—I mean, *Third* Blade Hamish sent me."

"You can set the tray on the table." Leith waved with his good hand. The trainee hurried across the room, circled to stay as far away from Leith as possible, and leaned over to set the tray down.

Leith rested his head against the wall. All the trainee saw was a First Blade who could lash out at him at any moment. Given Vane's lack of patience, Leith could only guess what the former First Blade had done to set the boy's hands to trembling and his eyes to darting glances at Leith through the fringe of hair.

Leith should be hard. Cold. He should make the trainee jump to attention.

He could do it. Ice lurked in his chest, waiting to form a numbing wall around his heart. He'd tapped that cold so many times over the years. He'd done it when he'd faced a fellow trainee, drawn his knife, and become a Blade. He'd done it again a year later when he'd leaned over a bed where a boy a few years older than him slept.

He was still a Blade. He still could kill. The chills on his back crept down his arms.

No. He wasn't going to become a First Blade like Vane.

"I'm not going to hurt you." Leith held his hands palm up. "What's your name?"

The boy eyed him as if waiting for Leith to change his mind and draw his knife. "Jamie. My name's Jamie Cavendish."

Perhaps being friendly was a mistake. But it was better than terrifying the trainee. Leith unbuckled the straps crossing his chest and the belt around his waist. "You're thirteen, right?"

Jamie bit his lip and nodded. A hint of red tinged the ends of his ears. If he was anything like Leith had been at that age, he was bothered by his lack of height. Leith could reassure him that'd he'd start growing again in a few years, but that was probably too friendly.

After setting his weapons on the floor beside the cot, Leith pulled his black shirt over his head. He gritted his teeth as his movement wrenched his wound.

Jamie's eyes widened and traveled down the length of Leith's right arm. His lips moved, most likely counting Leith's marks. Leith forced himself not to flinch. Thirty-six scars marred his shoulder and arm, the marks of thirty-six successful missions for King Respen.

"Help me with this bandage." Leith eased onto the cot. He tugged on the bandage Renna had wrapped around his shoulder three days ago. If he closed his eyes, he could still feel the gentle brush of her fingers against his skin.

His two-day ride across the stretch of prairie from Walden to Nalgar Castle had soiled the bandage. A spot of brown, dried blood stained the center.

Jamie stretched forward, his feet planted as far from Leith as possible. After a moment, he bit his lip. Had he realized the bandage was neater than Leith could've managed by himself with only one arm? Thankfully, the boy was only a trainee. He wouldn't dare say those questions aloud, especially not to the First Blade.

As they reached the final layer, Leith gritted his teeth. The bandage had darkened to a deep burgundy, so thick with dried blood the linen was no longer visible. When they worked the bandage free, it'd yank the scab off.

Jamie filled the basin with water, wet a rag, and handed it, still dripping, to Leith.

Leith pressed it to his shoulder and closed his eyes. The coolness filtered through the blood and bandage onto his burning shoulder.

When the bandage was as damp as he could make it, he dropped the rag, grasped the edge of the bandage, and tugged. The scab tore from his shoulder as if peeling away a layer of skin. With a final tug, the bandage dropped free.

Leith pressed his chin to his chest to look at his wound. The middle drooled blood, but the edges only oozed a clear liquid from the burns that had closed the wound.

When he raised his head, he found Jamie gaping at him. "You cauterized your own wound?"

Leith couldn't help the quirk to the corner of his mouth. "Yes, and I don't recommend it."

Shaking his head, Jamie dampened another cloth and handed it to Leith. Leith pressed it to his shoulder while Jamie laid out fresh bandages and worked the stopper from the salve.

Leith spread the salve over his wound and allowed Jamie to wrap the bandage around his shoulder and arm. If only Renna could tend the wound. But she was safely tucked away at Walden, and he wasn't about to wish her to Nalgar Castle.

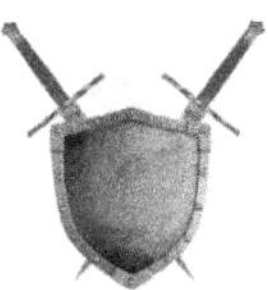

Renna Faythe plucked a weed that sprouted between two of the cornstalks growing in the kitchen garden of Walden Manor. The damp earth squooshed underneath her fingernails, darkening patches at the knees of her old, dingy dress.

Her eyes strayed towards the southwest. The prairie swelled into hills surrounding the town of Walden and its manor house, dotted with the blue, yellow, and white of daisies and bluebells. A breeze stirred the long grass into a muted rustle, rising and falling in pitch.

She touched the lump formed by the knife strapped to her ankle, a knife Leith had given her. Was he all right? Had he convinced King Respen that Harrison Vane was the traitor? Or had Leith been discovered and already killed?

Would she even find out one way or another? He was a Blade. Even if he survived, he'd be bound to wherever the king sent him. Perhaps he'd make the time to report to Lord

Alistair here at Walden but that didn't mean Renna would even see him.

Why did it even matter to her? She shook herself. Leith was a Blade. Did he even consider her a friend? Or just someone he had to protect out of obligation to make up for the past or repay her for saving his life during that blizzard? He'd been beyond stiff when she'd hugged him before he'd returned to Nalgar Castle.

The sun's heat slicked sweat between her shoulder blades and stuck her bodice to her skin. She yanked another weed from the ground. Stop thinking about him. And his green eyes. The slight wave to his black hair. The look on his face when he'd told her to keep his knife, like he'd been giving her more than just a piece of steel.

What was wrong with her? She hadn't been like this a week ago before Vane had tried to kill her. What had changed?

Nothing.

Everything.

She dug her fingers into the soil and jerked on a weed. Its roots clung to the ground and tugged at the cornstalk next to it. She clenched her teeth, pressed the cornstalk into the dirt with one hand, and ripped the weed from the ground with the other.

Something had changed. When? Was it when Leith hurtled through the window to save her from Vane? Or when she'd pressed her hand against his wound and felt his heartbeat? Perhaps it had happened when she'd hugged him goodbye.

The hug. Definitely that hug. It'd been innocent enough until his arms had almost wrapped around her and she'd felt safe. How long had it been since she'd truly felt safe?

"Renna!" Her thirteen-year-old sister, Brandi, burst around the corner of Walden Manor, her red-blond curls flying, her skirts hiked to her knees. Abigail Alistair, Lord Alistair's middle daughter, trailed at a more lady-like pace, her skirts only raised a few inches off the ground.

"What's wrong?" As Renna stood, the silver cross of her necklace bumped against her bodice. After so many years of burying that silver cross in the bottom of her jewelry box, the movement of it swinging around her neck tugged as oddly as the jumbled feelings in her chest.

"Nothing's wrong. At least, I don't know if anything's wrong." Brandi skidded to a halt and thrust her arm southwards. "There's two riders over there."

Renna's chest tightened as she spotted the two figures cresting the hill overlooking Walden. More messengers? Had someone else been killed by the Blades?

Or could it be Shadrach Alistair returning? Renna dug her fingers into her skirt. No. She might not know where the secret Resistance hideout was, but it had to be deep in the Sheered Rock Hills. It probably took longer than a week to make the round trip.

Brandi bounced on her toes and craned her neck to stare at the prairie. "I think it's Aunt Mara and Uncle Abel."

"Brandi, I know how much you want them to come for your birthday, but..." Renna studied the two figures as they drew closer. One of the shaggy, brown horses looked a lot like Stubborn, Uncle Abel's mule. And...was that a goat trotting along behind them?

Four of Walden's soldiers cantered their horses to

surround the newcomers, an extra precaution since Leith proved their security so weak. Renna twisted her gritty fingers together. Had Uncle Abel and Aunt Mara decided to visit? It was only a week until Brandi's birthday. Surely they'd make the trip for that, and to see for themselves that Brandi and Renna were all right.

From this distance, she couldn't make out their features. But Walden's soldiers didn't pull out their swords. They surrounded the riders and escorted them towards Walden Manor.

On her tiptoes, Brandi's head came nearly level with Renna's. "Is it them? Can you see?"

The morning sunlight flashed on a head of silver hair. The figure spotted them and waved, a wide, arm-swinging wave that Renna would recognize at any distance. "Yes! Let's meet them at the stables."

Brandi needed no other urging. She sprinted for the stables.

Abigail glanced at Brandi, then at Renna. "I'll let my mother know we have guests." She glided toward the kitchen door.

When Abigail had disappeared inside, Renna threw caution to the prairie wind and hiked her skirts up as high as Brandi's and dashed for the stables. She arrived, breathless, as the riders reined their mounts to a halt in front of the stables. Brandi was already there, giggling as a small, brown goat nibbled on her skirt.

Uncle Abel swung down from Stubborn. His cloak billowed dust, dulling the color of his light grey hair but doing nothing to diminish the brilliance of his blue eyes. Smiling at Renna, he reached to help Aunt Mara ease off a second mule. Uncle Abel must've borrowed it to make the six-day journey from Stetterly to Walden.

As soon as Aunt Mara's feet touched the hard-packed dirt, Renna jumped forward and hugged her. She smelled of the bellflower she added to her homemade soap. Her grey-streaked blond hair brushed against Renna's face.

Brandi wiggled into the hug. Uncle Abel wrapped his arms around all three of them. "You're both safe." His voice had a choked rumble to it.

Aunt Mara touched Brandi's hair. "We decided we couldn't wait for a note to find out if..."

If they'd survived the assassination attempt. Renna swallowed. "Not even scratched." She'd let someone else tell Aunt Mara how close Vane had come.

"Are you going to stay until my birthday?" Brandi tipped her face up, her blue eyes round and moist. Renna bit her lip. A person would have to have a heart of stone to resist Brandi's gaze, and even then, stone could melt.

Uncle Abel squeezed Brandi into a one-armed hug. "It's only a week away. Of course we'll stay that long."

But they'd have to leave shortly after that. Renna rubbed her fingers against her skirt. Their duties to Stetterly—Aunt Mara as healer and Uncle Abel as minister—called them back.

Should she be more like them? Here she was cowering in Walden when her duty as Lady Faythe should draw her to Stetterly.

Up until two weeks ago when Lord Alistair had asked, she'd never claimed the title. It belonged to her mother. The duty belonged to her father. It shouldn't belong to her.

Yet it did.

She was only seventeen. Surely she wasn't expected to lead Stetterly. Just survive.

"We have a lot to tell you but not here." Renna touched Uncle Abel's arm.

Uncle Abel released his grip on Brandi, though his arm remained draped across her shoulders. "All right. Please lead the way."

"I'll make sure Ginger is taken care of." Brandi grabbed one of the goat's horns, the one that had a strange curl to the end of it, and tugged Ginger towards the stable.

Ginger dragged her feet until the rattle of grain being served to the mules carried on the breeze. Ginger bolted towards the stable, nearly dragging Brandi over.

Rolling her eyes, Renna led Uncle Abel and Aunt Mara toward the manor. "Why did you take Ginger? Couldn't you find someone to take care of her?"

Aunt Mara shrugged her slim shoulders. "We tried, but the goat refused to be left behind."

Renna shook her head. Stubborn goat.

Lord and Lady Alistair greeted them on the front step of Walden Manor. Lady Alistair's dark brown hair lay in piles of perfect coils on her head, her petite features highlighted by her slim, green gown. Her wide smile didn't waver at the dust puffing from Aunt Mara's and Uncle Abel's clothes.

Lord Alistair stepped forward and shook Uncle Abel's hand. "Good to see you again, Abel."

"Our niece would never forgive us if we missed her birthday." Uncle Abel returned Lord Alistair's hearty handshake. "I gather a few things have changed since you visited Stetterly to ask about..." Uncle Abel trailed off, as if he wasn't sure what to call Leith.

"Ah, yes. Our mutual friend." Lord Alistair's mouth quirked beneath his beard. "Come inside. We have much to discuss." He led the way into the grand entry hall, the walls paneled with dark wood. The main staircase rose into a landing before dividing into two curving wings to the second floor. A large painting depicting a battle covered the wall above the landing.

Turning right, Lord Alistair led them down the hallway towards his study. As they entered, Lord Alistair waved Aunt Mara and Renna to seats in the leather chairs stationed in front of the desk while he headed for the wide, picture window. Uncle Abel's eyebrows rose as Lord Alistair inspected the curtains and checked the lock on the window.

Renna slid into a chair beside Aunt Mara, hiding her hands in her lap. She should've taken the time to wash them. She'd left fingerprints on her skirt.

"I take it you decided to trust Leith Torren?" Uncle Abel rested his hands on the back of Aunt Mara's chair.

"Yes. It turns out his information was correct. Respen attempted a wide-spread assassination attempt a week ago. I was able to warn the others, but even our preparations couldn't save everybody." Lord Alistair sank into his chair and bowed his head. "Lady Amber Dawson, Lord and Lady Westin, Lord and Lady Spencer, and Lord Hector Emilin were killed."

Aunt Mara pressed a hand to her mouth. "Poor Cecelia Emilin. Two children to raise all by herself. And Kurt Westin. He's only two, and already an orphan."

Two years old. Renna bit her lip at the ache building in her chest. Was it better or worse to become an orphan so young? He wouldn't even remember his parents while the night her parents died scarred her memory. "Who's taking care of him?"

"Lord and Lady Westin both had family living in Flayin Falls. They're still working out the details of who will raise him." Lord Alistair's gaze drifted to the map spread across the wall behind his desk. The dot marking the town of Flayin Falls lay a day and a half from Walden along Sheered Rock Hills.

At least he had family. Renna peeked at Uncle Abel and Aunt Mara. What would she and Brandi have done if their aunt and uncle hadn't been there to raise them? Renna prayed that the family who raised Kurt gave him as much love and care as Uncle Abel and Aunt Mara had given her and Brandi.

"We were prepared when First Blade Vane came after Renna and Brandi, but due to...complications, he got closer to Renna than we would've liked."

Uncle Abel reached over Aunt Mara's shoulder and clasped the hand Aunt Mara stretched towards him. "How close?"

Renna squeezed a clump of her skirt. Of course they'd asked. She'd have to tell them the truth now. "Vane came through my bedroom window, jammed the door's lock shut, and put a knife to my neck. He knew Leith was chasing him, so he waited to kill me until Leith got there. He wasn't paying attention to me, so I kicked him and swiped at him with the knife Leith had given me."

"Leith Torren gave you a knife?" Aunt Mara blinked at her. "When?"

"A few days before the assassination attempt." Renna

lifted her skirt a few inches, drew the knife from its sheath, and held it up. "He let me keep it afterwards."

Both Uncle Abel and Aunt Mara stared at her. For good reason. The Renna they'd known at Stetterly didn't have enough courage in her little finger to lift a knife, much less defend herself against a Blade.

But was she really different? She'd been desperate that night. If forced to do something like that again, would she? Or would she freeze?

"Leith fought Vane while I got the door open. Leith was wounded, but Shadrach shot and killed Vane." She shivered, hearing again a dull thunk. Was it the arrow striking Vane or Vane's knife sinking into Leith's shoulder that haunted her? "Leith decided to return to Nalgar Castle to continue spying. He planned to make King Respen believe that Vane was the one spying for the Resistance. We don't know if King Respen believed him or not."

"Do you trust him?" Uncle Abel's gaze turned to Lord Alistair. "It could've been part of King Respen's plan to plant a spy in our midst."

"I had thought of that, but I'm convinced that Leith's courage is sincere." Lord Alistair's mouth tipped upward. The sunlight beaming through the window twinkled in his eyes. "He now shares our faith."

Uncle Abel and Aunt Mara shared a look. Aunt Mara patted their clasped fingers with her free hand. "An answer to a prayer."

A prayer? Had Uncle Abel and Aunt Mara prayed for Leith when he'd been recovering from his wound at Stetterly? Renna shifted and stared at her feet. She hadn't done a lot of praying for Leith until recently. Or a whole lot of praying for anything besides safety.

Would she ever have courage like Leith? He'd fought Vane, saved her life, and, if that wasn't enough, he'd returned to Nalgar Castle, knowing he'd be tortured and killed if King Respen didn't believe him, to continue spying.

All this from a Blade whose faith in God could be measured in days. What did that say about her faith? What was wrong with her that she didn't have faith like that?

4

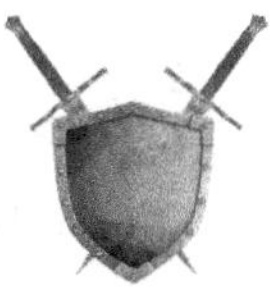

Leith called the trainees to assemble on the stretch of grass between the five-story Blades' Tower and the moat that surrounded the tower.

He bit back the tightening in his stomach. He'd been stuck here nearly two weeks, and still Respen hadn't sent him on any missions. Long enough for his shoulder wound to heal into a purple-red splotch, though the muscles below the skin remained weak.

Two weeks that the Resistance could've been preparing for the attack that was coming. Or had it already started? For all Leith knew, Walden might already have been attacked and overrun.

Were Renna and Brandi all right? What if they'd been killed while he'd been waiting for the right moment?

He tossed that thought away. He couldn't even contemplate a failure that horrible.

"They're assembled, First Blade." Twelfth Blade Altin's voice drew Leith's gaze back to the trainees.

The six trainees lined up by age, their black clothing stark against the yellow-green grass. Jamie, the oldest, eyed him as he rocked backwards on his heels. The next oldest boy, an eleven-year-old, gripped his knife, grinned, and leaned forward on his tiptoes. The four youngest boys hunched together, peeking at Leith. Altin stood behind them, his right hand still pressed to his chest in the Blade salute.

Boys. Too young to be taught to kill. If they were anything like Leith had been at their age, they were too thankful to be off the streets or away from families too poor to feed them that they didn't care that they trained to be Blades. They'd promised Respen their obedience, and that's what they'd give.

Leith swallowed and wrapped the dark cold around his heart. He drew his knife. It glinted in the pink sunlight streaming from the east. "Today, we're going to work on conquering fear. I know you've done this exercise before, but fear is hard to control. No matter how often you do this, you'll always have fear. You need to learn how to control it."

Six pairs of eyes widened. Altin dropped his hand from his knife and looked away.

Of course they feared him. Leith spotted the faint, white lines marring each of their necks from former First Blade Vane's knife. Scars that would've matched lines on Leith's own neck had the marks not faded with the years, though his had come from Respen's knife.

Even with the cold numbing his chest, Leith couldn't bring himself to scare the youngest ones further. He faced Jamie. Jamie clenched his fists but didn't move as Leith pressed his knife against the soft skin under Jamie's chin. "I know you fear my blade. You can't trust that I won't turn it and slit your throat."

Jamie's face blanched. His throat bobbed as if he wanted to swallow but couldn't. A shiver wracked his body and traveled up the knife into Leith's hand.

Leith couldn't do it. He couldn't torture any of the trainees like this. Training didn't banish fear. Only trust in God. Leith stepped back, his hand falling to his side.

Jamie's face relaxed only for a moment before he stiffened again. Leith sensed movement behind him as King Respen's voice slithered across his skin. "Is he ready?"

Leith's stomach scurried into his toes. He turned, clenched his fist, and thumped his chest, gritting his teeth as a throb shot through his shoulder. "Not yet, my king. He's young."

Respen tapped his fingers against the knife strapped to his waist. "You had killed at his age. He is not so young."

Leith eased himself a few inches to the left, placing himself between Respen and Jamie. Could he protect Jamie without giving himself away? "I had more years of training."

"None of my Blades have as much training as you, yet that did not stop any of them." Respen pointed at the youngest trainee, a boy of eight, and stared at Jamie. "Kill him."

The eight-year-old squeaked. Jamie glanced between the boy and Respen. His fingers closed over the knife at his waist, but he didn't draw it. His face turning the same gray-green as the dead grass along the moat's edge, Altin gripped the eight-year-old's shoulders, preventing him from running.

Leith had to intervene. Somehow. He couldn't stand

there while Jamie was forced to kill. But what could he do without getting both him and Jamie killed?

Jamie drew his knife and stared at it as if trying to picture himself plunging it into another boy.

A roaring filled Leith's ears. Act. Move. Do something. But his feet stuck to the grass, his hands immobile at his sides.

Jamie raised his chin, faced King Respen, and dropped his knife. "No. I can't kill him."

If Respen hadn't been standing there, Leith would've given Jamie a slap on the back. But that would have to wait.

Leith's stomach tightened even before Respen's mouth curved downward. "Then you are worthless to me. First Blade, kill him."

Jamie clenched his fists and held his ground. A breeze brushed his shaggy brown hair over his blue eyes. At that moment, warning the Resistance didn't matter. Preserving his cover didn't matter. Leith had to do what he could to save this boy who had the guts to stand up to Respen.

Time to use his role as First Blade. Leith strode forward and lowered his voice so only Respen could hear. "Respectfully, my king, I disagree that the boy is worthless. He has courage, something too many of the recent trainees have lacked. That courage merely needs the right hand with the correct amount of patience to turn it in the right direction."

Respen's fingers strummed against his knife's hilt.

Leith had him thinking. Now to drive the point home. "It took me longer than most to make my first kill. The boy will be the same way. Let me take him on a mission. It will be good experience for him."

Respen's drumming fingers halted. "Very well, my First

Blade. I will heed your counsel. Finish your training, then report to my study in an hour. I will outline your mission then."

Every muscle in Leith's body wanted to sag, but he held himself rigid. He clenched his right fist and pounded it over his heart. "Yes, my king."

Respen spun on his heels and marched away, sunlight glinting on his black hair and beard.

As soon as he was gone, Altin released the youngest trainee and pressed a hand against the Tower's wall, his face so green he looked about ready to vomit his breakfast into the moat. Jamie's face looked no better as he shook so hard his teeth clacked.

Leith would have chaos on his hands in a minute if he didn't take command. "All right. Back into line, everyone."

Altin straightened. The eight-year-old swiped at his face. The other boys stepped into line. The muscle at the corner of Jamie's mouth flexed, but he picked up his knife and took his place.

Leith split them into pairs and partnered Altin with Jamie to run through the basic knife-fighting moves. When the hour was up, Leith dismissed Altin and the trainees. Jamie lingered, shifting from foot to foot. Leith crossed his arms and waited for him to ask his question.

Jamie peeked at him. "Why didn't you kill me?"

Leith couldn't tell him the truth. "The king has lost too many Blades to waste all the training that's been put into you."

Jamie's eyes sharpened. He raised his chin. "I won't kill."

Would Jamie have been this defiant if he'd been facing

Vane instead of Leith? Probably not. "Perhaps not. Now go pack your things. You and I are leaving on a mission."

Jamie's mouth opened, like he was going to ask another question, but he snapped his jaws shut, whirled, and hurried away.

Leith touched each of his knives and strode across the wooden bridge that connected the Blades' Tower with the rest of Nalgar Castle. Below him, only an inch of sludge, more mud than water, filled the bottom of the moat. In a few more weeks, even that would dry up.

He passed under the arched entrance into the tunnel-like passageway that connected the cobblestone courtyard on the north side of the Great Hall with the grass-covered Queen's Court at the southern end of the castle. Across the passageway from the wooden bridge, a set of stone stairs rose into the darkness.

Drawing a deep breath, Leith strolled up the stairs and knocked on an oak door.

"Enter."

Leith pushed the door open. Respen stood in front of a wide window overlooking the cobblestone courtyard. Burgundy rugs muffled Leith's footsteps as he crossed the room and knelt at Respen's feet. "My king."

Respen flicked a hand at him. An order to stand. Leith stood and crossed his arms.

"I have received word that my northern army has taken Aven and is poised to strike Sierra. You and the boy will join them and assist in taking that town."

Sierra. The home of Lady Paula Lorraine and her daughter Jolene, the girl Leith's friend Shad was courting. Was Shad still in the Sheered Rock Hills? Or had he returned to Walden? Not that it mattered. Leith wouldn't have the time to ride to Walden to give a warning.

"How much did Vane know about the army?" Leith tried to sound as casual as he could. "If he knew about it, Sierra will be prepared."

Respen's dark eyes searched Leith's face. "Vane knew little about my army and my plans for it. I never entrust my entire plan to one person."

"A wise decision, my king." Leith bowed his head to hide his whirling thoughts. Even if Vane knew only a little of the army's existence, then according to the lies Leith had been spinning, the Resistance should know of its existence as well.

Or was Respen testing him? Telling him Vane knew about the army when he didn't? Or Vane knew more than Respen was telling him?

"Once you have finished at Sierra, I'd like you to go to Walden rather than continue with my army. How much did Vane know about your undercover work there?"

Most of it, though Leith wasn't going to tell Respen that. "He didn't learn of it until the Meeting of the Blades. I doubt he would've had time to report to Lord Alistair before he fled into the Sheered Rock Hills."

"Monitor Lord Alistair's response to the attacks and glean whatever information you can on Vane's whereabouts."

Leith had to bite his cheeks to stop his smile. He'd been ordered to Walden. Perfect.

The urge to smile faded. Respen's silence waited for him to ask the next question, the question a First Blade would ask. "Lord Alistair trusts me. If you wish, I will complete my failed mission and kill him."

Respen shifted his clasped hands. "If the lord of Walden were dead, Vane will report to no one. He will become harder to track and trap. No, we will capture Vane first. Alistair can watch his plan fail around him."

He stared at Respen's back and clasped hands, a cold sensation creeping into his fingers. He was alone with Respen and armed. Respen had his back turned. Leith's fingers crept to the hilt of his knife. He could draw it and stab Respen in the back. He could end this. Right here. Right now. No more battles. No more deaths.

He should do it. His knife slid a fraction in its sheath.

It would be murder. But would a murder to save lives be justified? Leith had lied to save lives. Was murdering to save lives any different?

With trembling fingers, Leith shoved his knife back into its sheath and dropped his hands. A knife in the back had been Vane's way of fighting. Respen's way. Not the Lord's way. Renna had chosen to spare Leith's life when it would've been smarter to let him die. Leith had to do the same with Respen and hope the cost in lives wasn't too high.

Besides, Leith had little hope of success. There was a reason Vane had never turned on Respen. Even Vane didn't dare chance it.

"You were always meant to be my First Blade. But you hesitated. You let Vane and Hess take the ranks of First and Second Blade away from you." Respen faced Leith. "Do not slip back into your old weakness. If the boy fails, he dies."

"Of course." Leith's tone rang as hard as the stones of the Sheered Rock Hills.

Respen believed he'd bled compassion out of Leith. That was Respen's flaw. He assumed, once he'd forced them to kill, they could never regain what they'd lost.

But he was wrong. God's grace was stronger than whatever bonds of blood Respen used on his Blades.

One day, Leith would show him how wrong he was. For now, Leith had to settle for getting Jamie out of this place of darkness before it captured him as it had once captured Leith.

5

Renna brushed her fingers along the broad leaf of one of the cornstalks. They were past her knees and growing taller each day. It'd been two weeks since Leith left. How tall would the stalks be when Leith returned?

If he returned.

A rustle accompanied Aunt Mara as she eased under the vine-covered trellis separating the flower garden and the kitchen vegetable garden. She knelt next to Renna, both knees popping. "This garden looks wonderful. You've done a good job with it."

Renna touched the leaf again. "It was mostly Le— Daniel's doing. Daniel is what that friend we talked about last night is called when he's here. He did all the planting and weeding at first. All I've done is keep it up."

Aunt Mara reached for a weed and eased it from the ground. Renna did the same. The cool air wrapped around them, so still that Renna could taste the sweet green of the growing corn and the moist earth.

After several minutes, Renna peeked at Aunt Mara. "When did my parents know they liked each other? They told us the story of how they met, and they always made it sound like love at first sight."

Aunt Mara pushed two cornstalks aside. Her gray-blond hair fell across her face. "In their case, it was near enough, I suspect. At least, your father knew right away that your mother was the one for him."

"And what about you?" Renna shuffled a few feet. Dirt caked the front of her skirt.

"When your Uncle Abel and I met, I didn't feel any interest at first." Aunt Mara's tone lowered. "I'd lost my patients—a woman and her baby—and I couldn't feel anything but guilt. But when Abel came back the next day to see if I was doing all right, that's when I felt he might be the type of Godly man I was interested in."

Renna picked at the dirt under her fingernails. That still didn't help the jumble in her chest. "But how do you know? How do you know if he's someone you should be attracted to or if you should fight it or if you're even attracted in the first place?"

Aunt Mara plucked another weed. "I can't give you an easy answer to that one. Because there isn't one. You feel attracted to him, yes, but also interested in his Godly character. He listens to you but is also willing to talk. He encourages you to be a better person and is in turn encouraged by you. You're comfortable with him."

Did Renna feel like that about Leith? He was a Blade. Dangerous.

But he'd encouraged her. And that last day he'd been at Walden, she'd felt safe with him.

Aunt Mara sat back on her heels. "Any reason you're asking all this?"

"No." Had she said that too quickly? Renna bit her lip and stared at the weed flopping in her hand. "Just curious."

Drumming hooves drew her gaze. A rider crested the hill above Walden and charged down the other side.

Renna scrambled to her feet. "Something's wrong." She gripped Aunt Mara's elbow and helped her to her feet.

By the time they joined the crowd in front of the manor, the dust-caked rider had jumped from his horse and tottered to Lord Alistair. "My lord, I beg to report that Aven has been overrun."

"Overrun?" Lord Alistair gripped the rider's shoulders. "What do you mean?"

"An army came from the south flying Respen's banner. Lord Donton and his family escaped, but most of his guards were killed." The rider coughed. Dust puffed from his hand. "The army left a small force to occupy Aven while the rest marched toward Sierra. I gave Sierra warning before riding here."

"You did well." Lord Alistair patted the man's back as Lady Alistair stepped forward, carrying a glass of water.

Renna tangled her fingers in her skirt. Aven overrun. Sierra threatened.

Walden was next. She could see it in the hunch of Lord Alistair's shoulders and the tightening of Aunt Mara's expression.

A shiver traveled down her arms into her fingertips. Why hadn't Leith warned them of this? Was he dead? An ache tore at her throat. No, he couldn't be dead. But what else could explain it?

A hand rested on Renna's shoulder. She glanced at Uncle Abel. His eyes had hardened to blue ice.

Lord Alistair faced the crowd. "This is hard news, but not unexpected. Plans for the defense of Walden will be put into place immediately. Please return to your duties until you receive further orders."

Aunt Mara patted Renna's arm. "Come. Let's find Walden's healer. Anyone can wield a sword, but only trained healers know what herbs to collect and how to prepare the poultices. Brandi knows enough to help too."

Poultices. For wounds. For war.

Renna eyed the rider one last time and shook.

War had come to Acktar.

6

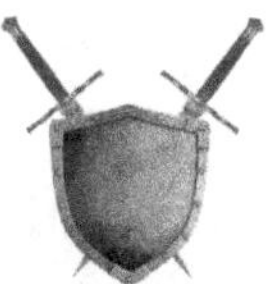

After scouting the army's position hidden in a valley south of Sierra, Leith rode Blizzard straight towards one of the sentries stationed at the perimeter. Jamie trailed him on a scrubby buckskin.

As they approached, the sentry straightened so fast his back cracked. Leith glared down at him, a hand near one of his knives. "Where's the Second Blade?"

"There, sir. By the command tent." The sentry's finger wavered so much Leith could only guess at the direction it pointed.

Leith didn't even nod in acknowledgement. A First Blade didn't waste courtesy on a common soldier. He nudged Blizzard. Blizzard snorted and trotted forward, tail raised like a battle flag.

As he and Jamie rode through the camp, soldiers halted what they were doing to stare, though they quickly ducked their heads if Leith turned his gaze in their direction. Vane would've reported them to their superiors for their insolence, but Leith settled for cold haughtiness.

The tan canvas of the commander's huge tent billowed in the center of camp. On either end, poles flew Respen's banner of black, crossed daggers across a dusty blue background.

A few yards away in a clearing formed in the middle of the soldiers' tents, as if no one dared encroach too closely, the three Blades assigned to the northern army had laid out their bedrolls in a neat triangle to protect each other's backs. Their horses ranged in the grassy stretch between their camp and the rest of the army tents. As Leith rode up, one Blade repacked his bedroll while another worked a sharpening stone along the edges of his knives.

Leith swung down from Blizzard and handed his horse's reins to Jamie. "Take care of the horses."

Jamie nodded and led the horses in a wide circle around the Blades.

Eighth Blade Kent pointed the dagger he was sharpening towards the commander's tent. "The Second Blade is in there with General Wentle."

Leith strode toward the commander's tent. The guards at the door opened their mouths as if to protest, but one look at his knives and black clothes snapped their mouths shut. Being the First Blade did have its perks. Few dared question him.

Brushing the guards and the tent flap aside, Leith stepped inside. Smoke from the oil lamps laced the stifling air.

As his eyes adjusted, he spotted Second Blade Craven

hunched over a table across from a slim, willowy man who hardly looked strong enough to raise a sword, much less fight. He had to be General Wentle. Both men looked up, and the lamplight fell across the general's pinched face, sharp nose, and squinty eyes.

"King Respen sent me to assist with the assault on Sierra." Leith sidled to the table.

"We were just discussing the final plans." Second Blade Craven tapped the sketch on the table. "Once it's dark, two thirds of the army will swing around and behind Sierra while the third will head straight north. The town will be surrounded and crushed."

Something Leith had to do everything in his power to prevent. He studied the sketch. "Do you know what defenses Sierra has? Thanks to Vane, they might be prepared for an attack."

General Wentle shook his head. His straight, blond hair flung out from his head, revealing small, rounded ears. "The Second Blade told me it's too difficult to get close enough to properly scout the town and manor."

Leith eyed Craven. Was it too dangerous, or had Craven taken one look at Sierra's defenses and decided it'd be too much effort? It's not like Craven cared one way or another if more soldiers were killed because he neglected to scout the town and manor first.

Craven's eyes flicked Leith's way, his forehead puckering.

Either way, it worked in Leith's favor. Leith focused on the map and pretended not to notice. "Not surprising. Lady Lorraine was canny enough to defeat former Second Blade Hess. She won't be taken easily."

Leith fought the urge to frown. Her wariness was both a blessing and a hinderance. It had kept the Blades away from the town, yet it'd also make any attempt by Leith to warn her difficult, if not impossible. Still, he had to try. "I'll slip into Sierra. Hold off the attack until I return."

General Wentle's mouth pinched even smaller, but he nodded.

Craven's eyes narrowed. "If we couldn't get through, what makes you think you can?"

Leith whipped out a knife, twisted Craven's arm behind his back, and touched the tip of the knife to the pulsing vein in the underside of his chin. "Did you want to challenge me after all, Craven? I survived Vane. I can survive you."

Craven met his gaze. "No, First Blade."

"Good." Leith withdrew and sheathed his knife. "I'll leave as soon as it's dark." Before either of them could question his plan again, Leith pushed from the tent. He stalked past the other Blades, grabbed a brush from Jamie, and set to work on Blizzard's dark gray fur.

Sheltered from sight between Blizzard and the other horses, Leith leaned his forehead on Blizzard's shoulder. A tremor shook Leith's body.

That threat to Craven had come too easily. When he'd reached for his former cold, it had hardened his heart in an instant.

Hadn't God softened him? Taken away his darkness?

Yes, but it still lingered, waiting. And while Leith played this double-life, he couldn't fully let it go. He needed it to keep up this pretense.

What choice did he have? If he left now, Lord Alistair

and the Resistance would be blind to King Respen's plans. Leith wouldn't be able to stop the next assassination attempt, the next attack, when it came. That was the whole reason he was a Blade, wasn't it? He was supposed to be used by God to save lives even if it cost his own.

But perhaps, his life wasn't the only thing this lie would cost.

ONCE DARKNESS WHISPERED THROUGH THE PRAIRIE GRASS, Leith slipped through the army camp and past the sentries. Not that he had to sneak, but it was good practice for getting into Sierra.

He didn't pause to take a deep breath until after he'd crested the valley's ridge and gone partway down the next side. He crouched in a thick clump of grass, a breeze whistling in a dry rasp. The day's heat radiated from the sand beneath his boots. A few crickets chirped, but most remained silent.

A rustle crackled the grass several yards in front of Leith. Leith held his breath and cocked his ear towards the noise. It came again, too loud to be an animal. It had to be a person.

Who else would be sneaking to Sierra? Leith ticked off where he'd last seen the other three Blades. All of them where accounted for.

When had he last seen Jamie? He'd been at supper. He'd lingered near the horses. Then, nothing.

Leith crept closer to the noise until a black shape sharpened against the gray-green grass. Jamie eased through the grass in a crouch. He glanced behind him, but his eyes swept past where Leith froze in a patch of shadow.

What was Jamie doing sneaking towards Sierra? Was he taking his chance to get away from the Blades? Though, he'd be better off waiting until he and Leith reached Walden instead of slipping into a town about to be attacked by the very Blades he was trying to leave behind.

Unless this wasn't simply about running away. The boy was trying to warn Sierra.

With the amount of noise Jamie was making, he didn't have a chance of getting past Sierra's guards, and his black clothing wouldn't help. The guards would probably see a black shape, kill him, and realize he was only a boy later.

When he was a few feet behind the boy, Leith crunched a clump of dried grass with his boot. Jamie froze. Before he had a chance to turn around, Leith launched from his crouch, slammed into the boy's back, and clapped a hand over Jamie's mouth.

Leith twisted as they fell so that he landed on the bottom instead of smashing Jamie between him and the dirt. He rolled them over, pinning Jamie beneath him where the boy couldn't reach his knife or any of Leith's.

"What do you think you're doing?" Leith withdrew his hand. His shoulder throbbed.

Jamie's jaw tightened. "I'm not going to tell you anything. You're going to have to kill me, First Blade."

"I'm not going to kill you." Leith bit back a growl. He didn't have the time to waste chatting with Jamie. "Sierra's guards would've done just that as soon as they spotted you."

"You're not going to kill me?" Jamie twisted his head to try to see Leith over his shoulder. "Why not? I was..."

Trying to sneak into Sierra, most likely. As First Blade, he should punish that. Perhaps he could pretend to be an ignorant First Blade.

Leith eased off Jamie. Since Jamie was here, he might as well be useful. "You can help me sneak into Sierra."

"No." Jamie crossed his arms and lifted his chin. "I'm not going to help you attack Sierra. So you'd better kill me."

How much did he dare tell Jamie? Was Jamie trustworthy? Or was this a trick?

But if he really was this determined to warn Sierra, then Leith could use his help. Sierra would be difficult to enter, even for him.

Was this the tension Lord Alistair and Shad felt when Leith first offered to join the Resistance? Words were cheap. Actions could be faked. In the end, it came down to a leap of trust.

Should he make that leap?

"Like I said, I'm not going to kill you." Leith drew in a deep breath. "Because I'm trying to warn Sierra too."

Jamie's body tensed. "How do I know you're not trying to trick me into helping you get into Sierra and then you'll kill me?"

They could be at this all night. Leith met Jamie's gaze. "If I'd wanted your help as the First Blade, I would've just ordered you to come along. Or I would've brought another of the Blades to help me sneak in. But I came alone because I don't want any of the other Blades to know what I'm really up to. Seems you had the same idea. Now are you going to help me or not? Because if you aren't, I'm going to tie you up and leave you here until I get back."

Jamie studied him. His eyes widened. "*You're* the Resistance spy."

Leith swallowed. Should he try to deny it?

No, he'd gone too far now.

"Yes."

With narrowed eyes, Jamie nodded.

Leith crept towards Sierra, Jamie crunching behind him. Unlike Walden, which was set in the bowl of several hills, Sierra Manor loomed on a hill with the town flowing down the hill to the east.

At the base of the hill, Leith crouched at the edge of the tall grass. The grass rising up the hill had been scythed short to deny the Blades cover if they tried to sneak close. Guards circled the manor in layers, following each other with only a fifty foot gap between them. Each ring of guards moved in the opposite direction so they could see anyone sneaking up behind the other guards.

Leith studied the guards, the timing, the manor. No wonder the Blades hadn't tried to sneak into Sierra. "Jamie, I'm going to need a distraction. If you could rustle through the grass headed west, I'll slip toward the manor from the east."

"All right." Jamie rose and turned to leave.

"And be careful. If they spot you, they could mistake you for a Blade."

Jamie disappeared into the blackness. Leith edged through the grass the other way. According to the report by the former Second Blade Hess a few weeks ago, Lady Lorraine's bedchamber lay on the second floor of the east wing where she could watch the sunrise each morning.

A section of grass waved and rustled a few yards in front

of a guard. The guard froze and peered into the grass. After a moment, he waved another guard over, creating a gap in the guard perimeter.

Leith slithered on his stomach and elbows across the open space. He froze as the guard going the opposite way came into view. Leith held absolutely still, a black patch in a blur of shadow. When the guard had passed Leith and his attention turned to the commotion by the tall grass, Leith wiggled forward.

After several more pauses, he reached the east wall below Lady Lorraine's window. He flexed his fingers and rotated his left shoulder. Two weeks wasn't enough time for the wound to completely heal, but he didn't have a choice. He'd have to grit his way through this and hope he had the strength.

A newer manor than Walden Manor, Sierra Manor was built of brick instead of stone. Most of the cracks between bricks were too small for him to grip. Instead, he used the shutters to boost himself onto the windowsill and from there onto the ornate molding on top of the window.

That put his head level with the sill of the second story window. He peeked into the room. A form lay under the filmy sheets on the bed across the room from the window, blond hair draped across the pillow.

Leith inspected the window. The panes swung inward, their hinges on the inside. He'd have to hope they didn't squeal when he pushed because he had no way of oiling them.

Hoisting himself onto the sill, he balanced himself with one hand on the molding while he eased his smallest knife between the panes. The latch caught on the tip of his knife. He lifted it and pushed the panes. They gave tiny squeaks.

He peered inside. Lady Lorraine still slept, the sheet rising and falling with her steady breaths. Easing through the window, he closed the window behind him and tiptoed across the room.

Lady Lorraine rested on her side, her long hair flowing across her pillow in a cascade.

He pressed his hand over her mouth, pinning her to the bed. Her eyes flared open, then narrowed.

Pain pricked his stomach. Leith jerked and caught sight of a knife gripped in the lady's fist.

Lady Lorraine's eyes flashed to Leith's empty right hand, and her knife paused in its thrust.

So that's how former Second Blade Hess died. He wasn't killed by Lady Lorraine's guards. He'd been stabbed by the lady herself when he'd bent over her with his knife in hand. Only Leith's empty hand had saved him.

Leith let go of her mouth and stepped back, both hands in the air where she could see them. A dribble of blood tickled his stomach. "I'm Lord Alistair's source in the Blades. I know I can't prove it, but I'm here to warn you."

She rolled into a sitting position, her knife poised in front of her. "There's one way to prove your loyalties. Sit." She pointed at a rocking chair a few feet away.

Leith hesitated. Waste time following her demands or waste time arguing? How much time would General Wentle give him before he moved the army into position?

Biting his cheek at the delay, he perched in the rocking chair.

She whipped the belt from the dressing gown lying

across the trunk at the foot of her bed and looped it around his shoulders before tying it tightly behind his back. Leith didn't resist as she blindfolded him, then tied his wrists to the rocking chair's arms.

Just cooperate. It had worked with Lord Alistair to prove his sincerity. Hopefully it'd work with Lady Lorraine too.

Her door opened and shut. Where was she going? The spot under his ribs throbbed. His shoulder ached after his climb. Was she fetching the captain of her guard?

The door's hinges creaked. As soon as Leith heard the rhythm of the second set of footsteps, he relaxed. "Shad, could you please convince your lady's mother not to kill me?"

Shad's footsteps halted a few feet away. "Wouldn't the other Blades like to see you now? Their First Blade, bested by a five-foot woman and trussed up with hair ribbons."

Hair ribbons? That must be what tied his wrists to the chair. "If you don't untie me quickly, that's exactly what's going to happen."

Someone reached behind his head and untied the blindfold. Leith blinked his eyes into focus. "I didn't expect you to be here, or I would've tracked you down instead."

Shad set to work on the ribbons holding him to the chair. "I decided to swing through Sierra before heading home to Walden. I arrived this afternoon. What are you doing here?"

"Respen has gathered an army under a general named Wentle. Three of the Blades are stationed with it. In less than an hour, it's going to surround Sierra and attack." Leith shook off the ribbons as Shad loosened the knots. "Respen ordered me to assist in the attack. Naturally, I volunteered for one last scouting mission."

Shad untied the knot in the dressing gown's belt. "What direction will they be coming from?"

Leith raised his eyebrows. "You aren't surprised? You knew about the army?"

Shad rested his hand on his sword hilt. "A few of the survivors from Aven made their way here, and the scouts we sent out failed to return yesterday. We got everyone out except for a few of us that stayed behind as rearguard in case anyone else from Aven managed to escape."

Lady Lorraine planted her hands on her hips. For the first time, Leith noted she wore a dark bodice and a divided riding skirt. Unusual attire for sleeping, unless she expected trouble. She speared him with a gaze as sharp as the knife now belted to her waist. "What information do you have for us, Blade?"

"The army is assembling a few miles from here. They plan to divide into three wings and encircle the town and manor, coming in from the southwest, southeast, and north." Leith fingered one of his knives but stopped when he spotted Lady Lorraine's hand shifting towards hers. "The army isn't supposed to attack until I return, but I'm not sure how long General Wentle will wait for me to get back."

Shad nodded. "Do what you can to delay them. The north wing of the army could pose a problem. We had planned a tactical retreat in that direction."

"Shadrach." Lady Lorraine's sharp glare swept between Leith and Shad. "Do you think it's wise to tell the Blade our plans?"

Leith hung his head. Would he ever be trusted based on his word alone like Shad was? Or would he always have to prove himself?

"He's trustworthy." Shad's voice carried a dangerous tone to it. "You owe him your life. In fact, every noble who survived the assassination attempt owes him their life."

"I see."

Leith felt her gaze prickling across his scalp as if she could tear through his skull and read his thoughts. He met those hard eyes and forced himself not to look away.

Her eyes and face didn't soften. "Are you the Blade who killed my husband?"

He should've expected the question. Of course she'd want an answer to that mystery, the same way Renna had wanted to know the details of her parents' deaths the night he'd met her. Answers soothed the itch of old scars. They didn't change anything, but they helped a person move on.

"No." One death he wasn't responsible for. Leith's hand crept to the tender spot on his stomach where she'd started to stab him. "Second Blade Hess killed him. If it helps anything, you killed Hess two weeks ago."

The glint of pain crossed her eyes. The iron in her spine flexed a fraction. "It does." After a moment, her posture straightened. "Will you be able to delay the army? Or at least give us some idea what the Blades stationed with the army will do?"

Shad grinned and shot a glance toward Leith. "I think the Blades are the least of our worries."

Leith pushed his right sleeve to his shoulder, revealing the long line of scars marching down his arm nearly to his elbow. "I'm the First Blade. The Blades will do whatever I tell them."

"First Blade." Lady Lorraine's eyebrows rose. "That does change the tactical picture, doesn't it?"

A knock rang against the door. Leith froze. Shad stepped between Leith and the door.

"Mother?" A girl's voice filtered through the wood.

Shad relaxed. Lady Lorraine hurried to the door, opened it barely wide enough for a girl to step through, and closed it quickly. The girl's long, golden blond hair draped down the back of the dark dress she wore.

"What's going on? I thought I heard voices." She glanced around the room. Her gaze turned towards Leith and Shad, a smile freezing on her face as her eyes widened. "Shad! There's—"

"It's all right. He's on our side." Shad strode to her side. "You'd better fetch your bow, Jolene. The army's going to attack tonight."

Leith faced Lady Lorraine. "I'll do what I can to delay the army and keep the Blades out of the action, though I can't do much without raising their suspicions."

Lady Lorraine reached for a set of saddlebags next to the door. "I need to assemble the men. Jolene, you'd better fetch your things from your room and join me."

When the door closed behind Lady Lorraine and Jolene, Leith met Shad's gaze. "When the fighting starts, I'm going to have to join them. I'll do my best not to kill anybody, but you can't hold back when you see a figure dressed in black. If you or your archers have a shot, take it."

Shad sucked in a breath, opened his mouth, then let out the breath in a whoosh. His shoulders sagged. "All right. It shouldn't come to that. We don't plan on staying long enough for a pitched battle. Whatever you do, stay out of the first ranks of men."

"Got it. Delay the army and stay back when the fighting starts."

Shad clasped Leith's forearm. "God go with you."

"And you." Leith eased the window open and swung over the sill. Both his arm and his stomach ached at the movement. As he dropped to the ground and belly-crawled the way he'd come, he prayed that God would protect both him and Shad that night so that neither of them ended up killing their best friend.

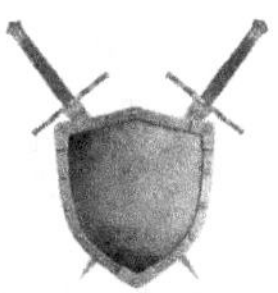

When Leith rolled into the deep grass at the base of the hill, he lay still for a moment. Where was Jamie? Had he been captured by Sierra's guards?

He touched the throbbing spot on his stomach right under his lowest rib. His fingers came away sticky with blood, but the wound didn't seem too deep. He smeared the blood across his hands. This might work to his advantage.

A subdued murmur rose from the manor house on the hill above. The clank of weapons handed out. The thud of boots on cobblestones. But no shouting. No panic.

A rustling a few feet away caught his attention. He rolled into a crouch and spotted a small, dark shape crawling through the grass. "Jamie."

Jamie jumped and cast about until his gaze focused on Leith. He crawled over. "Did you manage to warn them?"

"Yes." Leith glanced over his shoulder. "They already knew the army was coming, though they didn't know when."

He and Jamie slipped towards the army's encampment. At the crest of one of the hills above the camp, Leith halted Jamie. "We'll wait here. I want to give Sierra as much time as possible."

Jamie sank onto his stomach, folded his arms, and rested his chin on his hands. Leith eased to the ground next to him. So far, the wings of the army hadn't moved into position.

Nothing to do but wait as long as possible. Might as well put the time to good use. Leith eyed Jamie. "Any ideas on how to sabotage the army?"

Jamie stiffened and swallowed. "Let the horses loose?"

Leith tipped his head toward the camp. "That won't work. Can you see why?"

Jamie's mouth and forehead scrunched as he studied the milling army below. After a moment, he drew in a sharp breath. "They're already starting to saddle the horses. There aren't any left in the paddock."

"Correct." Leith eased a stick from under his stomach.

In the camp below, the mounted soldiers tossed saddles onto their horses' backs. The archers checked their bowstrings one last time. The three Blades remained in their huddle near the command tent, their horses already saddled.

"A Blade needs to be observant, and a Blade spying for the Resistance doubly so."

Jamie chewed on his lip and cocked his head. "Would fire work?"

Leith handed a stalk of grass to Jamie. "How dry is this?"

Jamie broke it into tiny pieces. "Really dry."

"And what do you think would happen if we started a widespread fire?"

"A wildfire." Jamie tossed the bits of grass onto the sand. "Not a good idea." Jamie rested his chin on folded arms. "That's it for my ideas, short of whacking General Wentle on the head and hoping no one notices he's missing until he wakes up."

Leith raised his eyebrows. "I think that might be a little hard to explain."

Jamie ducked his head. "It's what I thought of doing to you so I could sneak away."

"You considered knocking the First Blade on the head?" Leith shook his head. Jamie had guts. And nerve.

Jamie winced. "That's why I decided it was a bad idea."

"Good choice."

Down below, General Wentle stalked from the command tent toward the huddled Blades. His arms waved in the air. Probably shouting at them about Leith's tardiness. Craven faced General Wentle, and the general backed off.

Leith held still. He and Jamie had a few more minutes. "What's brought all this on? I never guessed you were anything other than a willing Blade trainee until you stood up to Respen."

Jamie rubbed a pebble between his fingers, his head bowed so his mop of hair covered his eyes. "I'm not sure I should tell you."

"You already know my biggest secret. In fact, you know enough to get me killed." Leith's stomach knotted with that thought. He'd had to place a lot of trust in Jamie over the span of one night. What if he betrayed Leith?

No choice now but to stick with this trust and see where it played out.

Jamie straightened his shoulders. "My parents were

Christians from Mountainwood. Lord Beregern turned them over to King Respen. They were executed. I wasn't."

Jamie must've shown some streak of defiance back then. That's how Respen picked his Blades. He'd spot a boy with a fighter's spirit, and he'd mold that spirit into something sharp and vicious.

"I learned I wasn't going to escape easily. Too many guards. Too many Blades watching." Jamie tossed a pebble into the sand, picked it up, and tossed it again. "I hoped I'd get good enough to...to escape."

If he'd dared make that much of a movement, Leith would've patted Jamie on the back. "Don't worry. When we get to Walden, I have a few friends who can protect you. You'll never have to return to Nalgar Castle again."

Jamie nodded and stared straight ahead. Not the reaction Leith would've expected from a boy who'd spent the past two years plotting his escape. Perhaps he still didn't fully trust Leith. Leith couldn't blame him. He wouldn't readily trust a First Blade either.

"You aren't alone, Jamie." Leith swallowed. Another secret, another risk. But Jamie needed to know. "God is with you."

Jamie's eyes shot towards Leith, then swiveled to the ground. He shoved the pebble through the sand with his finger. "I used to think so. Now, I'm not so sure."

Leith hung his head. Shad would know exactly what to tell Jamie. Brandi would come up with the perfect Bible story. But Leith? What sort of wisdom did he have for Jamie? "Sometimes we have to pray for the courage to be sure."

Jamie chewed his bottom lip.

Movement in the army camp in the valley below caught

Leith's gaze. General Wentle stomped from the command tent again.

Leith eased into a crouch. "Time to practice your sneaking skills."

He led Jamie down the hill, showing him where to place his feet and how to move to make the least amount of noise. The clouded stars cast a few shifting, deeper shadows in the darkness. The night lay so still Leith heard every squeak of his and Jamie's boots on the dirt and every whisper of their clothes against the grass.

At the edge of the camp, Leith froze. He could march right in, but mysteriously appearing out of nowhere behind the general was more intimidating.

With the army assembling in the clearings, Leith slipped into camp in the darkness provided by the deserted rows of tents. Jamie tiptoed in his footsteps, leaving only a single trail of bent grass for the two of them.

After crossing the stretch of ground between the last row of tents and the command tent, Leith leaned against the center support post by the tent entrance. Jamie slipped towards the horses.

"He should've been back by now!" The force of General Wentle's shout drew the general onto his tiptoes. "If he's not back in one minute, I'm going to—"

"You'll do what?" Leith lowered his voice into a growl.

General Wentle spun on his heels, craning his neck until his gaze latched on Leith. "What took you so long? We were supposed to begin moving an hour ago!"

"I'm the King's First Blade. You do not question me." Leith straightened and pushed the tent flap open. "Get inside."

He marched into the tent. General Wentle stalked inside, his entire body stiff. "What did you learn?"

"Your army would've been in trouble had you gone with your original plan." Leith tapped the map. Now, to tell enough of the truth to be convincing. "Sierra was warned. They have archers stationed in the top floor. The approaches from the north and south are open ground. The army would be cut to pieces coming from those directions. Only an approach from the east has some protection by slipping through the town."

General Wentle leaned over the map. His slim face twisted.

Leith held his breath. Would this be enough?

"Fine. We'll attack from the south and east." General Wentle straightened and stormed from the tent. Even before the flap fell back into place, he shouted instructions at his division commanders.

Leith strode from the tent to the three Blades. "Second and Eighth Blades, you'll go with the wing of the army going through the town. Tenth Blade, you and the boy will be with me."

The other Blades nodded. Leith strolled to Blizzard and swung his saddle onto his horse's back. When had things gotten so muddled? He'd known it'd be difficult spying for the Resistance in the Blades, but he'd never expected he'd ride into battle against the very people he was trying to protect.

Should he have remained in Sierra? Was this the moment he had to leave the Blades for good?

But if he did, he wouldn't be able to warn of the army's next move. He'd failed to warn Aven and he'd barely managed a warning for Sierra. He wasn't going to fail to warn about the next attack, especially if Walden was the next target.

Leith swung onto Blizzard and nudged him into position beside General Wentle. Not exactly his first choice of places to be when riding into battle, but he had little choice.

With groaning leather, clanking metal, and the rumble of several thousand feet, the army marched from its camp toward Sierra.

Had Leith done enough? Would Lady Lorraine, Jolene, and Shad retreat safely? Or would the circling army capture them? Or worse, would General Wentle ask Leith to send the Blades after them?

The army reached the line of tall grass at the foot of Sierra's hill. The manor house above them loomed dark, the town beyond it black as well.

Torches flared along the line, signaling to General Wentle that the wings of his encircling noose had marched into position.

Leith gripped Blizzard's reins so tightly Blizzard pawed and tossed his head. Jamie drew and sheathed his knife over and over again, his face pale as the moonlight dripping down on them like silver blood.

"All right. Forward. Double time."

The captains relayed General Wentle's commands to their troops. The first ranks of soldiers stepped from the tall grass into the open area.

And promptly disappeared.

Screams howled at the half moon above. The next rank of soldiers, unable to stop with the press behind them, disappeared after the first, their cries mingling into an eerie nightsong.

Leith swallowed. So that's why Shad had warned him. Whatever lever that had been keeping the coverings stable must've been pulled as part of Lady Lorraine's retreat. Instead of the solid ground Leith had crawled over, a thin layer of dirt covered hatches balanced over deep trenches dug around Sierra Manor, the bottoms covered with sharpened stakes.

Before General Wentle could reorganize his men, arrows lanced from Sierra Manor's upper story. Soldiers toppled and screamed in the rows lined up before the trench. Arrows speared the ground on either side of General Wentle.

Leith eased his horse between the manor and Jamie. His skin tightened as if that muscle spasm could stop an arrow from piercing his chest.

"Forward!"

Soldiers jumped the trench, only to be cut down by the arrows from Sierra. Shouts rumbled from the east. Men streamed through Sierra, the buildings providing the cover that the soldiers in front of Leith lacked.

Leith patted Blizzard's neck. Never thought he'd be thankful to be a Blade.

The arrows from the manor halted. General Wentle waved at the men. "Keep moving!"

More soldiers jumped the ditch and flocked towards Sierra Manor, their commanders yelling to be heard over the shrieks of wounded men, the screams of frightened horses, and the stamping crunch of the soldiers' boots.

Pinpricks of fire streaked down from Sierra Manor and landed on the rooftops of the town. Timber flared so quickly they must've been smeared with grease or layered with straw. In a few minutes, ten buildings burned away the night.

Lady Lorraine had guts. No one messed with fire on the prairie.

The soldiers charging through the town halted and stared at the buildings going up in flames around them.

"Put out those buildings!" General Wentle stood in his stirrups, his hands strangling his horse's reins. "We can't let that fire spread!"

A shift of the wind, a stray spark, and the whole prairie could go up. The army's camp and all their supplies could be burned, not to mention all of Sierra and its manor.

General Wentle halted his horse at the edge of the trench and pointed at Leith. "First Blade. Round up your Blades and search the manor for those archers."

Leith raised his eyebrows at General Wentle and didn't move.

General Wentle scowled. "Fine. If you would be willing, could you please order the Blades to search the manor?"

Leith tipped his head toward General Wentle and snapped his hand at Jamie. "Come."

Jamie nudged his buckskin into position next to Leith. Leith kicked Blizzard into a gallop towards the ditch. Blizzard sailed over the four-foot gap and thundered along the manor-side of the ditch.

The Tenth Blade joined him from the west. The other two Blades appeared from the smoke-filled town.

Second Blade Craven jerked his head back the way he'd come. "They knew what they were doing. They'd cleared the ground to dirt around the buildings they picked to burn."

Leith would've expected nothing less from a lady who

slept with a dagger under her pillow. The fires would take men to fight, but they wouldn't spread out of control if dealt with properly.

Leith swung off Blizzard and dropped the reins onto the ground. "Second Blade, take the Tenth Blade and look for a back door." Hopefully, Shad and the others were long gone.

The Blades saluted and slipped along the manor wall. Leith pressed his back against the wall next to the front door. Jamie huddled next to him while the Eighth Blade crept to the other side.

Keeping his body pressed against the wall, Leith lifted the latch and flung the door open.

A sharpened spike speared the place his stomach would've been if he'd stood in front of the door to open it. A leather string tied it to the latch. Another of Lady Lorraine's tricks.

Leith rested a hand on his knife. If Vane were here, he'd send in Jamie first. A small loss if the trainee were killed in a trap. "Eighth Blade, take point. I'll be rear guard."

Nodding, the Eighth Blade tiptoed through the door. Jamie glanced at Leith. Leith winked and drew his knife. Jamie did the same and crept through the door.

Partway down the hall, they met the Second and Tenth Blades. The floorboards creaked below Jamie's boots. Leith froze, but the manor remained silent. Empty.

"Should we pursue them?" Craven flexed his fingers on his knife's hilt.

"No." Leith sheathed his weapons. "Your orders are to remain with the army and mine are to take the trainee to Walden to aid the search for Vane. Odds are, you'll run into them again."

Craven scowled. "Might be a while. The general told me his orders are to head to Mountainwood for reinforcements before turning south. It'll be a while before we're ordered north toward Walden."

A knot he'd been carrying around for weeks eased. Walden was safe.

For now.

8

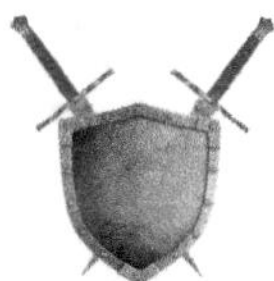

Renna moved her piece on the Raiders board. Brandi smirked. A bad sign for Renna's piece.

Abigail hunched over the board, her forehead and mouth squinched. Next to her, Jeremiah read a book while waiting for his turn.

Lydia tapped her foot, the rhythm increasing the longer Abigail studied the board. The youngest Alistair sibling Esther played with her doll and tea set next to Brandi. Somehow, Brandi managed to pretend to drink tea, keep Esther amused, and play Raiders all at the same time.

On one of the couches, Shadrach had his arm wrapped around Jolene, her head tucked against his shoulder. Ever since Lady Lorraine, Jolene, and Shadrach had arrived yesterday, Jolene had been pale and shaky. What had she seen? Or done? Renna wasn't sure she wanted to ask.

Across the room, Lady Lorraine, Lord Alistair, Uncle Abel, and Aunt Mara talked in low voices.

Renna tore her gaze back to the game. Brandi bounced in

her seat as she knocked one of Renna's pieces from the board. "Another for me."

Renna shrugged. At least Brandi was enjoying her birthday. Even if it was an afternoon break from the preparations for war.

Abigail moved her piece as the door creaked. Probably another report for Lord Alistair on the progress of the defenses.

"Am I interrupting anything?"

Renna held her breath and raised her head. Leith leaned against the doorframe, dressed in prairie-gray homespun. His black hair waved across his tanned forehead. His green eyes swung towards her.

He was alive.

Alive.

Her pulse drummed in her ears.

"Lei—Daniel!" Brandi shot to her feet so fast her thigh smacked the table and sent their board and pieces flying. She dashed across the room and barely slowed before running into him with such force that he stumbled backwards several steps. She wrapped her arms around his waist and squeezed. "You came!"

"Came for what?" Leith hugged her.

Brandi stepped back and cocked her head. "My birthday, of course. I'm fourteen today."

"Your birthday?" Leith rested his hands on her shoulders. "I didn't bring you a present. But, I did bring you a friend." He reached into the hallway and pulled a boy into the room. The boy looked to be about Brandi's age, with blue eyes peering up through a fringe of shaggy, dark-brown hair. "This is Jamie."

Brandi's grin glowed across her face. "Nice to meet you, Jamie. Do you like to play Raiders? We're partway through a game, but I think I just scattered the pieces all over the room." She dragged Jamie into the room by his arm.

Renna slipped to her feet, her mouth dry. She tried to swallow, but her tongue clogged the back of her throat. She should welcome him. Or hug him like Brandi had.

No, bad idea. She tucked her arms across her stomach.

Lord Alistair shook Leith's hand. Leith tipped his head toward Jamie and said something to Lord Alistair in a low tone. Lord Alistair nodded. Leith would probably have to make a full report later.

Renna eased away from the center of the room. Brandi chattered away at Jamie. Shad clasped Leith's hand as Uncle Abel, Aunt Mara, and Lady Lorraine gathered for introductions. She should join them. But her feet stuck to the floor.

Lady Alistair swept into the room. Her gaze paused a moment on Leith and Jamie, but if she wondered about the addition of two new guests, her features remained smooth. "Cake is served."

At her wave, a servant pushed a cart into the room. A three-tiered cake spread with a thick, buttercream frosting towered on the cart. Sugared flower petals topped the buttercream.

Brandi tugged Renna forward. "Come on."

As the servant dished slices onto plates, Brandi shoved two plates into Renna's hands. "Take a piece to Leith."

"Why me?" Renna glanced toward Leith. He'd backed against the wall, his eyes flicking around the room. A flash of something, both cold and hot, darted through her stomach. "Why not you?"

Brandi grabbed two more plates and waved one towards Jamie. Jamie stared at the room, eyes wide. "I'm taking a piece to Jamie. After all, he's my birthday present."

She waltzed across the room and brandished one of the plates. "Have you ever had cake, Jamie? It's about the best thing ever, after Aunt Mara's maple sugar cookies. Those are the best ever."

Jamie jumped, his hands waving in the air as if in surrender. "Not in a few years."

When Renna turned, Leith's eyes rested on her. Her breath caught in her chest and fluttered there, papery thin.

She could do this. She shuffled one foot forward, then the other. A few feet from Leith, she held out the plate. "Would you like a piece of cake?"

"Yes, thanks." His smile carved dimples into his cheeks.

Not fair. Her heart thumped in her temples and drooled heat down her arms. The plate in her hand bobbled as Leith reached for it. He lunged forward and caught the tipping plate, sticking a hand into the cake's frosting. The fork grated across the plate and thumped onto the rug.

For a moment, they stared at the fork. Renna peeked up at Leith. A smile crept across his face. "At least I caught the cake. Less of a mess."

Her chest relaxed. Why had she been so nervous? A smile broke onto her own face. "I'll fetch a new fork."

She retrieved the fork from the floor and crossed the room. Out of the corner of her eye, she spotted Leith holding out his frosting-covered fingers and glancing around the room. He popped his fingers into his mouth.

She swiped a fork and two napkins from the cart and

returned to Leith. He halted partway through licking a speck of frosting and yanked his finger from his mouth.

"Brandi helpfully shoved plates and forks into my hands, but she forgot napkins." Renna held out the fork and napkin.

Leith took them, nodded his thanks, and poked at his piece of cake with his fork. "Are you doing all right? After what happened with Vane?"

Was she all right? If anything, she was too all right. She'd watched a man die. She should be more traumatized by that, shouldn't she? But it wasn't like she mourned Vane. He'd killed her mother. He'd threatened to kill her several times. "I'm fine. And you? How's your arm?"

With a glance around the room, he angled his shoulder towards the wall and pushed up his left sleeve until she could see the bowl of his shoulder and the purple-red splotch from his knife wound.

Renna leaned closer, her fingers itching to probe the wound and check the amount the muscle had healed below the skin. "The wound closed nicely. It might take a few months or longer before the color fades to white. How's the muscle feel? Can you move your arm all right?"

Before he could answer, her eyes snagged on the single red line across the top of his shoulder. This time, her hand made it most of the way to his shoulder before she caught herself. "Your mark of failure."

"The only mark I'm not ashamed of." He dropped his sleeve, hiding the mark once again.

She'd seen the marks marching down his right arm nearly to his elbow. His past, etched into his skin. So much shame displayed in a way he never could erase. It could only be covered, hidden.

Forgiven.

She'd forgiven him for the role he'd played in the deaths of her parents and one of her cousins. So what now? What happened after forgiveness? Trust? She already trusted him. Friendship? What would a friendship with Leith look like? Not like the one he had with Brandi. Hers with him was more than that. Or less. Or something.

Silence stretched between them. Not a bad silence, but not exactly comfortable either. She wasn't sure what to call it. She held up her plate, her cake only missing a few bites. "How do you like the cake?"

He held up his piece, also missing only two bites. "It's good. Really good. Not something Respen feeds his Blades."

Renna smiled. Leith's answering smile shot warmth into her fingers and toes.

"Renna. Daniel. You two." Brandi's voice cut through the silence. "If you're done talking, it's time to open presents."

Renna turned. Every person in the room was staring at her and Leith. Uncle Abel had his arms crossed. A different heat flashed across her face and neck. She ducked her head, scurried across the room, and slipped into the seat next to Brandi.

Uncle Abel produced a small box. "This was something we should've given you years ago."

Renna touched the silver cross dangling from a slender chain around her neck.

Grinning, Brandi yanked the ribbon from the box and flung the top open. She drew out a thin chain. A silver cross tinkled along the chain and swung at the end as she held it up. Her eyes and mouth formed matching Os. "It's just like Renna's."

Aunt Mara rested a hand on Brandi's knee. "Your mother always said it was a reminder of where to look when you needed strength."

Brandi clasped it around her neck and met Renna's gaze. Renna touched her own necklace again. When Brandi flung herself at Aunt Mara and Uncle Abel for breath-stealing hugs, Renna found her gaze drifting towards Leith. He and Jamie leaned against the wall in the far corner.

His gaze met hers. Her face heated. As she ducked her head, she caught sight of Uncle Abel's bright eyes watching them.

9

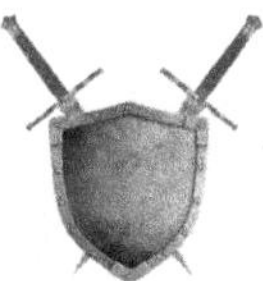

Leith rolled out of his blanket in the cold damp of pre-dawn. Jamie still curled in his blanket on the cot across from him. Leith shook him. The boy groaned and rolled over. Leith shook him harder. "Jamie. Time to get up."

Jamie blinked, then bolted upright so fast he banged the back of his head on the wall. "First Blade. Sorry. I'm awake."

Leith knelt. "You should know by now I'm not like First Blade Vane."

Jamie straightened his shoulders. "I know. I just...for a moment, I forgot."

Leith hung his head. Leaning over Jamie like that, he'd probably triggered a memory of Vane. Leith had endured enough of his own beatings at Vane's hands. Sometimes Vane had kicked him awake so hard he'd had black bruises spread across his ribs.

He patted Jamie's shoulder and stood. "Grab breakfast and tend the horses."

Jamie nodded, straightened his clothes, and hurried from the room. Leith strode from the room a moment later.

The cooks passed him a slice of bread as he strolled through the kitchens and out the door. The crisp morning air tiptoed along his skin. Too soon, the sun would burn the hint of dew from the grass.

Leith trailed his fingers over thigh-high cornstalks. The scratchy leaves tugged at his clothes. Someone had tended this vegetable patch in his absence. He couldn't find any weeds that needed plucking.

When the kitchen door opened and shut, Leith didn't turn around. Most likely Renna. Had she been the one to take care of the garden?

A boot crunched on the grass. A heavy tread, not Renna's light patter. A man's foot.

Leith whirled. His hand closed over thin air where his knife's hilt usually rested.

Abel Lachlan stood a few yards away. "A little jumpy."

Leith swallowed. Lachlan had every reason to be suspicious. Perhaps not of Leith's loyalty to the Resistance. He'd proved that to Lord Alistair, and through him, to Lachlan.

But Lachlan was perceptive. And thanks to Brandi, everyone had seen Leith and Renna talking and staring at each other last night.

Lachlan crossed his arms. "What's your interest in Renna?"

Yep, Brandi had done a good job of making sure everyone noticed. Leith ducked his head. "I have no interest in Renna."

"We both know that's a lie." Lachlan's voice sliced the

morning air. "You might lie to Respen, but you should at least tell the truth here."

Leith dragged in a deep breath. He could face Respen. Surely he had the courage to face Lachlan. Leith widened his stance and met Lachlan's gaze. "Fine. Yes. But it makes no difference. I'll never pursue it."

"Why not?"

"I'm a Blade. I have blood on my hands." The words carved into his chest. He'd helped kill Renna's parents. He'd killed her cousin. Yes, she'd forgiven him. But forgiveness was one thing. Courting was something altogether different.

"If Renna and Brandi are to be believed, you're a Christian. Is the blood on your hands more powerful than the blood of Christ?" Lachlan's gaze stabbed at him.

"No, it isn't. I know it has been forgiven." Leith crossed his arms as if to stop his chest from crumbling. He hung his head, unable to hold Lachlan's gaze any longer. "What I'm doing is dangerous. It wouldn't be fair to Renna to drag her into it any more than she already is, and...I know I'm not going to survive this war."

"How can you know that?" Lachlan's tone softened. "Only the Lord knows each man's time."

"When Respen finds out, he'll kill me. And he will find out. One day, I'll make a mistake. No one never fails, not even me. When that happens, I will die." His throat burned.

It did him no good to dream of the future. He'd never have it. The best he could hope for would be to make sure Renna and Brandi got their future. That's why God had placed him in the Blades, wasn't it? Not to save himself, but to save everyone else.

"Your life is in God's hands, not Respen's."

Leith released a slow breath. "I know."

"Both Brandi and Renna are going to need your friendship. Mara and I will be leaving later this morning." Lachlan dropped his arms to his sides. "Be gentle with Renna. She's been through a lot."

Leith flinched. He'd been the one to inflict much of it on her.

Lachlan stepped closer. "I can't protect them. I never had the skill. But Renna and Brandi will need a protector."

Leith met Lachlan's gaze and held it. "I promise I will protect them with my life."

Lachlan rested a hand on Leith's shoulder. "Thank you." With a groan, Lachlan eased onto the grassy slope beside the garden. "Sit."

Something in Lachlan's eyes told Leith he had more to say. Leith sat on the grass a few feet away. What else did Lachlan want to say to him?

Lachlan stared at the waving line of cornstalks in front of them. "A number of years ago, I was the minister in Blathe."

Leith's breath caught. He tried to ask when, but the word died in his throat. Lachlan could've left Blathe long before Leith had been born. He might be telling Leith for any number of reasons.

"I was there the night your mother and father died."

"My mother killed herself." Leith spat the words. His stomach churned with memories he'd locked in the past.

"Did Respen tell you that?" Lachlan draped his arms across his knees.

"Yes." Leith squeezed his eyes shut. He'd screamed for his mother, but she'd never come. She hadn't loved him enough to even try to get him back when his father had sold him to the lord of Blathe.

"Respen lied."

"What?" Leith blinked at Lachlan.

"She didn't kill herself. She died saving my life."

Leith's muscles froze. Nine years of pain. A lie. He cleared his throat, but his voice still came out scratchy. "What happened?"

"When your father sold you to Respen, Lena, your mother, came to me and Mara to ask us to intervene. She had nowhere else to turn. We approached your father to plead with him to try to get you back. Orn refused." The rising sun glinted on Lachlan's silver-gray hair. "Orn leaped to false conclusions and grew angry. He drew a knife and would've stabbed me if Lena hadn't stepped between us. I'm not sure if she intended to take the knife or just stop Orn."

Leith hung his head. Too many questions. "Why did my mother stay with him? Or even marry him in the first place?"

"I don't know." Lachlan leaned his head back and stared at the sky. "Perhaps she wasn't willing to say she'd made the wrong choice. Maybe she thought she could change him or maybe, deep down, she still loved him. I don't think she'd anywhere else to go or anywhere to turn. When Mara and I tried to reach out to her, it took a long time before she was willing to accept even a small charity."

A memory sparked. Leith closed his eyes. "She told me, the night before she died, that we were going to go to church in the morning. Do you think...before she died..."

"I have hope that God worked in her heart before she died. I can't be sure, but I like to think she died with hope."

Hope. She hadn't had much of it in her life. An ache in

Leith's chest eased. A scar, perhaps, finally healing. She hadn't willingly abandoned him. She'd tried to get him back and died while trying to rescue him. "Why didn't you tell me any of this while I was at Stetterly?"

"The same reason I'm confessing this to you now. I failed back then. I promised Lena I'd look after you." Lachlan's shoulders curved as if the weight of the past bore down on him. "But Respen refused to give you up. When I tried, he used circumstances in Blathe to force Mara and me to leave town. He had his own reasons for wanting us gone. In my cowardice, I never went back. I told myself you were better off with Respen. When I caught a glimpse of you the night Laurence and Annita died, I knew I'd made a horrific mistake. Instead of protecting you, I'd turned my back and let Respen turn you into a killer."

Something inside Leith tilted. "That's why you didn't toss me out into the snow or let the sheriff kill me." Lachlan had called on principles as his reason for helping Leith. It'd been the truth, but only part of the truth.

"I feared that if I told you, you'd grow angry. Angry enough to turn us in to Respen. Or you might've become disillusioned and stopped searching the way you were."

Maybe he would have. Or maybe it wouldn't have made a difference. Leith couldn't be sure.

He couldn't feel anger. Not toward Lachlan. His confession had soothed some of the raw edges of Leith's past. "You aren't at fault for what happened to me or the choices I made. I knew what I was doing when I killed the first time, and I made the decision again and again to obey Respen. The responsibility is mine."

After a pause, Leith raised his head. The growing dawn

spread fingers through the cornstalks and shooed away the dew. "What would you have done if Respen had let me go?"

Lachlan shrugged. "Brought you to Stetterly."

What would it have been like to have been raised in Stetterly? Grown up racing down the halls, wiggling through church services in the white church down the road from the manor, getting patched up by Mara Lachlan whenever he got into some kind of scrape.

Would the Lachlans have adopted him? Leith couldn't bring himself to ask. They'd never had children, so he had a feeling they probably would've.

That would've made him Renna and Brandi's adopted cousin. Which would make the things he felt toward Renna a whole lot more awkward.

No, it was probably best things had turned out the way they had. As much as a past in Stetterly glowed with the same golden blush as the rising sun, he was where God had placed him. He was a Blade for a reason.

He stumbled to his feet. "I should go look for Jamie. It's his first day here. He doesn't know his way around yet."

He tried to keep his pace casual as he retreated. When he reached the stables, he ducked inside and leaned against the wall in the shadows. As his eyes adjusted, he picked out hooves shuffling through straw, crunching teeth on hay, and the long, low snorts of horses clearing dust from their nostrils.

"Blizzard loves apples." Brandi's voice rang from the back of the stable.

"Blizzard?" Jamie's tone dipped.

"Daniel's horse. He let me name him."

Leith couldn't help but smile at that. Brandi hadn't given him much choice.

"What's your horse named?"

"Named?" Jamie sounded even more confused. "I don't know."

Leith could picture Brandi's eyes rolling. "I get it. It's a horse. It doesn't have a name."

"Um, how about Buck?"

Brandi gave such a huge sigh that Leith could hear it even from his place in the shadows. "Buck? Really? Every buckskin horse is called Buck. It's not a creative name at all."

"Well...I kind of call him...in my head you see...I call him Buster."

"Buster? That's the best you could come up with?"

Leith slipped out the door. He didn't need to worry about Jamie. Brandi would look out for him. Or, at the very least, get him so confused he wouldn't be able to get into any trouble.

10

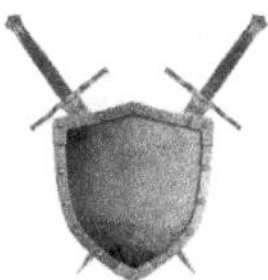

Renna swallowed her tears for the thousandth time that morning. Uncle Abel led the second mule from Walden's stables while Aunt Mara stood next to Stubborn. Brandi alternately squeezed the breath from her and strangled their goat Ginger with hugs.

Uncle Abel paused next to Renna and rested a hand on her shoulder. She sniffed and scrubbed at her eyes. "Why do you have to go so soon?"

He rubbed her back. "Stetterly needs us, and we can't risk having Respen's army cut us off."

"Stetterly isn't at risk, is it?" Renna twisted her fingers into her skirt. Stetterly should be safe. It hadn't been attacked by the Blades last time. Surely it wouldn't be attacked this time either.

Uncle Abel patted her shoulder, but his gaze grew distant. "Yes, we'll be fine. We are in God's hands."

Renna didn't dare ask what he wasn't telling her. She leaned into his hug. "When will you be coming back?"

Uncle Abel glanced at Brandi, then tightened his hug. "We won't be back. Acktar is getting too dangerous for you and Brandi to stay here much longer. Lord Alistair will send you to the Resistance hideout in the Sheered Rock Hills. And we'll stay at Stetterly."

A shiver raced along Renna's skin. Uncle Abel and Aunt Mara planned to stand with the town until the end.

Shouldn't that be Renna's duty? Lady Lorraine had been the last to leave Sierra. If the war came to Walden, Lord Alistair would do the same. Yet, Renna had been the first to flee.

Tears burned her throat. Would this war ever end? Would she and Brandi see Uncle Abel and Aunt Mara again? She buried her face against Uncle Abel's shoulder. "I'll miss you."

"And we'll miss you." Uncle Abel's voice cracked. He held her for several minutes until he pulled away to hug Brandi.

Renna wrapped her arms around Aunt Mara. "I'm going to miss you so much."

"Me too, dear." Aunt Mara gripped Renna tighter. "Take care of yourself and Brandi."

"I will."

Nothing more to be said. No more hugs. Uncle Abel and Aunt Mara swung onto the mules, and Uncle Abel grabbed the lead for Ginger. Too soon, the mules trotted from the yard and up the hill, disappearing into black dots over the horizon.

Brandi swiped at her eyes. When she turned to Renna, her smile wobbled across her face. "I'm going to the stables for a while."

She trudged toward the building. Renna took one step to follow her, but that Blade trainee, Jamie, trailed after Brandi.

He seemed like a nice enough boy, and Leith trusted him, so Renna left them alone. Sometimes, a friend could help more than a sister.

Renna slipped into the flower garden and sat on a stone bench next to the fountain in the center. An inch of water lay still and hot in the bottom, the rest of the fountain silent and dry. At this part of the summer, Lord Alistair wouldn't waste the water to keep his fountain going when the crops needed the water more. Around her, the flowers that had bloomed so vibrantly a few weeks ago had dried into husks. Only the prairie daisies and bluebells continued to bloom.

A footfall crunched on the pebbled path winding through the garden. She turned and spotted Leith, dressed in the dust-colored homespun he wore for his peasant's disguise, shifting from foot to foot a few yards away. Had he purposely made noise so as not to startle her?

"Are you all right?" His green eyes flitted over her, as if he wanted to meet her gaze yet didn't dare.

She drew her feet onto the bench and hugged her knees. "Not really."

Leith eased onto the rim of the fountain a couple of feet away. It couldn't have been comfortable perching on the scalloped rim, and if she'd attempted it, she would've overbalanced and landed on her back in the scummy water on the bottom.

Perhaps she should offer him the seat next to her on the bench. It would be the nice thing to do.

But the more she thought about doing it, having Leith sit so close to her she'd feel the heat radiating from his skin and see the lines of color threading through his green eyes, her breath caught and her own skin flashed as hot as the pebbles baking in the noon sun.

Whatever this feeling—attraction or love or something in between—it was getting worse.

Leith ducked his head. "No, of course you aren't all right. I just meant...I wanted to make sure..." He shook his head, his knuckles whitening against the lip of the fountain.

She ran her tongue across the backs of her teeth. Of all the people at Walden, he'd been the one to come after her. Not Lydia. Not Jolene. Not even Shadrach. But Leith.

What should she say? What could she say that wouldn't come out strange as the patter in her chest?

She studied the scuffed leather tips of her shoes peeking from under her skirt. A different sort of weight dropped into her stomach. "I feel like I'm losing my family all over again. I know I'm not the only one. So many people are leaving their homes and losing loved ones. When will it end?"

"I don't know." When Renna risked a peek, Leith's head hung. "Shad would have some sort of wise answer."

"Or Brandi would come up with some Bible story for this." Renna wiggled her toes and watched the cracks in her leather shoes widen and close. "She's probably telling one to Jamie right now."

They lapsed into silence. Renna rocked back and forth, but the motion didn't inspire her tongue. What should she say to him? Or should she say anything? Why wasn't her tongue—or brain—working?

He stood and jabbed his thumb towards the flat area where Walden's soldiers gathered for drill. "Lord Alistair asked that Jamie and I join drills, and I probably should go."

Renna dropped her feet to the cobbled path. Aunt Mara

and Uncle Abel wouldn't want her to spend all day moping. If she couldn't stand strong with Stetterly, she should at least accomplish her small duty as a healer here. "And I should get back to helping the healer."

When she glanced up, Leith had his hand held out to her. "Can I walk you inside?"

She placed her hand in his to let him pull her to her feet. His hand was rough with callouses across his palm and the pads of his fingers. A shock traveled up her arm and curled in the pit of her stomach.

His grip was strong. Sure.

Safe.

11

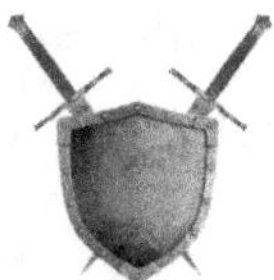

Leith adjusted his grip on the wooden sword he'd been given. The guardsman he'd been assigned as a sparring partner stepped forward and swung his wooden sword at Leith's head.

Leith tried to lift his sword, but the unfamiliar weight on his wrist tugged the sword half-out of his grasp. Ducking, he managed to block the blow, but the force sent his wooden sword spinning from his hand. It clunked to the ground, the wooden blade thwacking his shin on the way down.

He sucked in a breath and shook his fingers. Good thing this wasn't Respen's version of learning weaponry, or he'd be using a real sword. He'd be missing his leg from the knee down.

His left arm ached with the weight of the small shield he carried. The nearly healed wound in his shoulder twinged every time he'd been forced to raise that shield to block a blow.

"You almost had it that time." The guardsman picked up

Leith's fallen practice sword and handed it to him. "You have a good sense of balance and a good eye for fighting techniques. You just can't seem to handle a sword for some reason."

Plenty of reasons, but Leith couldn't explain. Of course he had good fighting instincts. He was a trained fighter. But not with a sword.

Out of the corner of his eye, he spotted Shad's gaze. A hint of a smirk played at the corner of his mouth. Payback for all of the times Leith had laughed when Shad had attempted to learn knife-fighting.

Payback Leith deserved. He hadn't gone easy on Shad.

A crack cut the air next to him. Jamie raised his practice sword again and parried a guardsman's thrust.

After a week of drilling, Jamie could hold his own during the basic maneuvers. Leith grimaced. He had knife-fighting ingrained into his muscles and memory for nine years. Jamie only had two years of training. Not so much to unlearn.

Not that Leith really wanted to unlearn his knife-fighting skills. This was only a ruse, both for the men around him and the Blades lurking at the edge of the Sheered Rock Hills. To these guards, he was nothing more than the peasant Daniel. To the Blades, he supposedly dressed as a peasant and participated in drill to count Walden's guards, assess their level of training, and discover Vane's whereabouts.

As Leith gritted his teeth and raised the sword again, a dust cloud to the south drew his attention. Not big enough to be Respen's army. Perhaps several riders or one rider coming in fast.

Shad turned to the dust cloud as well. When a single dot solidified over the crest, Shad faced the drilling guards. "Dismissed. Get cleaned up, grab something to eat, and take an hour's rest before reporting to the ditch digging crew."

Leith handed his practice sword to Jamie. "Can you return my sword too?"

Jamie nodded and took the sword. Leith slipped away from the rest of the guards. Entering the flower garden, he tiptoed along the paths until he reached the study's broad window.

A few minutes later, one of the panes swung open. After a glance around, Leith boosted himself through the window and onto the windowseat. Shad swung the window closed even before Leith had rolled into a crouch on the floor.

The study door gave a tiny creak. Leith pressed into the shadow next to the curtains. Lord Alistair's voice boomed inside. "Shad?"

"Just checking that the window is secure." Shad locked it. As he turned, he shot a smirk in Leith's direction. "We wouldn't want any Blades to get in."

Leith fought to hold a scowl on his face.

Shad strode across the alcove and drew the curtains closed behind him. Leith peered around the edge of the curtain as Lord Alistair waved a slim, dust-covered man to a seat. The man still huffed and tottered, the glass of water in his hand spilling down his arm.

Lord Alistair steepled his fingers. "Take your time and catch your breath."

The rider slurped water between gulps of air. He plunked the glass onto the oak desk. "I swung towards Keestone as instructed."

Lord Alistair moved the glass to a stack of papers and

swiped at the ring of water it had left on the desktop with his sleeve. "What did you learn?"

"Clarbon was overrun a week ago. Lord Hartley was killed, but he and his men bought enough time for his family to flee to Keestone."

Leith flinched. Clarbon attacked. A lord killed. He hadn't warned them in time.

He'd failed. Again.

"As I rode past, Keestone was under attack." The rider scratched at his hair. Dust trickled down his neck. "It won't hold, but I ran into a rider from Duelstone. Most of the citizens of Keestone got out and Lord Farthen has some sort of plan to fall back to Duelstone and from there to Uster. Refugees from Clarbon, Keestone, Duelstone, and Uster are headed to Walden as we speak."

Lord Alistair tapped his fingers against his chin. "We'll be ready."

"I swung by Mountainwood on the way back. I spotted most of the northern part of the army, with reinforcements from Mountainwood, swinging south. They'll probably meet up with the southern army at Duelstone."

Some good news at least. As Leith had guessed, Respen had given his commanders instructions to wait before attacking Walden. The armies would cut off Walden from the other towns and possible reinforcement before they attacked.

But when the attack came, Walden would feel the full might of Respen's army, both northern and southern branches.

Respen wanted to be sure Walden fell.

"Thank you. You may go. Report to the kitchen. The cook will see that you're fed." Lord Alistair waved his dismissal.

The rider creaked to his feet and staggered out the door. As soon as the door closed, Leith crawled around the edge of the curtain and rose to his feet.

Lord Alistair had his head bent, lines digging into his face. "Both Dently and Flayin Falls were spared. It seems Respen isn't attacking the towns where his Blades were successful. With Respen's armies positioned where they are, we're cut off from the towns to the west."

"I'm sorry." Leith gripped the back of one of the chairs in front of Lord Alistair's desk. "I should've provided better warning."

"You did the best you could." Lord Alistair's shoulders hunched. "The extent of Respen's plan took us by surprise. All except Paula Lorraine. If I'd listened to her advice years ago, Walden would be more prepared. But, in the end, it won't matter. We have plans for withdrawing into the Sheered Rock Hills."

Their secret base. The one buried so deep in the Sheered Rock Hills even the Blades hadn't stumbled across it. What plans did the Resistance already have set up? A memory sparked. "The Leader is almost ready."

Shad's head snapped up. Lord Alistair's hands slapped onto his desktop. "Where did you hear that?"

"I read it in a note you'd sent Abel Lachlan this past winter." Leith flexed his fingers against the chair. "It's one of the things I didn't tell Respen when I returned from Stetterly."

"I see." Lord Alistair relaxed. "Yes, the Leader's readiness is a factor in our plan."

Who was the Leader? One secret Lord Alistair wouldn't trust to Leith. Then again, probably best Leith didn't know. He could cause too many problems if he let anything slip to Respen.

"Right now, the Leader doesn't matter." Shad straightened and waved at the map hanging on the wall behind Lord Alistair. "We have to decide what we're going to do in the meantime."

Lord Alistair swiveled in his chair. "We'll have to send the refugees coming here on to..." He trailed off and glanced at Leith. "On to Eagle Heights."

Eagle Heights. The name of the Resistance base. "You can't send them right now. There are three Blades scouring the Sheered Rock Hills looking for Harrison Vane. While I can prevent them from getting too close to Walden, I can't stop them from following the refugees to Eagle Heights."

"That could pose something of a problem." Shad crossed his arms. "You mentioned the next Meeting of the Blades is in a week and a half, correct?"

"Yes." Leith nodded. Shad was on the right track. All the Blades would leave the Sheered Rock Hills to attend the Meeting of the Blades. "If you send the refugees out three days before the Meeting of the Blades, you should be safe. Split them into small groups and send them by different routes. There'll still be tracks, but hopefully it'll be scattered enough and old enough that few of the Blades will be able to follow."

Martyn still could. Leith swallowed the burn in his stomach. Martyn would be looking for Vane. Surely he'd ignore five or six day old tracks made by a group.

A sharp pain twisted Leith's chest. "Will you send Renna and Brandi along with the refugees?"

Lord Alistair stroked his beard. "Not sure. It'd probably be best. Their presence in Acktar is no longer necessary, and they'll be safest in Eagle Heights."

He should be thankful they'd be safe. Wasn't that what he wanted? Renna and Brandi safe and far away from Respen. He'd joined the Resistance to make that happen.

So why did a hollow ache pour through his chest?

Leith opened his mouth, but at first the words clogged in his throat. He drew in a deep breath. "I'm the First Blade. I report directly to Respen. Alone. When I return to Nalgar Castle, I could...I could kill him. I've had opportunity already. I'll have the chance again."

Lord Alistair leaned back in his chair. His eyes hardened. "I'd never give you that order. You're the Resistance spy, not the Resistance assassin."

Leith's shoulders relaxed as some of his tension eased. Not that he'd really believed Lord Alistair would ask it of him, but he had to be sure. "I know. I just wanted to make sure I wasn't failing by not killing him."

"You're not failing." Shad dropped his arms back to his sides. "You've done the best you could."

The leather in Lord Alistair's chair squeaked as he rested his elbows on his desk. "I'll admit, it's something I considered when you returned to Nalgar Castle. And, if I thought it'd help the Resistance cause, I'd be tempted to ask you regardless of how right or wrong the action might be. But, it wouldn't help, and it wouldn't be right."

Leith sagged. At least he hadn't failed yet again when he'd decided not to kill Respen. "Why not?"

"The problem with fighting for a cause is that the rules of the cause dictate how we fight. And if we sacrifice the cause to win a few battles, we'll ultimately lose the war." Lord Alistair tapped his steepled fingers together. "In this case, the Resistance was founded on the principle that Respen has usurped the throne. He assassinated King Leon, Queen Deirdre, and their sons. He was crowned without the proper Gathering of Nobles."

"I see." Leith hung his head. He'd killed one of those royal sons. "And if I were to assassinate Respen, the Resistance would be doing the same thing."

"Exactly. We can't kill him and prop up our own ruler in his place. Our ruler will have to be acknowledged by the entire Gathering of Nobles, and Respen must be dealt with using the justice God has bestowed to a rightful government."

"Even beyond that, killing Respen wouldn't stop the war." Shad rubbed the hilt of his sword. "Can you imagine the uproar among the nobles? The country would erupt into civil war. Yes, we have war now, but at least this war has sides and a way to end it. A civil war in the wake of Respen's death would last for years as noble after noble tried and failed to claim the throne."

"The Blades would scatter and align themselves with whatever noble happened to be winning." Leith grimaced. "Never thought Respen being alive would be a good thing."

"That's politics for you." Shad straightened. "We'd better get something to eat before we go on ditch digging duty. But first, I have something to show you."

Leith followed Shad from the study, down the hall, and up the broad staircase. Taking a left, Shad pushed open the door to his room. Leith raised his eyebrows. Had Shad continued to practice the knife-fighting skills Leith had tried to teach him last time he was in Walden?

As he stepped inside, Leith swept his gaze around the room. A mountain lion skin covered the floor next to a blocky, four-poster bed. A rack with arrows in various stages of completion took up most of one wall.

Leith halted in the center of the room and studied the only change since he'd been there last. A broad, wooden shield leaned against the wall across from the bed. Nicks marred its surface. Not long slashes, like Leith would've expected if Shad used this shield against a sword. These knicks looked more like a knife stabbing the shield. "What've you been up to?"

Shad grinned so broadly his skin pulled taut across his square jaw. He drew a bundle from under his bed and tossed back the wrapping.

Leith stiffened. Vane's knives gleamed in the lamplight, their blades cleaned, polished, and oiled. His shoulder throbbed with the memory of one of those knives slamming through his skin into flesh and muscle.

Shad hefted one. "Stand back and watch this."

Leith stepped to the side of the room. Shad cocked his arm back and tossed the knife. It flew, end over end, until it slammed into the shield. Leith's eyebrows rose. The throw hadn't been perfect. The knife hit the shield low and off-center, but even that much was impressive. "You've been practicing."

Shad shrugged and picked up another knife. "After seeing what Vane could do with throwing knives, I didn't want to be at that kind of disadvantage again."

Leith pulled out one of his own knives, pinched the tip between his fingers, aimed at the shield, and whipped the knife forward. It spun, flashing, before it crashed next to the shield hilt first. "That's the extent of my knife-throwing skills."

Shad's eyes narrowed. "Perhaps it has something to do with my archery training. I'm used to figuring out distances and stuff like that. It took some tweaking, but I didn't have to start from scratch."

"I'd probably be hopeless at archery too if I tried it." Leith shrugged and retrieved his knife. "About as hopeless as I am with a sword."

Shad grinned, strode forward, and threw his knife at the shield. This time, the knife struck high and to the right. "So when are you going to start courting Renna?"

"What?" Leith paused with his knife half out of its sheath. "I can't do that."

"Why not?" Shad drew another knife, stepped back, and threw again. The knife thunked into the shield's center.

Leith grimaced and tossed his knife. It plunked against the wall and slid to the floor. "I'm still a Blade. I'm going to ride away from here soon, and there's no guarantee I'll come back."

Shad drew another knife. "We're living in risky times. I have no better chance of surviving than you do, and both Jolene and I know it. But it's better to take the risk of being hurt together than avoid truly living. I'd rather have loved Jolene even a short time than not at all."

"It's different for you." Leith paced as far away from Shad as he could in the confined chamber. Two steps and he reached the foot of the bed. Two steps the other way and he swerved around the head of the mountain lion rug. "You aren't responsible for the death of Jolene's father. I helped kill Renna's parents. What kind of man helps kill a girl's parents, then courts her?"

"Abel Lachlan didn't seem to have a problem with the idea."

Leith blinked at Shad. Had Shad seen them talking? "What gave you that impression? He didn't give me his blessing, nor did I ask for it. He asked that I protect Renna and Brandi."

"Exactly." Shad smirked, the corners of his eyes crinkling. Another knife thunked into the shield. "If he'd had a problem with you being close to Renna, he would've warned you away. What do you think he meant by asking you to protect her?"

"I think it was a warning. A warning to protect her heart as well as her person." Leith ground his teeth together. Heat flared in his chest. "I'm not about to break her heart."

He'd seen the results of a broken heart. He'd watched it every day in his mother's dark, pained eyes when she'd tried so hard to please his father, only to have him belittle her. Or worse, hit her. She'd given her heart to Orn Torren, and he'd done worse than break it. He'd ground it beneath his fist and drank it away to nothing until Leith had had no trouble believing she'd killed herself rather than face another day.

Leith wasn't about to do that to Renna. Perhaps it'd be better to love her even for a day than not at all. But, Leith would rather not love her at all than see her heart broken even one moment.

12

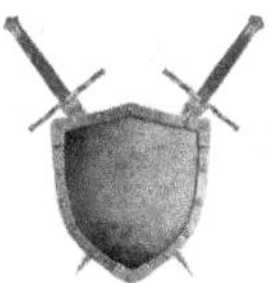

Leith stabbed a shovel into the ground again. A shallow trench now extended in a large ring around Walden manor. A hump of dirt no bigger than a prairie dog mound rose next to the trench.

Next to him, Jamie heaved another shovelful from the ground and dumped it onto the pile.

After a glance around to make sure no one was in earshot, he laid a hand on Jamie's shoulder. "I'm going to leave tonight to return to Nalgar Castle."

Jamie froze, a spark cringing across his eyes.

"You don't have to come with me." Leith knelt so he could look Jamie in the eye. "You can stay here and leave Walden with one of the refugee groups. I'll tell Respen I was forced to kill you, and he won't look for you."

Jamie's eyes flicked toward the town. Leith followed his gaze. Rows of makeshift canvas tents dotted the hillsides around Walden for the refugees from Clarbon, Keestone, and Duelstone. Keestone had fallen. Duelstone would crumble any day, if it hadn't already. Only Uster remained before the entire army would swing north for Walden.

Jamie squared his shoulders. "I want to return to Nalgar Castle with you."

Leith raised his eyebrows. "Why?"

Something flickered in Jamie's eyes. "I want to help the Resistance."

Leith searched Jamie's face. He couldn't see any deception, but what if Jamie had been a spy for Respen all along? When they returned, he'd report Leith to the king.

But if he was telling the truth, then Jamie was the bravest thirteen-year-old Leith had ever met. And Leith couldn't ignore that bravery if it was real.

"All right. But first sign of trouble, and you get yourself out of there."

Jamie nodded, but that did nothing to ease the knot in Leith's gut. If Leith slipped up, he'd get both himself and Jamie killed.

RENNA TWISTED HER FINGERS THROUGH HER SKIRT. THE cotton scraped against her fingers.

Across the room, Lord Alistair gave Leith a few more instructions before shaking his hand. Brandi chattered to Jamie as if trying to stuff his ears with enough words to last for however long he'd be gone.

Shad slapped Leith on the back. They exchanged a few words too low for Renna to hear.

Then Leith stood in front of her. She couldn't breathe. Would she ever see him again? He was leaving for Nalgar

Castle. In a few days, she'd leave for the Resistance hideout, never to return until Respen was defeated. If he ever was.

She tipped forward onto her toes. When he'd left last time, she'd hugged him. And she hadn't been able to forget the feel of his strong shoulders.

Perhaps she'd better not hug him this time.

"Renna." Leith's deep, green eyes met hers.

Her heart bumped in her throat. What was he about to say?

"Stay safe."

Her breath whooshed as her heart thumped back into her chest. "You too."

No more words would come. But they weren't needed. Brandi was there. She hugged Leith so tightly Leith winced. "Don't break my ribs. I'd have a hard time explaining that to Respen."

Brandi grinned, but the grin only lasted seconds. "Take care of Blizzard."

"I will." Leith hugged Brandi back.

Renna ducked her head and focused on her fingers, which were strangling the life from her skirt. When had it become so natural to see Leith hug Brandi? As if he was already a part of her family in some way. Though what was he, exactly? Brandi's brother, but what did Renna feel about him? Brother didn't fit.

Leith gathered Jamie, and the next moment, they slipped out the window.

Renna's knees buckled. She stumbled backwards into one of the chairs in front of Lord Alistair's desk. Would she ever see him again?

And why did that hurt so much?

13

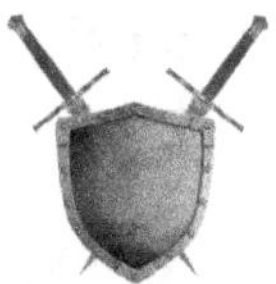

Riding through Nalgar Castle's gates was like riding into the gates of darkness itself. Leith choked on the stale air that clung to the castle. The flags above the battlemented towers hung limp while heat waves danced over the cobblestones.

He swiped at his hair and grimaced at the slick, wet texture of the strands. His black shirt glued to his back and chest. At this point, the dank coolness inside the thick, stone walls of the Blades' Tower sounded almost welcome.

He glanced at Jamie. Jamie stared straight ahead, his jaw tight. Something burned in his eyes, sending a pang through Leith's stomach. What was Jamie planning?

Halting in front of the stables, Leith dismounted and handed Blizzard's reins to a stableboy. He couldn't figure out Jamie's problem now. He had to be the First Blade, not Daniel, and trainees were too below a First Blade to notice outside of training sessions.

Leith strode into the passageway connecting the two

courtyards and over the wooden bridge that led to the Blades' Tower. At this time of summer, the sun had reduced the moat to a dry ditch with a patchwork of cracks in the bottom.

On the grass strip between the Tower and the moat, Twelfth Blade Altin drilled the remaining five trainees in their basic knife-fighting skills. As Leith passed, Altin nodded before turning back to the drills.

Stepping into the Tower, the stone-cooled air swiped cold fingers down Leith's back. His sweaty skin prickled.

A servant scrubbed a table in the main floor common room, panting, as if he'd just run up and down several flights of stairs. Leith bit his cheek to stop his frown. The servant had probably done exactly that the moment Leith had been spotted entering the castle.

As First Blade, Leith couldn't feel pity. He couldn't even acknowledge the servant. He brushed past him and headed up the stairs. His calves burned by the time he reached his room on the fourth floor of the tower.

He tried not to shiver as he crossed the threshold, as if Harrison Vane's ghost still lingered in the shadows carved in the cracks in the stones.

He hung his saddlebags on a hook and glanced around the room. His blankets lay undisturbed on the bed. A lamp already glowed on the small table, its flicker struggling to penetrate the gloom. Washing up at the small basin and pitcher of water the servant had left for him, Leith changed into fresh, black clothes. Time to make his report to King Respen.

Trudging down the four flights of stairs, Leith strode out the tower and across the wooden bridge once again. Instead of heading back to the cobblestone courtyard, he turned and strode up a set of stone stairs that led to King Respen's chambers.

Leith knocked on the carved oak door that led to the king's apartments. A curt reply ordered him to enter. He lifted the latch and stepped inside.

The plush burgundy rugs muffled his footsteps. Large, arched windows overlooked the cobblestone courtyard to his right. Padded chairs occupied a circle around the fireplace at the far end of the room, pillows clustered against the armrests in case the stuffing was not plush enough for the occupant. Wood paneling covered the walls, hiding the stone beneath a layer of oak.

Respen sat at a desk below one of the windows overlooking the cobbled courtyard. A clerk stood at his elbow, scribbling notes on a piece of paper. Leith waited while Respen finished up his business.

After dictating a few more notes, Respen waved his hand. The clerk bowed and scurried past Leith without looking at him. Poor fellow. What had he done to get the job of liaison between the king and the administrative officials that lived and worked in the office wing of Nalgar Castle?

"Report." Respen flicked his hand at the rug next to the desk.

Leith knelt on the rug, his knees sliding into the indents pressed into the rug from the time the former First Blade had spent on his knees reporting to his king. As Leith met Respen's eyes, a jolt surged down his back.

"Harrison Vane isn't hiding in Walden Manor. I was able to search the manor and didn't see him." That much of his report was true. Vane wasn't in Walden Manor. He was buried next to it. "The Resistance has a hideout deep in the Sheered Rock Hills, a place they call Eagle Heights."

Respen stroked the tip of his pointed, black beard. "That's where he is. Even if my Blades could find it, he'd kill them before they could report to me. Better to lure him out of his hiding place."

"Most likely, my king." Leith allowed himself only a brief pause. "I was able to train with Walden's guards. While Lord Alistair has a core of trained soldiers, most of his men are farmers and townsfolk with little training or fighting experience. Their numbers continue to grow."

Even though Lord Alistair had given his permission, Leith's chest ached as if he'd betrayed the Resistance by giving King Respen even that much information.

Respen lowered his hand back to the arm of his chair. "Well done, my First Blade. How did your experiment with the young trainee progress?"

"He was an asset to me when I sneaked into Sierra before the attack and again at Walden where his youth made others less wary around him."

"Good. When do you think he will be ready?"

Never, but Leith couldn't say that. "Soon."

Respen nodded, his dark eyes focused on the window overlooking the courtyard. "Very well. Report to me when the rest of my Blades arrive."

"Yes, my king." Leith pounded his clenched fist over his heart in a salute, stood, and strode out the door and down the stairs.

At the bottom of the stairs, he leaned against the wall. His hands were shaking. The lies. The half truths. Each word weighed against the other stories he'd already spun.

How much longer could he manage without slipping?

Leith cracked open the Tower door and settled down to wait. From this vantage point, he could see the door to Jamie's room in the outer wall next to the moat and the bridge to the rest of the castle.

Maybe that look in Jamie's eye had been nothing but determination. Perhaps he was seeing phantoms in the dark. But Leith couldn't take the chance. If Jamie had something up his sleeve, Leith would find it.

Several hours into the night, a dark figure slipped from Jamie's room. The half moon provided enough light for Leith to make out the silhouette, though he couldn't see the face.

What was Jamie doing? If he'd planned to betray Leith and the Resistance, then he had a lot of guts to wake Respen to make his report. Unless Respen knew about this plan and was awake and waiting.

Jamie tiptoed toward the bridge, his steps a mere crinkle in the yellowed grass. Leith tensed, one hand on the door, the other flexing at his side. He couldn't let Jamie step onto the bridge. If Leith tried to grab the boy there, both of them would be silhouetted and the creaking wood would warn Jamie of Leith's presence. Too early, and Jamie would notice the Tower door opening.

Jamie glanced toward the door, but his gaze swept past without pausing. He turned and reached one foot for the bridge.

Leith swung the door open, stepped forward, and

wrapped a hand over Jamie's mouth. Before Jamie could do more than jump, Leith pinned Jamie's arms to his sides and dragged him into the Tower.

Leith shoved him into a chair he could only dimly see in the moonlight filtering through the open door. "Stay."

When Jamie didn't move, Leith lit a lamp, set it on the table, and closed the outer door so none of the other trainees would overhear them should they wake. Only Altin remained in the Tower, and his room was on the third floor. When Leith had tiptoed past, he'd heard the steady sound of Altin's breathing.

Leith stalked back to Jamie and glared at him. "What were you doing?"

Jamie hunched in the chair and shook his head.

Heat flared in Leith's chest, though ice streaked down his back. "Look at me. What were you planning to do? Betray the Resistance?"

Jamie's head snapped up, his blue eyes wide. "No! I'd never do that."

Leith searched Jamie's face and eyes. He couldn't see anything but sincerity, but that didn't mean anything. Respen couldn't see Leith's lies in his eyes either. "Then what were you doing?"

"Doesn't matter." Jamie's jaw tensed.

"Yes, it does." Leith fought the rush of cold that poured through his chest. What was he willing to do if Jamie proved untrustworthy? To protect Renna, was he willing to kill Jamie if necessary? "Can I really trust you?"

"Yes." Jamie clenched his fists. "I wouldn't betray the Resistance."

"Then prove it. What were you doing?" Leith planted his

hands on the table and leaned towards Jamie. What possible motive could Jamie have for sneaking out if it wasn't to betray the Resistance?

"I..." Jamie gnawed on his bottom lip, swallowed, and met Leith's gaze. "I was going to kill King Respen."

"Respen has enough tricks up his sleeve to keep the former First Blade in line. He'd be able to kill you in a heart-beat, surprised or no." Leith gaped at Jamie. "What put the notion in your head to kill Respen?"

"He killed my parents."

That night sitting in the tall grass outside Sierra filtered through Leith's mind. *I hoped I'd get good enough to...to escape.*

But that had been a lie. Jamie had trained to kill Respen. He'd returned from Walden to kill Respen.

Leith perched on the table and crossed his arms. "If you were so determined, why did you refuse to kill earlier? You could've become a Blade and gained more freedom of movement."

Jamie kicked at a tableleg. "Respen is the only one I want to kill."

Leith bowed his head. Hadn't he felt that same kind of anger? He'd hated his father enough to contemplate killing him when he grew big enough. "Jamie, your parents wouldn't want you to kill Respen for revenge. It isn't right."

"I know, but..." Jamie clenched his fingers. "It isn't right that Respen isn't punished for what he did. And he keeps on hurting people. What if he hurts Brandi? She's my friend."

So that's what triggered Jamie to make his move now. "I know. It isn't right. That's why I'm doing my best to help the Resistance fight him."

"How is fighting him different from getting revenge?" Jamie's hands squeezed so tightly his knuckles whitened.

How was it different? Was one just as much a rebellion and distrust of God as the other? Some in Acktar seemed to think so. Lord Hector Emilin had died because he'd refused to fight Respen. "The motive is different. Revenge is done out of hatred, but resistance is done to stand up to evil. And the method is different. Revenge takes the fight to Respen while resistance only counters whatever move Respen makes. It's defensive, not offensive."

"So if you're fighting for the Resistance, why haven't you killed him by now?" The lamplight cast shadows across Jamie's face.

"If it were the right thing to do, I would've tried it by now. Lord Alistair doesn't want Respen killed just yet. It'd do more harm than good right now."

Jamie's eyes flashed up before flicking back to his boots. "I guess so."

Leith tensed. A defiant light still shone in Jamie's eyes. If Leith didn't get through to him now, who knew what Jamie might try next.

"My father killed my mother." Leith gripped the edge of the table and hung his head. Would he ever be able to contain the pain of those words? "If he hadn't died that night too, I probably would've killed him."

Jamie gaped at him.

Leith pushed up his right sleeve, revealing the rows of scars on his arm. "When I killed for Respen, I drew on that pent up anger. My father may have killed my mother once, but I killed him in my heart over and over and over again. When you plot to kill Respen, you've already killed him in your mind. You claim you'd never kill for Respen, but that's what would happen eventually if you held on to your anger toward him."

Jamie dragged in a shuddering breath. "So what do I do instead?"

Leith studied the set of Jamie's jaw and shoulders. "You said your parents were Christians, but what do you believe?"

Jamie shrugged. "Not sure. Sometimes I still pray. But a lot of times, I'm just too angry."

If only Leith knew the words to tell Jamie, but odds were that, growing up with Christian parents as he had, Jamie had probably read more of the Bible than Leith had. If Shad were here, he'd know what to tell Jamie. Or Brandi.

A smile twitched Leith's mouth. There was one set of Bible stories he knew very well. "Do you know the stories about Daniel?"

Jamie shrugged. "Of course."

"Daniel was just a boy when he was taken away from his parents. But he didn't get angry at God. He kept praying and trusting." Praying and trusting. How well was Leith doing that? Was he trusting?

Jamie hung his head. "I'm not much like Daniel."

"Courage like Daniel's only comes from God." Leith leaned a hand against the tabletop. "Daniel didn't keep praying and trusting because he had courage. He had courage because he prayed and trusted."

"But what about King Respen? What happens to him?"

The lamp sizzled and huffed. The common room spread too far for the light to reach, casting the corners and under the tables in darkness. Leith studied the shadows but didn't see any sign that Altin had woken. "We wait for justice. God might use the means of the government the Resistance intends to set up or He might wait, but Respen will face justice."

Jamie nodded at that. He probably understood better than Leith did.

"It doesn't mean we're not going to do anything. There's plenty for us to do."

Jamie's forehead furrowed as he nodded. "Some of the other trainees aren't happy either. Some of them would want to leave if I talk to them."

"Good, but be careful." Leith eased to his feet and reached for the lamp. He'd pushed Jamie enough for one night. "Time to head back to your cot."

Jamie bit his lip and rocked back and forth. "Do you think Brandi is all right? I wouldn't want anything to happen to her. I haven't really had a friend before."

Leith patted Jamie's shoulder. "I don't want anything to happen to Renna or Brandi. Don't worry. By the time Respen sends us out again, both of them will be long gone from Acktar."

14

Renna slipped her hairbrush into the saddlebag she'd set on her bed. Only two saddlebags, yet she didn't even have enough to fill them. Just a spare dress, a brush and a few of those kinds of essentials, her jewelry box, and her Bible.

She glanced around the room she'd had for the past couple of weeks. Lavender curtains hung across the window with a matching quilt on the bed. Braided rugs in a darker shade of purple covered most of the wooden floor. Home, and yet, not. Would anything ever feel like home again? Or would she always be living somewhere temporary? Somewhere not hers?

Lydia glided into the room and perched on the edge of the bed. Her long, brown hair brushed the waistline of her leaf-green dress. "Packing?"

Renna nodded. "Are you leaving too?"

Lydia shook her head. "Mother decided that we'd stay behind. There'll be other times to leave, and getting the refugees out is more important. Father wasn't exactly happy, but we're sending Abigail, Esther, and Jeremiah away so they'll be safe."

Renna chewed on her lip. Was she being a coward running to the Resistance hideout? She was the niece of the late King Leon. Her mother had been a princess of Acktar. Should Renna step up and stay behind to rally the remnants of the Resistance?

Jolene poked her head into the room. "Need any help packing?"

Renna held up the saddlebags, then let them plop onto the bed. "All set."

With the scuff of her buckskin divided skirt, Jolene swept into the room and plopped into the plush chair a few feet away from the bed. The arrows in the quiver strapped across her back rattled.

Renna scrubbed her fingers along her skirt. Why couldn't she be more like Jolene? Jolene had a bow and arrows she'd used in defense of Sierra. Renna had a knife she couldn't use strapped to her ankle.

Lydia's slim mouth curved into a smile. "So, that peasant farmer that's been hanging around lately. What's his name? Daniel?"

Renna stilled. "What about him?"

"You looked good together at Brandi's party." Lydia's smile grew to a grin.

Renna flopped onto the bed next to Lydia. "He's..." A Blade, but Renna couldn't say that. "He's a wandering farmer. There's a war coming, and I'm leaving."

"And what does that have to do with it?"

Not a whole lot. Renna blew a strand of hair from her

face. It flopped across her eyes. "I'm not sure he even sees me as anything other than a sister the way he does Brandi. Besides, he left last night, and I don't know when he'll be back. With this war coming, I might never see him again."

"We're cut off from most of Acktar now." Jolene reached over her shoulder and touched the fletching on her arrows.

Lydia's voice lowered. "We don't know what's happening to the western towns."

Western towns, like Arroway where Lord Philip Creston lived. A lord Lydia had been attracted to when he'd visited for her birthday party four weeks ago.

Renna swallowed. Cut off from the towns to the west. Cut off from the towns to the south. Including Stetterly. Uncle Abel. Aunt Mara. Had they arrived at Stetterly safely?

A call came from downstairs. Renna drew in a deep breath and hoisted her saddlebags to her shoulder. Time to leave.

Renna's shoulder ached with the weight of her saddlebag. Beside her, Brandi switched her saddlebag to her other shoulder and shifted from foot to foot.

The tents that had dotted the hills around Walden collapsed as each group packed up their things and moved out. One group headed east to follow the Spires Canyon before turning north. Another headed straight north, another west.

So many people leaving. Still, more poured into Walden each day. More people fleeing Uster and the last stragglers from Duelstone and Keestone. Even a few Christians from

Mountainwood who'd somehow managed to remain hidden for years in a town controlled by a lord loyal to King Respen.

Partway up the hill, Lady Lorraine and Jolene both stood straight, their matching blond hair floating in a slight breeze. Lady Lorraine clasped the hand of an old woman. Jolene hugged a child. At the edge of town, Lord and Lady Alistair did the same thing for the citizens of Walden who were leaving.

Lady Lorraine, Lady Alistair, Jolene, Lydia. They'd all made the choice to stay behind as long as they could to help prepare Walden for the coming battle.

Renna shrugged her aching shoulder. She was doing it again. Letting others make her decisions for her.

Only a few weeks ago, she'd faced First Blade Vane. She'd found a small measure of courage, enough to strike at him when he'd held a knife to her throat. Had she already lost that courage?

What was she supposed to do? Was it her duty to leave or to stay? She squeezed her eyes shut and tried to pray, but the words wouldn't come. Nothing besides the jumble inside her chest.

Lord Alistair strode toward her. "Your group is gathering. It's almost time to go."

Leave or stay? Safety or danger?

She pressed her finger against the buckskin of her divided skirt. It wouldn't be that much danger. If it were, Lord Alistair wouldn't allow Lady Alistair and Lydia to stay.

If Lydia and Jolene had the courage to stay, then surely Renna did too. Right?

Renna straightened her shoulders and let her saddlebag fall to the ground. "I'm not going."

Lord Alistair's eyes searched her face. "It'll be safer if you and your sister leave now."

It would be safer. She should listen to Lord Alistair. Surely he knew best.

But if she did, she'd be doing what she always did. Run. Hide. Let others make her decisions for her. Renna stiffened her spine. "You once asked me to step into the role of Lady Faythe of Stetterly, and my duty as Lady Faythe is to stand beside you and Lady Lorraine to prepare Walden for battle."

Something glinted in Lord Alistair's eyes. He dipped his head toward her. "Very well. You'll stay here until my wife and daughter leave. Brandi—"

Brandi dropped her saddlebag so quickly it thunked on the stone and bounced down the front steps. "If Renna's staying, then I stay too."

Renna wrapped her arm around Brandi's shoulders. "We stay together."

"All right." Lord Alistair turned to head back to the town. "I believe the healer has a few more things to finish up if you want to continue to help there."

Brandi's nose wrinkled. "Isn't there something more interesting to do? Like make arrows or something?"

For the first time that morning, Lord Alistair's eyes twinkled. His mouth managed a small quirk. "Well, we're losing most of our ditch digging crew. Perhaps you'd like to help with that?"

Brandi planted her feet and held out a hand. "All right. Where's a shovel?"

15

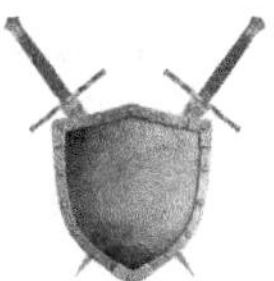

"You are failures." Respen's voice boomed around the dark meeting room.

Leith flinched with the rest of them. While he'd been unable to gain information about Vane, he'd brought information back from Walden.

"You are my Blades. You are better than this. No Blade has ever been able to run from me. No Blade has ever been able to hide." Respen pounded the table. The two candles flickered with the vibrations shooting through the tabletop.

Next to Leith, Martyn swallowed hard and reached toward his hip where his knife normally rested. His eyes shot toward the far wall, where all the Blades' weapons hung on pegs.

"Twelfth Blade Altin."

Altin knelt in front of King Respen. "I aided the First Blade in training the boys. When the First Blade left for Sierra and Walden with the oldest trainee, I continued the training on the rest. All of the boys progressed well."

"Well done, my Twelfth Blade."

Altin's shoulders sagged as he pushed up his right sleeve. Respen leaned forward and slashed a line across Altin's upper arm.

As Altin returned to his seat, Leith struggled to pay attention through the rest of the reports. As First Blade, he'd heard the short version of all of these reports once already. How did Respen manage to remain so alert while hearing these reports for the second time?

Leith clenched his fists below the table. Another way Respen kept his Blades in check. A Blade might be able to lie once, but to lie twice—once to the First Blade and once to Respen's face—increased the chances the lie would be noticed. Or, in Leith's case, he had to lie to Respen's face twice.

"First Blade Torren." Respen's voice shuddered through the shadows.

Leith stood. He only had to take a single step and kneel now that he sat in the first seat on the king's right. He thumped his right hand over his heart and met Respen's eyes. "I trained the boys for two weeks before I was sent to Sierra to aid in the attack. I sneaked into Sierra Manor, but they were already roused. After the attack on Sierra, I rode to Walden. While there, I was able to learn that the Resistence hideout in the Sheered Rock Hills is called Eagle Heights and that Harrison Vane is most likely hiding there."

"You have executed your orders, but not as successfully as I know you can." Respen's dark eyes stabbed into Leith. "Still, you have done enough to earn a success."

Leith suppressed his sigh of relief as he rolled up his right sleeve. His thirty-seventh successful mark. He didn't wince as the sharp edge sliced into his skin, drawing a line of blood. After so many years and so many marks, the feel of the king's knife on his skin was more familiar than his mother's touch.

Respen leaned closer until his breath hissed across Leith's face. "Twice my First Blade has failed to kill the ladies Rennelda and Brandiline. Do not fail me this time, my First Blade."

Leith had expected Respen would eventually order him to kill Renna and Brandi, but he hadn't realized it'd be this soon. At least they'd be long gone from Walden by the time he arrived. "Of course, my king."

Respen leaned back in his chair. His fingers drummed against the armrest while his dark eyes contemplated Leith. "After you kill them, I want you to stay in Walden. Vane seems to have developed a particular fascination with those girls. Their deaths will spur him out of his hole and into our trap. Take the boy along. It will be a good lesson for him."

"Yes, my king." Leith saluted and stood when Respen waved his dismissal.

"The rest of you, your orders are same as before." Respen stood. "The next meeting will be held four weeks from today." He swept from the room, the door banging against the stone behind him.

As the Blades shoved to their feet, Leith turned to Martyn. "You look beat."

"Been riding through the Sheered Rock Hills for a month. You're lucky I took a dip in a creek a few days ago or I'd smell as bad as I look. I collapsed into bed when I got in without bothering to clean up or shave." Martyn rubbed a hand over the scruff on his face. "Rough country up there.

Had a run in with a mountain lion." He pulled up his shirt and showed Leith the healing wounds on his back.

Leith winced. His friend had been hurt trying to find a man who was no longer alive. If only Leith could end this useless hunt without giving himself away. "Wish I could say rest up and get a hot meal, but looks like you've been assigned the same patrol."

Martyn dragged his fingers through his hair. "Where do you want us positioned?"

Leith closed his fingers around the space where one of his knives' hilts normally rested. Where should he position the other Blades that'd be the most convenient for the Resistance without being suspicious?

"Stick towards the west and prepare to swing to the east to cut Vane off once he enters Walden. Stay well clear of Walden. We don't want him to catch sight of you if he does make the journey from Eagle Heights to Walden. I'll let you know once I've killed the girls."

"Right." Martyn slapped him on the back. "Good luck. You're going to need it. I'm beginning to think those girls must hold a curse or something to have survived this long."

Leith nodded. When Martyn strode across the room to gather his weapons, Leith shook his head. "Not a curse. A blessing."

16

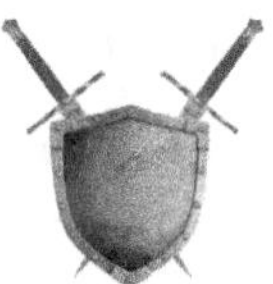

As the sun stretched its arms into the sky, Leith and Jamie led their horses to the hilltop overlooking Walden Manor.

Even in the few days they'd been gone, the trench around the manor had deepened until it almost could be called a ditch. Any deeper and they'd need a bridge to get their horses across.

In the town, houses and shops were being disassembled board by board so the timber and beams could be used to construct defensive walls around the manor.

Since Leith and Jamie were dressed in their homespun clothes, the guards circling the manor paid them no mind besides asking a few basic questions. Leith headed straight to the study while Jamie took care of their horses.

When the guard at the door announced him as Daniel and pushed the door open, Lord Alistair and Shad looked up. Both of them stood in front of the map hung on the wall behind Lord Alistair's desk. Tacks had been pushed into the wood, and Shad's hand hovered over Uster as if about to push in another tack.

Shad grinned. "Welcome back."

Leith checked that the door was closed. "Respen ordered me to kill Renna and Brandi."

Shad crossed his arms. "Not unexpected."

"No. Respen hopes to use this to lure Vane out of hiding. It'll be hard to explain if Vane doesn't make an appearance. I think it's a test." Leith placed a hand on one of his knives. "Respen's already suspicious of me. He's testing if I'll carry out this order or not. But it doesn't matter. Renna and Brandi are long gone."

Lord Alistair frowned. Shad rubbed his sword's hilt. "Actually, Renna and Brandi decided to remain here."

"What?" Leith's muscles froze. What was he going to do now? He couldn't carry out his orders, and now he didn't have an excuse for failing.

His heart lurched. He'd be able to see Renna one more time.

"This could be the time to pull you out." Lord Alistair sank onto his leather chair. "You've done much for us already."

Leave Nalgar Castle forever. He could be free of orders and marks and spilled blood. He'd be able to attend church each Sunday instead of Respen's twisted Meeting of the Blades. He could go to Eagle Heights with Renna and Brandi and spend time with both of them. Leith closed his eyes. Was it possible for a dream to hurt this much?

Of course it hurt when he couldn't claim it.

Leith opened his eyes. "Any information I can give you

will be useful. At the very least, I can use my position as First Blade to keep the rest of the Blades away from Walden."

"So what are we going to do?" Shad rested his hand on the hilt of his sword.

Leith shrugged. "Not sure."

Lord Alistair tapped his beard. "Respen hopes to lure Vane out of hiding?"

"Yes." He'd told Lord Alistair that information once already.

"And he plans to attack Walden sooner or later." Lord Alistair leaned his elbows on his desk. "Are the Blades back with the army?"

"Yes, the Blades left when I did. Three to the northern division, and two to both the southern and western divisions like before. The other three are waiting in the Sheered Rock Hills northwest of Walden to cut off Vane if he should show up, or at least, that's what I led them to believe."

Lord Alistair's eyes gleamed as a smile crept across his face. "So, we fake Renna and Brandi's deaths and make Harrison Vane reappear."

"Reappear?" What insane plan did Lord Alistair have growing this time?

"The best way to fool Respen is to give him exactly what he expects. Respen gets what he wants: Renna and Brandi's deaths and Vane's reappearance. We get what we want: Renna and Brandi out of Walden before the army's attack and the other Blades distracted."

Shad nodded and scratched his chin. "I see." He glanced at Leith. "It might work."

"What will work? How do we make Vane reappear?"

Leith wasn't sure he'd like the answer. He'd be just fine with leaving the man dead and buried.

"In about a week and a half, after we've given enough time for Vane to have supposedly heard of the deaths and returned to Walden, you'll impersonate Vane and train our soldiers. Respen will hear the rumors and believe Renna and Brandi are dead and Vane has returned long before you ever report to him." Lord Alistair's smile bloomed into a grin.

Shad eyed Leith. "We won't tell our soldiers Leith's name. Only that he's a Blade. Maybe have him wear a hood or something. Give him an air of mystery. There's nothing like a secret to get everyone talking."

Leith could see one major flaw with their plan. "The Blades waiting in the Hills to trap Vane will come here to try to help me catch him."

"You'll have to be both Harrison Vane and Leith Torren." Lord Alistair waved the objection away.

Leith frowned. If they went with this plan, then at least two of the three names he wore were trying to kill each other. He wasn't sure how many more people he could handle being. He was Leith Torren, First Blade of King Respen, and Daniel, the itinerant peasant farmer. Now he was also going to be Harrison Vane, former First Blade and spy for the Resistance.

Except that Leith Torren was the spy, Vane was dead, and Daniel didn't exist.

Lord Alistair continued as if he hadn't noticed his discomfort. "You'll only train the men during the middle of the day when no one can sneak too close to the manor, and you'll be surrounded by our men. After you're done working with them, Vane will disappear until the next day."

Leith spun on his heels and paced across the room. If he pressed onward with this, he'd have to deny the disquiet in his heart. More cold. More masks. More lies.

But if he refused to train Walden's men, how many of them would die because they lacked proper training? How many would fall to a Blade's knife because Leith had refused to give them his help? In a few weeks, an army would descend on Walden along with five Blades.

He hung his head. The choice wasn't much of a choice at all. When it came down to it, he'd rather have more lies than more deaths on his conscience. He turned back to Shad and Lord Alistair. "All right. So how do you propose we fake Renna and Brandi's deaths?"

Lord Alistair steepled his fingers. "If we want rumors to reach Respen, we won't be able to tell our guards what is happening. We can't have anyone slipping and accidentally telling the truth."

"That will make things tricky." Leith paced away from the desk, running the positions of the guards and the available cover through his mind. "Thanks to your tightened security, I think I can slip from the manor to the line of trees outside the garden without being seen, but I won't be able to get any farther, especially not with Renna and Brandi with me. And if you make any sudden changes to the guard rotation to provide me with a gap, someone will notice, and that's just the sort of speculation we want to avoid."

Shad rested his hand on the hilt of his sword and joined Leith in pacing. "What if we sneaked you out in disguise during the daylight? Dressed as workers getting more wood from the Hills or something? We could splash blood around their rooms to make it look like they'd been killed, but you'd already be past the guards."

Leith shook his head. "That's an option, but I'm not sure it'd work. A little blood scattered around isn't going to convince everyone, and a party of workers mysteriously disappearing into the Hills might be noticed. And, while I gave orders for the Blades to stay well to the west and away from Walden, I can't guarantee that all of them followed my orders. If a Blade decided to circle south and check on Walden, he'd be expecting to see me with dead bodies."

"So what do you suggest?" Lord Alistair tapped his chin with the tips of his steepled fingers.

Leith planted his feet and faced Lord Alistair. "We don't sneak them out at all. We sling their dead bodies across my saddle, and I ride boldly out of here."

Both Shad and Lord Alistair shook their heads. Shad crossed his arms. "It'll never work. Our guards would attack you."

"I don't think they will." Leith hurried on as Shad's jaw tightened. "Shooting at a First Blade at a distance is one thing. Facing him on equal ground is another. Especially with the shock of seeing Renna and Brandi dead."

Shad's arms remained crossed, a scowl darkening his face. Of course Shad stood by his men. A commander's loyalty demanded nothing less.

But Lord Alistair's frown had relaxed into a line between his eyes. "It's possible they'll hesitate. They hesitated a few weeks ago when facing Vane. But, what if Shad is right and they attack?"

Leith shrugged. "If I'm right and they hesitate, this plan'll work. Any watching Blades will see exactly what they expect to see, and it'll give an excuse for why you suddenly decide to have Vane train your guards, who will be more inclined to listen if they know they've failed once. But, if Shad is right and they do attack me, I'll simply surrender. They'll take me to you, and we'll come up with another plan."

The silence stretched. Finally, Lord Alistair nodded. "All right."

As they gathered around the desk to hash out the details, Leith couldn't banish the weight in his stomach. For all his confidence, he couldn't be sure Walden's guards would react as he expected. Nothing prevented one of them from putting an arrow in his back. For the past weeks, Lord Alistair and Shad had trained their guards to fight Blades with information he'd provided.

But if this plan worked, then it'd prove that training hadn't been enough. And if Walden's guards couldn't fight Blades, then none of the towns stood a chance.

17

Renna shoved her shovel into the mound of dirt and straightened. Every bone in her back cracked with pain.

Beside her, Brandi stabbed her shovel into the ground and levered another clod of dirt onto the mound. Why had she ever let Brandi convince her to take a break from inside work to join the digging crew?

All along a wide circle around Walden Manor, other people, both men and women, also wielded shovels and picks. The deeper the ditch, the higher the mound and the better protection the defenders of Walden would have.

Axes thunked as men hacked sharp points onto the ends of logs. Others dug holes and dropped the logs into them with the points set at an angle facing outward from Walden Manor. On Walden's front step, a group of archers, including Jolene and Lady Lorraine, crafted arrow after arrow.

Lydia dropped into the ditch next to them. Her hands

sported red blisters. "Father asked that you join him in his study."

"All right." Renna dropped her shovel and scrabbled over the mound of dirt. Brandi scowled at her and heaved another shovelful from the ground.

Renna stopped at the pump outside the kitchen to wash her hands and scrape some of the dirt from her boots before she tromped into the manor. Not that it mattered. All the rugs had been rolled up and stored away. She followed the path of dirty bootprints down the hallway and into Lord Alistair's study.

Lord Alistair perched behind his desk while Shadrach leaned against the book cases next to him. But Renna's gaze snagged on the third person leaning against the bookcases a few feet away from Shadrach. "Leith."

His mouth quirked, but he didn't say anything. Something in his gaze tightened her stomach. What was wrong?

"Have a seat, Renna." Lord Alistair pointed at the seats in front of his desk.

She slipped into the nearest one. "You wanted to speak with me?"

Lord Alistair's gaze softened. He rested his elbows on the desktop. "I know you were determined to stay here as long as possible, but circumstances have changed. I'm afraid you and Brandi are going to have to leave."

"We're leaving?" Renna stared across the desk at Lord Alistair. She'd finally gotten up the courage to take on her duty as Lady Faythe. Now she'd have to leave anyway. "Why?"

Leith's dark hair swished across his forehead. "Respen has given me orders to kill you and Brandi. We have to make you disappear once and for all, otherwise he'll keep sending Blades after you until one of them succeeds."

Clasping her hands tighter, Renna nodded. Each failure to kill them only increased Respen's determination to see them eliminated. "When do we leave?"

Lord Alistair sighed. "Tomorrow morning at dawn."

She sagged in the chair. Was it wrong to be relieved that she wouldn't have to keep being courageous? She glanced at Leith but found she couldn't meet his gaze. "You won't be coming with us, will you?"

He shook his head. "No. After we stage your deaths, Shad and I will take you partway into the Hills. Someone from the Resistance will take you and Brandi the rest of the way."

"And you'll be returning to Nalgar Castle to make sure he believes we're dead." Renna's heart clenched. Each time he returned, it increased his chances of being discovered.

His mouth tightened into a line. "I've been ordered to stick around here after I kill you. But I'll be returning to the castle after a month."

She swallowed hard. "I'm sorry I caused all this hassle. If I'd gone with the refugees like I was supposed to, I wouldn't have caused all this trouble."

Lord Alistair waved his hand. "We've come up with a workable solution that fits with our plans."

Shadrach straightened. "I'll see to the horses you'll be taking. If you and Brandi can pack your things, I'll be taking them to a spot in the foothills tonight."

Renna nodded. As Shadrach left, she pushed herself onto shaky legs. "I should go tell Brandi." She stumbled from the room.

Once outside the door, she pressed her back against the

stone to stay on her feet. She'd tried to do the right thing. And it had gone wrong. She should've listened to Lord Alistair and left. But no, she had to go and try to be Lady Faythe.

What a poor excuse for a lady she turned out to be.

The door to the study opened and closed. "Are you going to be all right?" Leith's voice eased around her as gently as falling snow.

"No." The word croaked out of her throat.

He took a step closer, his eyebrows tilted. The sight took the rest of the starch out of her knees. As she wobbled, he put an arm around her, so solid and strong she leaned her head against his shoulder. "I tried to do my duty, to be Lady Faythe, but all I did was cause a mess. I even tried to pray about it, and I thought it was the right thing, but I must've thought wrong."

Leith held still as the cliffs above Walden Manor. "Respen used to tell me that duty was obeying his orders. But my true duty is to obey God, to deny myself to help others the best I can in the position God has placed me."

She'd done that, right? "Then why is it so tangled up?"

"When we're so tangled, it's hard to see God's direction. Perhaps we can't see it or He doesn't give it. I don't know."

She should know. She'd grown up with a minister for an uncle. She should have all the answers.

But she was so tired. If she could have a month or even a day without being hunted, perhaps she'd have the time to get it all straight in her head.

18

"Renna, wake up." Brandi's voice pierced into Renna's brain.

She forced her eyes open, wincing as her eyelids scratched her eyes. Shafts of light blurred through her eyelashes. "Is it time to get up already?"

"Yep." Brandi bounced back, her white nightdress swirling around her bare ankles and feet. The light from the lamp in her hand jittered across the wall.

Groaning, Renna threw back the covers. She already wore her shift and underthings underneath her nightdress. She resisted the urge to tuck in the strands of hair that had frizzed out of her braid while she'd slept. She had to look like she'd been dragged out of bed. Correction. Her dead body had to look like it had been killed in bed.

Someone knocked on the door. Brandi waltzed over and flung it open. Leith stuck his head in. "Are you ready?"

Renna nodded, staring down at herself. Her face heated as she wrapped her arms around her stomach. Her thick nightgown and all her underthings beneath provided more than enough modesty. Still, Leith was seeing her in her nightgown. A downright embarrassing situation. But for this to work, every detail had to be taken into consideration.

Leith stepped into the room, holding an animal skin bag. Undoing the cap, he poured a puddle of thick, red liquid onto the mattress. He flung a few drops onto the wall and dribbled some onto the floor.

The musty scent of blood filled the room. Renna grimaced. The appearance of a murder was necessary, but they were leaving a mess for the servants to clean.

Leith stepped back and eyed his handiwork. She tightened her grip around her stomach and turned away. He knew how a murder should look. How the blood should spray and pool if he'd slit her throat. Was he bothered now as he used that knowledge to fake the blood pattern across her bed? She couldn't tell. His face set in a cold, hard expression.

The face of a Blade. A First Blade.

Recapping the animal skin, Leith turned to them. His gaze met hers. Bowing his head, he closed his eyes and took a deep breath. Renna clenched her fists. Her face must be contorted in a horrified expression.

She shouldn't picture him as a killer. Saved by Christ, Leith wasn't that man anymore. This was a mask.

A mask he wore too easily.

"Take these." Leith handed her and Brandi dark blankets. "I'll tell you when to put them on."

Renna hugged hers. This night couldn't end fast enough.

Leith led the way from her room. Occasionally he'd flick

drops of blood on the floor. Renna winced. Blood soaked into wood, nearly impossible to scrub out.

How many hours had it taken Aunt Mara to clean the blood left behind after her parents' murders? By the time Uncle Abel had deemed it safe for the girls to return from their hideout in the Spires Canyon, Stetterly Manor had been spotless. No sign of the events of that night remained. Only the loss.

Tiptoeing down the stairs, Leith held the door to Lord Alistair's study open for them. Brandi skipped inside. Renna followed closely behind. If only she had even an ounce of Brandi's enthusiasm.

A crowd waited for them in the study. Lady Alistair, Lady Lorraine, and Jolene sat in the three chairs while Lord Alistair leaned his hands on the back of Lady Alistair's seat. Lydia perched on a corner of Lord Alistair's desk, her skirts draped neatly.

Leith stood to the side in the shadows, his face tilted down. Lydia, Jolene, and Lady Alistair glanced at him, but their gazes quickly switched back to Renna and Brandi.

Renna swallowed. They'd said their goodbyes after dinner, but apparently everyone needed another round. If only Uncle Abel and Aunt Mara were there to give her a hug. Better yet, come with them to Eagle Heights.

She shook her head. Stetterly needed her aunt and uncle. The people of that town couldn't afford to lose their minister and healer too. After tonight, they might believe she and Brandi were dead. Lord Alistair would try to send a message to reassure Uncle Abel and Aunt Mara, but two divisions of Respen's army stood between them and Stetterly.

Lady Alistair stood and turned to Renna. "I'll be praying for you."

Renna gave Lady Alistair a smile, unable to speak past the clump of tears in her throat. She swallowed. She wasn't going to cry tonight. Surely God had a plan in this sudden departure as well.

Lydia hugged Renna. "It won't be long before we'll join you."

Jolene stepped in for a hug as soon as Lydia backed away. The arrows in her quiver rustled. "We'll miss you until then."

Lord Alistair spoke quietly with Leith, most likely going over a few last minute details. Leith nodded, and Lord Alistair clapped him on the shoulder.

Renna tiptoed closer and glanced at Lord Alistair. "Thank you for taking us in for the past few months. And all the trouble you're going through to keep us safe."

Lord Alistair smiled, though lines remained trenched around his eyes and mouth. "It's been my pleasure to protect you as much as I'm able."

After a last round of goodbyes, Leith led them to the alcove at the back of the room. He closed the curtains behind them. "Wrap the blankets around your shoulders. It'll hide your white nightdresses."

Renna flung the blanket around herself and gripped the corners. The warm wool settled around her shoulders. Brandi wrapped herself in her blanket, grinning.

Leith cracked the window open and peeked out. Climbing out, he hunched below the window in the shadows.

After a moment, he popped up and waved at Brandi. She knelt on the windowseat. Gripping her around the waist,

Leith swung her out of the window and onto the ground. He placed a hand on her back and pressed her into the shadows. Renna spotted a guard walking the perimeter of the garden.

When the guard had moved past their position, Leith eased to his feet once again. Renna knelt on the windowseat. Leith's strong hands closed around her waist. Her breath caught. She held her breath as Leith swung her out of the window. As her feet landed on the ground, she crouched in the shadows next to Brandi.

After the next guard had passed, Leith led them around the flower beds and past the decorative fountain. They crept along the thick hedge.

Renna's heart remained in her throat as she padded barefoot behind Leith and Brandi. What would happen if a guard discovered them?

Reaching the back hedgerow, Leith halted them. He peered through a gap in the hedge. When the guard had passed them and neared the far corner, Leith motioned Brandi through. Brandi eased through the hedge, dashed across the cleared space, and disappeared in the darkness of the trees beyond.

Renna waited next to Leith. She held her breath as a guard rounded the corner and started towards them. Leith placed a hand on her back. She tensed, struggling to stay still, until the guard passed a few feet away from them on the other side of the hedge.

When he was fifty yards away, Leith motioned for her to slip through. Renna shoved her way into the tangle. Twigs scratched her face and tugged at her braid. Sticks jabbed her bare feet. Breaking through the hedge, she nearly fell onto her knees. Had the guard heard all her noise? Staggering, she flung herself across the open grass and into the trees.

Brandi popped out of the darkness. She grabbed Renna's arm and steered her behind a large tree. "You'd make a lousy Blade. Even I managed to be quieter than that."

No argument there. Renna crouched next to her sister, shivering. Cold laced through her fingers. Her feet stung with the dew she'd picked up in her dash through the long grass.

A dark shape joined them. Renna stifled her shriek. It was only Leith. He led them through the trees and into a dense stand of scrub brush. In the darkness, the trees screened them from the guards.

Jamie stood waiting with two horses, a small buckskin and Blizzard. Brandi tromped to them and rubbed each horse's neck in turn.

Renna gripped the wool blanket and tugged it tighter around her shoulders. "What happens now?"

Leith glanced toward the east, and Renna followed his gaze. A faint tinge of gray spread into the sky in that direction. He touched the animal skin tied to his belt. "Now we bluff our way past the guards."

19

Leith pulled out the animal skin bottle filled with goat blood and grimaced. They weren't going to like the next step. "If people look too closely, the two of you don't look dead. We need to make you so bloody no one will notice."

Renna's face paled to the same color as her nightdress. Brandi eyed the animal skin bag. Leith wasn't about to tell them that even with the goat blood he was going to pour over them, it'd be less blood than would've spurted from their wounds if he'd really killed them.

Leith approached Brandi. "Hold still."

Brandi squinched her face up. Leith gripped her chin and tipped it up. Starting under her chin, he poured a stream of the blood from the animal skin. The blood ran down her neck and rippled onto her white nightdress.

Leith took the blanket from Brandi's shoulders. "Put your arms down by your side."

Brandi pressed her hands to her sides and stood straight

like a guard lined up for drill. Leith wrapped the blanket around her. To anyone watching, it'd look like Leith had bundled Brandi's body in a blanket to make it easier to carry out of the manor.

Jamie swung onto his horse and nudged it next to Leith and Brandi. Picking Brandi up, Leith placed her across Jamie's knees with her head and feet hanging down.

Brandi giggled as she tried to squirm into a better position. "This feels funny."

Leith knelt next to Brandi's head. "Sorry. It's going to get worse. Take a breath and close your eyes."

Brandi squeezed her eyes shut. Her cheeks puffed as she held her breath. Leith pinched her nose and poured the blood under her chin. It flowed over her face and into her hair. Her body convulsed in suppressed giggles.

Taking his hand from her nose, he stood up and stepped back. "Try to pretend you're dead."

Brandi's mouth twisted with a smirk. Leith grinned back even though she couldn't see him. He met Jamie's eyes. Jamie placed a hand on Brandi's back. His mouth flattened into a firm line.

Leith turned to Renna. She clutched the blanket tighter, her eyes fixed on Brandi. She trembled. "It looks so real. She looks dead."

He couldn't let her panic now. Stepping into her line of sight, he gripped Renna's shoulders. "She's a rather lively, giggling corpse."

Renna drew in a breath and nodded. Her gaze strayed past him and her shoulders relaxed. She pointed. "You're right. I don't think most corpses do that."

He glanced over his shoulder in time to catch Brandi

sticking out her tongue. Leith shook his head. Brandi would regret that when she got blood all over her tongue. She wouldn't be able to rinse her mouth until they were safely away from Walden.

Leith turned back to Renna and held up the animal skin. "Your turn."

Renna wrinkled her nose, but she held still. Tipping up her chin, he poured a stream of blood down her neck. It spread over her white nightdress, stark in the dawn's growing light.

Leith swallowed a rush of memories. A moonlit room. The look of terror in a teenage boy's eyes. His choking death.

"Is everything all right?" Renna's voice tugged him from his memories.

He drew the cold wall around the memories. He wasn't about to tell Renna he'd been thinking about the night he'd killed her cousin. "I'm fine."

Somewhere in the trees, the first bird twittered the world into wakefulness. The goat's blood worked its way down the front of Renna's nightdress. If God hadn't touched his heart, it could've been Renna's blood Leith spilled.

He shook himself. He didn't have time to waste on the lives he'd taken. Right now he needed to concentrate on the lives he could save.

Taking the blanket from her, he wrapped it around her while she held her hands down at her sides. He picked her up. Huffing, he slung her as gently as possible over the front of his saddle. She made a sound in the back of her throat and squirmed. Leith walked around Blizzard and knelt next to her head. "Sorry. That can't be comfortable."

Renna grimaced, a strange expression with her head

hanging upside down. "If I were dead, I wouldn't care, would I?"

"Nor would you care about this either." Leith uncapped the animal skin. "Take a deep breath and close your eyes."

Like Brandi, Renna scrunched her eyes closed and sucked in a breath. Leith pinched her nose and poured the blood over her chin and face. The dark red, almost black liquid gurgled from the skin bottle and globbed over her cheeks and into her hair.

Renna's throat constricted, like she was fighting the reflex to gag. At the edges of the layer of blood, her skin took on a gray-green cast.

Leith's own stomach churned, but he shoved the sensation away. Now was not the time to develop a revulsion to blood.

When the blood had stopped running, Leith let go of her nose and stood. He scowled at the blood, both dried and wet, that coated his hands. But he resisted the urge to wash them. The blood would convince his audience he was the cold-blooded killer he portrayed.

Swinging into the saddle, he adjusted Renna across his knees. He tried to touch her as little as possible, but there just didn't seem any way that wasn't awkward. She squirmed like a hooked worm.

When she was finally settled across his saddle and knees, he pulled a black cloak from his saddlebag. Clasping it beneath his chin, he flipped the hood over his head so the cloth covered his eyes and half his face. Turning his head, he spotted Jamie doing the same with his own cloak.

They were as ready as they could be. Too much later, and

the sunlight on Blizzard's fur would turn him a recognizable gray instead of black.

Leith nudged Blizzard and swung his head towards the pink and purple bands stretching across the eastern horizon. Jamie's horse fell into step behind him.

Renna's body was warm and soft against his thighs and knees. He yanked his mind away from its wandering. He needed to concentrate. He was a Blade. Renna was a dead body draped over his saddle. Nothing more.

They broke out of the treeline a few yards away from the mound and ditch that circled Walden Manor. A gap had been left in the mound of dirt for workers to easily go in and out.

Two guards strode in opposite directions on either side of the ditch. Both of them froze and raised their weapons.

Leith kept Blizzard walking forward and flipped the corners of his cloak over his shoulder so his knives were clearly visible.

The guards' eyes widened and flicked between Leith, his knives, Jamie, and the bodies slung across the front of their saddles. Leith eased Blizzard to the side to make sure both guards could see Renna's bloodstained face and long, blond braid. Stricken lines tore across the guards' faces.

Leith had to deny any emotion besides cold. He pitched his voice into a low growl. "I am the First Blade. The ladies Rennelda and Brandiline are dead."

One of the guards stepped forward. His face twisted, as if Leith had yanked the man's heart from his chest. Perhaps he had. Renna and Brandi were the heart of Acktar. As long as they lived, there was hope that King Respen's reign would end.

The guard's sword wavered between raised in attack and lowered in defeat. The other guard had already lowered the tip of his sword to the ground. With a glance at his companion, the first guard lowered his sword as well, his shoulders slumping. "Please, at least leave us the bodies."

Blizzard shifted. Across Leith's knees, Renna stiffened and whimpered. He risked a glance down. Blizzard had stepped on the end of her braid. Squeezing with his knees, Leith managed to get Blizzard to step forward again.

"And have you turn their graves into a memorial?" Leith's scornful tone was so cold he gave himself shivers. "They'll be buried deep in the Hills where you'll never find them. Don't try to follow us. If you do, I won't give them even that much courtesy."

They'd talked long enough. Any longer, and the next set of guards would step into sight. Leith pressed his left hand against Renna's back, flicked the reins, and dug his heels into Blizzard's sides. His horse lunged into a gallop. Gathering his powerful hindquarters, Blizzard leapt the ditch. Leith ducked his head to keep the hood in place.

Renna flopped against the saddle. Leith felt more than heard her gasp. He kept an eye on her braid. If Blizzard stepped on her braid at this speed, it wouldn't be good.

Another set of hoofbeats pounded behind them. Leith glanced over his shoulder as Jamie on his buckskin sailed over the ditch. Brandi bounced. Her head bopped against the buckskin's leg.

When they crested the hill overlooking Walden, Leith halted Blizzard, grabbed Renna's braid, and tucked it under the blanket. Then he urged Blizzard into a steady lope. He and Jamie needed to gain distance from Walden.

Leith kept to his easterly course for a mile before he angled north. By the time they reached the foothills, Renna's stomach pressed against his knees every time she panted a breath.

Blizzard lunged up a grassy slope. Leith slowed him to a canter, then a trot as they wound around outcroppings of rock and stands of pines and cedars.

At a sheltered warren of rocks, Leith halted Blizzard. The horse's nostrils flared, but his sides weren't heaving even after the exertion of loping the distance with the weight of two riders on his back.

As Jamie halted a few yards away, Leith swung from the saddle. He rested a hand on Renna's back. "Stay dead for a while longer. I'm going to scout for other Blades. Jamie, keep watch in case we were followed."

Leith slipped from the rocks and climbed up a promontory. Lying on his stomach, he studied the land spread before him. To the southwest, the hills fell away into the rolling prairie only broken by the buildings of Walden. A cluster of black dots rode towards the Hills, though they veered towards the east.

From here, Leith didn't see any signs of a campfire or other shapes moving amongst the Hills. Still, he hiked a wide circle down and around until he was sure the area remained clear of Blades.

He returned to the cluster of boulders. The horses remained nearly as he'd left them, Brandi and Renna draped across the saddles, the reins trailing on the ground. Both had their heads raised, ears pricked towards him. With a snort, Blizzard returned to cropping at the sprigs of grass and weeds that grew in the boulder's damp shadows.

Jamie slid down a boulder and landed on his feet a few yards away. "The guards from Walden are still looking in the wrong direction."

"Good. No Blades around either." Leith strode towards Blizzard. "You help Brandi. I got Renna. They'll be dizzy after hanging upside down for so long."

Reaching Blizzard and Renna, he tapped Renna's shoulder. "I'm going to help you slide off."

She nodded the best she could. Her braid came loose from the blanket again, and its end flopped onto the ground.

Leith straightened and frowned. He didn't have a lot of options that weren't awkward. At this point, neither of them had a choice. She couldn't ride the whole day draped across his saddle.

He gripped her around the waist. Her arms, still held to her sides by the blanket, tensed beneath his fingers. He lifted and pulled her towards him, curling her body to swing her head upright. As he took a step back, her legs and feet slid up and over the saddle. She fell against him, her legs buckling.

She formed a warm, blanket-wrapped bundle in his arms, and he found he wasn't in any hurry to let her go. He could come to enjoy this. Who was he kidding? He enjoyed holding her now.

What if he didn't return to Walden? If he continued on to Eagle Heights with Renna and Brandi? Would he dare court Renna as Shad had suggested? Would he have more moments like this?

He drew in a deep breath and choked on the musty, sour stench of blood coating Renna's hair. Here she was covered in blood, unable to see or open her mouth, dizzy, and he was taking advantage of it. She was probably wondering why he stood there with his arms around her far, far longer than necessary.

He took a step back but kept a grip on her shoulders as she swayed. The blanket came loose, and Renna tugged her hands free. He guided her hands to the saddlehorn. "Hold on for a moment while I fetch water to clean the blood from your face."

She nodded, wrapped her fingers around the saddle-horn, and rested her head against the saddle. Blizzard planted his hooves and leaned in her direction to compensate for her weight against him.

Leith pulled his canteen and a cloth from his pack. Wetting the cloth, he scrubbed her face as gently as he could.

"Eww! That's so disgusting." Brandi's voice sputtered somewhere behind him. "Blood tastes awful. Ow! My side hurts. Your saddlehorn dug into my ribs the whole way."

Something tight eased in Leith's chest like the release of a breath he hadn't realized he'd been holding. Their limp, silent bodies had nearly been enough to play tricks with his mind.

Renna scrunched her face and pried her mouth open. She patted the air, her eyes still caked shut. "Let me."

He poured water on the cloth again and handed it to her. She scraped the dried blood from her eyelids until she could peel them open.

"Here, try this." Leith poured half the canteen over her head.

She scrubbed at her face until only a few brown flakes peppered her nose and crusted in the lines around her eyes.

Blood still matted her hair and coated the front of her nightdress.

Leith took the bloody cloth from her. "I'm sorry. That's the best we can do for now."

Renna's nose wrinkled as she picked at the blood in her hair. "Thanks. At least I can see."

"And talk." Brandi's tone left no doubt that she considered that the worst torture of all.

Renna laughed, grimaced, and pressed a hand to her side. "That was the most uncomfortable ride ever. We'll be sitting upright for the rest of the way, won't we?"

"Yes." A risk, but the girls couldn't ride the whole distance slung over the saddle like that. As long as they stuck to the east and the Blades stayed to the west as Leith had ordered, they'd be fine. Leith waved at the saddlebags tied behind his saddle. Her saddlebags, not his. "You and Brandi can change behind those rocks over there. Try to be quick. We need to keep moving."

He folded the blanket that had wrapped around Renna while she fished in a saddlebag and hurried toward the rocks.

After adjusting the saddlebags and placing the folded blanket across the space he'd made behind his saddle, he drew one of his knives and chopped a small hole into the ground. Jamie collected several good-sized rocks and set them next to the hole.

"All right. We're set."

Leith turned around. Renna now wore a light blue shirt and what looked like wide, buckskin trousers. She held out a bundle of white cloth and red-brown blood. "What do you want us to do with these?"

"We're burying them." Leith pointed at the hole he'd dug. Renna dropped her and Brandi's nightdresses into it, and Leith shoved the dirt and sod over them with his foot. He piled the rocks Jamie had fetched to prevent animals from digging them up.

Brandi bounded to Jamie's horse and swung herself into the saddle. "Are we in a hurry, or not?"

Leith knelt by Blizzard and laced his fingers together. When Renna placed her boot into his hands, he boosted her into the saddle. She scooted back until she sat on the folded blanket. Leith reached for the saddlehorn and placed his foot in the stirrup. As he swung on, he had to crimp his right leg to avoid kicking Renna as he swung it over the saddle.

As he found the stirrup with his right foot, Renna wormed her arms around his waist. He caught his breath. Her body pressed against his back.

He gave himself a severe shake. Friends. Just friends.

Blizzard shifted, and Renna's arms tightened into a strangling squeeze. He patted her hands. "I won't let you fall."

He glanced at Brandi and Jamie. Brandi hung onto Jamie with one hand and waved at Leith with the other.

Jamie's eyes were wide, his shoulders moving in tiny shudders as if he were afraid to breathe.

Breathless and girl-shocked. Leith could relate.

20

Renna held her breath as Blizzard set out at a walk. Sitting nearly on the horse's rump as she was, each stride tipped her one way, then the other.

She tightened her grip around Leith's waist. The hilts of the knives strapped to his belt dug into the insides of her arms. She wrapped her fingers around the leather straps crossing his chest, though the straps across his back scratched against her face.

Still, this was an improvement from earlier. At least her stomach and ribs no longer bashed against the saddle.

"Stay as quiet as you can." Leith's voice rumbled in his chest.

She peeked over his shoulder. He held Blizzard's reins loosely, mostly letting the horse choose their path along the sloping side of a mountain. Leith sat straight in the saddle, his left hand resting on his thigh. She would've thought the posture casual except for the feel of his muscles tensing in time with Blizzard's strides.

Closing her eyes, she leaned her forehead against Leith's back. Her father had ridden like that. Comfortable in the saddle. On their trips to visit Walden, she'd ask to ride double with him so she could relax in his steady, safe guidance of his horse.

Would her father have liked Leith? Considering Leith had played a role in his death, probably not. But without that?

She sighed and clung to Leith as Blizzard lunged up a steep section. It didn't matter. Her father wasn't here, and Leith probably didn't see her as anything other than a friend. Was she even that? Maybe he only saw her as a burden.

Had he noticed how she'd leaned against him when he'd pulled her from Blizzard earlier? He'd probably wondered why she'd taken so long to stand on her own two feet. She should've leaned against Blizzard. That would've been the smart thing to do. But when she'd stumbled from the saddle, unable to see or open her mouth, he'd been so solid she'd soaked the feeling in.

As she was doing now.

Leith's elbow knocked against her arm. "Look."

Renna raised her head. To their left, the mountains fell away into a wide, grassy meadow surrounded by oaks and maples. A stream sliced through the center. Far below, a herd of elk grazed the grass, some lying down, some standing. The mountains rose around them in rocky cliffs and stands of juniper, cedars, and pines, stretching as far as she could see into the gray distance. A wild, lonely land.

The size of the place drummed through her, as if here the sky stretched bigger, the rivers deeper, the trees stronger, and the earth more alive than anywhere she'd seen before.

With the mountains gnawing at the sky around her, it seemed impossible that the flat roll of Acktar's prairie still existed somewhere to their south.

"This is beautiful."

"Yes." Leith nudged Blizzard, and the horse eased into a walk once again.

"How do you know where you're going?" Renna peered over his shoulder. While there might've been a faint worn spot in the gravel and rocks that Blizzard followed, it couldn't be called a trail.

"Shad gave me the directions I need to head to find the campsite he's setting up for us, and I've travelled through here before." Leith shrugged. "In those early years, Respen had us track down the Rovers, and Martyn and I spent a lot of time wandering the Hills in search of Rover hideouts."

She'd heard of the Rovers. Her parents had told stories about the times the bands of rustlers and outlaws had plagued Acktar. But Martyn wasn't someone Leith had mentioned before. "Martyn?"

"My best friend in the Blades. He's now the Third Blade." Renna felt more than heard Leith's sigh. "He's loyal to Respen."

"More than he's loyal to you?"

Leith's shoulders sagged. "I'm not sure. Years ago, we pledged we'd watch each other's backs. I don't know if that pledge will hold once he learns what I've done."

Renna squeezed her arms to give him a hug. She hadn't considered what joining the Resistance would cost him. Only what it'd cost her if he didn't. Leith stood to lose more than just his life. If the truth ever became known, he'd lose a friend.

He'd made that choice. For her. For Brandi and Shad and all of them.

What had she ever sacrificed like that? Any sacrifices she'd ever done hadn't been her choice. Her parents, her safety, her home. They'd all been ripped from her against her will.

Blizzard's stride covered the miles along craggy ridges, down into wooded gorges, and across gurgling streams. Leith gave them a few short stops to allow the horses to rest, graze, and drink, but the stops weren't enough to stretch the aches from Renna's legs and back. After a few hours, even the novelty of the landscape and the herds of elk and bison wore away with the pain shooting through the insides of her legs.

The rhythm of Blizzard's hooves lulled her eyes closed. She rested her head against Leith's back. A weight pressed at the space between her eyes. She yawned.

The swaying rhythm stopped. Renna blinked and shoved herself upright. Somehow, dusk had settled across the mountains. "Why are we stopping?"

"You're falling asleep." Leith turned in the saddle and balanced sideways. Laying the reins across Blizzard's neck, he reached an arm around her waist and pulled her onto his lap.

"What are you doing?" She stiffened.

"Relax. I'm just making sure you won't fall off when you fall asleep." He tucked her against him, his left arm supporting her back.

Perhaps she should've protested. But her eyelids couldn't resist the weight pressing against them any longer. She leaned her head against his shoulder. One of the knives strapped to his chest poked her side. *This would be a lot more comfortable if he wasn't a Blade.*

Blizzard set off again. His gait rocked her. She tucked her fingers against Leith's chest.

She was warm. Almost comfortable. Tired.

And protected.

21

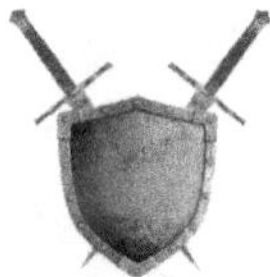

Renna woke to the grating sound of a crow cawing somewhere above her. Shivers prickled along her arms.

Brandi lay beside her, sprawled on her back, mouth open. A snore battled with the crow for the most obnoxious noise. A network of branches and poles laced above and around them.

She pushed herself up. A wool blanket wrapped around her, but under that, a layer of pine boughs protected her from the ground. She must've been tired last night.

Pulling the blanket around her shoulders to ward off the morning chill, Renna crawled from the lean-to shelter and stood. The shelter leaned between two trees at the edge of a small meadow set in a bowl of cliffs along two sides.

Across from her, the meadow dipped into an especially thick patch of trees, a faint gurgling and whooshing sound coming from that direction.

In the center of the meadow, five horses wandered

between their favorite patches of grass. Short lengths of rawhide hobbled their front hooves to prevent them from going too far.

"Good morning."

She whirled and spotted Shadrach perched on a log next to a small fire a few yards away. A swathe of needles and leaves had been cleared away from a ring of rocks beneath the thick branches of a pine. The smoke from the fire curled through the branches, scattering into nothing but hot puffs of air.

Renna walked over and sank onto a log on the opposite side of the fire. A breath of smoke washed against her face along with the rich scent of frying cornmeal. "That smells good."

"Figured something hot might be appreciated after that long ride." Shadrach flipped one of the flat cakes. The grease in the pan spit and popped. "Leith scouted the area this morning and didn't see any signs of Blades, so he said a small fire would be fine."

Renna spread her fingers toward the fire. The heat tickled her palms. "Where's Leith? And Jamie?"

Shadrach motioned toward the trees at the far side of the meadow. "There's a stream and small waterfall in that direction. They're washing up."

Renna drew her fingers through her hair. Flakes of dried blood rained onto her blouse and divided skirt. "Do you think Brandi and I could at least wash our hair later?"

Shadrach grinned and raised his eyebrows. "You'd better before someone does mistake you for something dead."

"At least it should be easier to wash out than the paint you poured on my hair when I was eight. Both Lydia and I had streaks of blue and green in our hair for months." Renna matched his smile. How long had it been since she'd felt comfortable enough around Shadrach to tease him? The past four years of hiding at Stetterly and fooling herself into thinking she was attracted to him hadn't helped matters any.

Shadrach speared a corn cake, put it on a tin plate, and held it out to her. "Father made the vegetable garden my responsibility shortly after that. Kept me so busy I didn't have time to get into any more trouble."

As Renna took the plate, Brandi crawled from the lean-to. Her red-blond hair frizzed into a ball around her head, except for the places matted down with dried blood. "Is that breakfast? It smells good, and I'm starving."

Shadrach reached for a stack of tin plates next to him. He dumped a corn cake onto a plate and handed it to Brandi.

Voices drew Renna's attention. She turned and spotted Leith and Jamie strolling towards the fire from the direction of the stream, their hair still damp. Jamie's hair stuck out in all directions while Leith's was semi-straight, as if he'd tried to finger comb it.

Leith took a seat on a log to Renna's right. When he glanced in her direction, their eyes met. She jerked her gaze away, but not before she glimpsed Leith's smile. What should she say to him? Should she say good morning? Ask how he'd slept? She'd been fine talking to him on their ride yesterday. Why couldn't she talk to him now?

That ride made it worse. She'd spent a whole day with her arms tucked around him. She'd fallen asleep with her head against his shoulder. Should she apologize for that? Pretend she hadn't noticed his heartbeat and the way her own pulsed in response?

She gripped the plate in her hands tighter. She'd taken too long. If she said something now, it'd sound strange.

Whatever her thoughts over the day before, Leith didn't seem affected by it. He grinned at Brandi and accepted his plate of food from Shadrach. "I'd forgotten how convenient it is to travel with a lord's son. They do all the cooking."

"That's because Blades never seem to stop long enough for a hot meal." Shadrach handed Jamie a plate before dishing the last corn cake onto a plate for himself.

Renna grimaced and shifted her aching legs and rear end. All they'd had yesterday was hard corn bread and dried meat on one of the times they'd stopped to rest the horses.

Shadrach prayed for all of them, then they bit into the meal. Brandi inhaled hers and scraped her plate clean with sand by the time Renna finished.

Once Renna finished cleaning her plate, Renna and Brandi gathered clean underthings from their packs. As Renna exited the tent, Leith leapt to his feet. "I'll walk you to the waterfall."

"Thanks." Renna followed him across the meadow, Brandi skipping beside her. Skirting the horses, they eased down a rocky slope to the stream. The waterfall gushed between two rock ledges in a white fury, plunging several feet into a wide pool. The sun glinted on the pine needles, skimmed across the wet rocks, and prismed through the white foam.

"It's beautiful." Renna halted on a ledge.

"One of many like it in the Hills." Leith sat on a rock with his back to the stream. A stand of firs screened the waterfall from his perch. "I'll keep watch here so you aren't disturbed."

"Thanks." If she or Brandi screamed, he'd be there in an instant.

Brandi gripped her arm. "Come on!"

Shoving through the fir trees, Renna approached the waterfall. She set her stack of clothes a safe distance from the spray floating in the air around the falls. She peeled her dress away from the blood that still stuck to her skin and underclothes.

Down to her underthings, Brandi jumped into the pool. Her head submerged for a moment before she popped back to the surface, flinging her strands of wet hair out of her face. "I have just decided I love waterfalls."

Renna tiptoed to the edge. "It looks cold." She touched the water with a toe. The water had to be about fifty degrees. Maybe less. She shivered and stepped back.

Brandi clambered out of the water. "Come on, Renna. It isn't bad once you get used to it."

"Maybe I'll just sit here and wash—" Brandi hugged her and flung both of them off the ledge. A shriek tore from Renna's mouth as she slapped into the water. She clawed to the surface, sputtering. Brandi popped above the surface a few feet away. Renna shoved a wave of water at her. "Brandi!"

"Are you all right?" Leith's voice called from his perch.

"We're fine!" Renna glared at her sister. "See what you did? You nearly had him walking in on us to see if we were being attacked by a mountain lion or something."

Brandi smirked. "You're the one doing all the screaming."

"Only because you tackled me. I couldn't help it." Rolling her eyes, Renna undid her braid and finger-combed her hair. Dried blood glued chunks of it together.

Grimacing, she swam to the waterfall and dunked her

head under it. While the water pounded onto her head, she scrubbed at her hair. She and Brandi took turns rubbing at each others' hair until the last of the encrusted blood pounded away with the waterfall's current.

Teeth chattering like rabid squirrels, Renna rolled out of the pool and lay on a sun-warmed rock. She closed her eyes as the sun played over her face and arms. How long had it been since she could relax and enjoy the sun on her face without worrying about dying or Blades or war? If only they could live in this meadow forever.

Nearby, Brandi's feet splashed and squished against the rocks. Cold water dripped onto Renna's face. "Brandi!"

"Are you just going to lie there all day?"

"Guess not." Renna rolled to her feet. After she dried herself off as much as she could, she changed into fresh underthings. She pulled the blue bodice over her head and tugged on her divided skirt. She laced up her knee-high boots and strapped the knife Leith had given her to her ankle. There. Much better.

Renna gathered her pile of soiled clothes. She turned to Brandi. "We'd better—"

Perched on a limb above the creek, a huge, tawny cat stared down at Brandi with yellow eyes, its tail twitching back and forth. It padded an inch forward along the branch.

Renna's heart galloped around her chest. Her fingers trembled so much she barely managed to draw the knife from its sheath. "Brandi, don't move."

Brandi placed her hands on her hips. "Why not?"

"Please, just don't make any sudden moves." Renna glanced at the mountain lion crouched over her sister's head.

She tightened her hold on her knife. Not that she could do anything if the mountain lion decided to attack.

Brandi's eyes flicked to the knife and widened. "All right. I won't move."

Renna gritted her teeth. Her knees wobbled. She couldn't do anything, but surely Leith could. "Leith? Can you come here?"

Out of the corner of her eye, she spotted him round the stand of firs, a knife already gripped in his hand. He eased into the space between Renna and Brandi, his eyes fixed on the mountain lion. "Brandi, walk to Renna slowly."

Brandi tiptoed forward. When she passed Leith, she glanced over her shoulder, squeaked, and walked faster. Renna stepped forward and hugged her. Somehow, everything was better when they were together.

Leith held his arms out from his sides. His black clothes made him look big and menacing. He stepped forward, brandishing his knife and holding the cat's gaze. The mountain lion stood up and backed along the branch.

Renna's heart pounded harder. What if the mountain lion attacked Leith? It'd sink its fangs deep into Leith's throat while its claws ripped his body apart. How much defense would Leith's knife be?

Leith broke a twig off a scrub bush growing out of the rocks along the river. With a yell, he threw the stick at the cat, bouncing it off the mountain lion's face and front paws.

Yowling, the mountain lion scrambled backwards, leapt down from the tree, and dashed away into the woods. For several minutes, scratching and cracking sounded from the slope of the mountainside.

When the noise faded, Leith relaxed and turned back to them. He sheathed his knife. "It's gone."

Renna's legs collapsed beneath her. Her knife clattered to the stone next to her. Her whole body shook. "We could've been killed."

Leith knelt next to her. "You're safe now. Mountain lions are normally shy and wary of humans. They don't attack unless you wander into their territory or near their young."

"So why did this one get so close?" Renna hugged her knees.

Leith glanced at the pile of ruined clothes she'd dropped on the ground. His mouth quirked. "I suspect because you smelled like a dead goat."

Renna gaped at him. Behind her, Brandi snorted and burst into a fit of giggles. "He must've thought we were funny looking dead goats."

Leith's mouth quirked. "That's probably why he didn't pounce right away and sat watching you instead. You didn't look like any dead goat he'd ever seen."

Perhaps it was the relief that they were all alive and unhurt. Maybe it was the image of the mountain lion cocking its head in puzzlement, trying to figure out why two dead goats were taking a bath in a waterfall. Renna couldn't help it. A giggle wormed up her throat and out her mouth. Tears leaked from the corners of her eyes.

Leith stared at her as if the mountain lion had made off with her sanity. Renna didn't care. When had she last laughed like this?

22

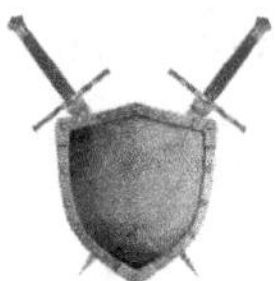

As dusk settled around the meadow, Renna sat near Leith around the small campfire he'd deemed it safe enough to risk. He and Shadrach were discussing what to do if Shadrach's Resistance contact didn't show up in the next few days. She glanced toward the trees where Jamie and Brandi brushed each of the horses in turn.

Blizzard's head jerked up. The horse froze, ears pricked towards the northwest, a tuft of grass sticking forgotten out of his mouth.

Leith tensed. His eyes darted around their clearing. "Someone's coming. Take cover near the horses."

Renna hurried across the clearing. Jamie was already motioning Brandi into cover behind a large tree. Renna leaned against a tree near Blizzard and peered at the clearing. Had a Blade discovered them?

Shadrach and Leith took a stand behind the first row of trees in front of the horses. Leith had knives in both of his hands, his eyes hard, while Shadrach strung his bow and nocked an arrow to the string. Jamie crept into position beside Leith and also pulled out a pair of knives.

Renna shuddered. All of them, even Jamie, were prepared to fight, and perhaps kill, to protect her and Brandi. Would it come to that?

"It could be the person who's supposed to meet us." Shadrach fixed his gaze on the tree line across the meadow.

"Or it could be a Blade that stumbled on our camp." Leith's gaze darted back and forth.

Renna held her breath. A danger or a friend? She trembled. A swarm of Blades might burst from the trees at any moment.

Blizzard snorted softly, his eyes fixated on the trees across the meadow. A dark brown horse broke from cover, its rider an indistinct mass on its back. He halted his horse by their fire ring and swung down. Renna caught sight of the quiver of arrows and unstrung bow strapped to his back. A sword glinted among the packs on his saddle. He didn't look like a Blade. They never carried any other weapons besides knives.

"Hello the clearing!" The man's voice boomed against the surrounding rock face.

Shadrach grinned, placed the arrow back in his quiver, and unstrung his bow. "He's one of ours." Stepping from his place behind a tree, Shadrach strode towards the stranger. "Hello yourself!"

Renna tiptoed out of hiding as Shadrach and the man shook hands. Leith's hands, still gripping his knives, hovered above his sheathes. He glanced at her. She shrugged, not sure what to tell him.

Shadrach waved them forward, a grin splitting his face.

Brandi bounded from the trees towards the newcomer. Renna started forward. Even if the man was a threat, she wasn't going to leave Brandi out there by herself. Behind her, two sets of knives whispered into their leather sheathes.

"And this is Renna." Shadrach tugged her forward. "This is Walter Esroy. He used to serve in the army before Respen took over. He's going to be your guide to Eagle Heights."

Walter bowed towards Renna. He looked to be in his mid-fifties with abundant wrinkles and sparse patches of hair covering the back of his head. Equally sparse bristles dotted his cheeks and chin. Muscles still clung to his stocky frame, proving time hadn't diminished his skills. His blue eyes danced with merriment, though Renna detected a sharp edge to them. Beneath the happy exterior, this man could be deadly. She smiled at him. "It's a pleasure to—"

Before she could get any farther, Walter's arm swept her behind him while his other hand yanked his sword from its sheath. "Shad, behind you!"

Her pulse ticking with fear, Renna peered around Walter's back. She spotted Leith standing halfway between them and the trees, his hands in front of him, palms up, to show he wasn't a threat. She breathed out a sigh. No danger.

Shadrach spun, then relaxed. "He's on our side."

Walter straightened and stuck his sword back in its sheath. "I heard you had turned a Blade, but I didn't put much stock in those rumors."

"They're true, but the less everyone knows, the better." Shadrach glanced at Leith, who crossed his arms.

Renna swallowed. What if King Respen heard those rumors and pieced the truth together? Currently he believed that the former First Blade was the spy and still living with the Resistance. If the king ever learned that Leith was the real spy...Renna's stomach churned. Leith risked torture and death each time he returned to Respen's castle.

If only Leith could go all the way with them to the Resistance hideout in the mountains. He'd be safe there. He'd never have to return to King Respen's castle. He could keep her and Brandi safe.

She shook her head. He had too much courage to join her in taking the coward's way out.

23

The next morning, Leith saddled the brown horse Renna would be riding, checking and re-checking the saddle, the girth strap, the bridle.

A lump settled into his stomach and clogged the back of his throat. After today, he might never see Renna again. While Respen yet reigned, she could never return.

Until his secret was discovered, Leith couldn't leave.

And if Respen discovered his deception, Leith wouldn't be able to leave. He'd most likely end up chained to the wall in the top room of the Blade's tower, tortured until he begged for death, then killed by whatever Blade Respen ordered to do the deed. A sour taste twisted his stomach.

He drew in a deep breath. Until the time came, he couldn't dwell on thoughts of capture. He had to believe God would bless his efforts and would provide a means of escape. In the Bible story, God had protected Daniel in the den of lions. He'd protect Leith in the den of Blades he faced.

Leith led the brown horse into the clearing, patting its

neck. Near the campfire's ashes, Jamie held Sunshine, the palomino Brandi had adopted as her own at Walden. Still holding the horse's reins, Leith straddled one of the logs, motioning for Jamie to sit also. Jamie perched on the next log, eyeing him. Leith met Jamie's gaze. "You can go with them. You'd be safe with the Resistance."

Jamie looked down. He toyed with the palomino's reins, twisting them over and through his fingers. When he met Leith's gaze once again, Jamie's jaw tightened. "No. I'm going to stay with you. I know I almost messed up last time, but I won't do it again."

Leith patted Jamie's shoulder. He was volunteering to face the same terror Leith struggled to face. He'd have to do a man's job and have a man's courage, but he was up to the task.

Jamie tilted his head towards the lean-to. "Do you think they'll be all right?"

"They should be." Leith adjusted his grip on the reins as the brown horse tugged away from the cleared dirt towards a patch of grass. "I ordered the Blades to stay to the west, and I haven't seen any sign that they've wandered back this way yet. And God will protect them."

"How can you be sure?" Jamie chucked the half-burned end of a branch into their fire ring. "He didn't protect my parents."

Leith shifted and stared at his boots. What had Renna, Shad, and Brandi told him all those months ago when he'd been searching? One of them would know something wise to tell Jamie.

"There's a lot of darkness and pain in this life, and we don't always understand why things happen. But that's where trust comes in. We have to trust that God can see the full landscape better than we can."

Jamie's eyes and chin still drooped with a frown.

What could Leith tell him that would make sense? And not sound like empty words? Brandi would come up with some Bible story. Leith would have to make do with the ones he knew. "The Daniel stories in the Bible wouldn't be miracles if Daniel wasn't thrown into the lions' den and his friends weren't thrown into the furnace. As much as we might not like it, we can't skip the lions' den part to get to the happy part."

Jamie chewed on his bottom lip and nodded.

With the rustling of boots through grass, Renna exited the lean-to shelter, carrying a small bundle of her personal items. Her blond hair swung in a long braid down her back. She wore the same light blue shirt and divided skirt she'd worn yesterday.

Leith jumped to his feet and stumbled over the log he'd been sitting on. He dragged the horse by the reins and snagged her bundle as if he'd purposefully lunged forward. "Let me help you with that."

"Thanks." Her smile did strange things inside his chest.

Turning, he strapped the bundle to the back of the saddle. For good measure, he checked the tightness of the saddle's girth yet again.

Brandi skipped from the shelter. Her red-blond braids slapped against her back and the nearby trees. Jamie helped her strap her bundle to the back of her saddle.

She bounced over to Leith and flung herself into a big hug. "Take care of Blizzard."

He grinned and hugged her back, even though his voice

scratched his throat. "I will. Take care of Sunshine. That's a good horse you have there."

She nodded and pulled away. Far too short for a forever goodbye, but Leith had to pray this wasn't the last time he'd see her. Maybe he'd survive long enough to join them at Eagle Heights.

Leith turned to Renna. What should he say? They'd said goodbye before. He should be well-practiced by now. But he couldn't bring himself to move. This time was too final.

Renna stepped closer. "Leith, I..." She swept a strand of hair behind her ear.

"Do you still have the knife I gave you?" He bit the inside of his cheek. She was trying to say something, and he brought up knives. Real smooth.

She nodded and patted her right ankle. "I never go anywhere without it."

"Good." Of course she still had it. Why wouldn't she?

"Leith." Renna stepped forward and hugged him, resting her head against his shoulder. "I'm going to miss you."

Leith managed to wrap his arms around her before his brain shut off. If only he were free to leave Respen's darkness behind once and for all. Perhaps Shad had been right. Leith should've pursued Renna more when he'd had the chance. Now he'd never know.

He pulled back and forced himself to smile. He swiped at the two tears that meandered down her cheeks. "We'll see each other again." The words tasted as bitter as the lies he told Respen.

As Walter and Shad approached them, Renna pulled back, her cheeks reddening. Leith cleared his throat and knelt to help her mount. She scrambled onto the horse's back, nearly kicking Leith in the face as she pulled herself the rest of the way into the saddle.

In a few moments, the last goodbyes and Godspeeds were exchanged. The horses trotted across the meadow, the last waves from the treeline.

Then they were gone.

As he, Shad, and Jamie rode from the meadow in the opposite direction, Leith glanced back one last time. A sense of foreboding wrapped around him as if the time he'd spent in that meadow was the last bit of happiness he was going to experience for a long, long time.

24

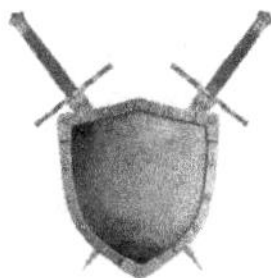

Renna bit her lip at the ache in her muscles. Her ankles throbbed from the hard leather of the stirrup rubbing against her boot. Her clothes stuck to her, and when she rubbed her face with her hand, her hand came away sticky from her perspiration. Even in the elevation of the mountains, the forest steamed with heat. All she wanted to do was collapse into a soft bed.

She glanced forward. Her sister still perched on her horse, a grin splitting her face. At the front of their small line, Walter Esroy swayed easily with the rhythm of his horse, at home in the saddle.

All morning, Brandi had chattered with Walter about the trees, the rocks, the birds flying overhead. Only now that it was approaching noon did her sister's mouth slow down as hunger took over.

Renna clung to her horse as it lunged up a small incline. She had to get everyone talking again to distract herself from her discomfort. "So what is Eagle Heights like?"

Walter half-turned in his saddle to nod at them. "You'll like it there. I can't tell you too much yet, but it's a place where Respen'll never hurt you again. You'll like the people there. We've all had to hide from Respen."

Safety from King Respen. Could she really be safe?

"There's a number of people who'll be happy to see you. Many of the old army have fled there. Most of them knew your parents." His head bobbed in rhythm with his horse. "I knew your parents back when they first met. You've all heard that story, haven't you?"

Brandi nodded. "Mother and Father used to tell it to us all the time. Were you there? Were you the tracker who helped Father find Mother?"

"I was there, but I wasn't the tracker." Walter's face deepened with more wrinkles. "I was one of the Rovers."

"You were?" Renna blinked at him. Had a few of the Rovers joined the Resistance? She could see why the Rovers wouldn't like King Respen. He'd spent the last couple years having the Blades wipe them out, but Rovers weren't exactly the kind of people the Resistance recruited. They'd done their share of murdering and plundering before King Respen took over.

Brandi grinned and urged her horse closer to Walter's. "Tell us the story. It's been years since we've heard it."

Walter scratched at the patches of grey hair on his head. "Well, we'd heard there was going to be this big to-do over the wedding of Lord Farley Alistair's son and one of Princess Annita's best friends. The prince and princess were going to show up along with most of the nobles. Sounded like a place that'd have lots of rich wedding gifts."

"So the Rover leader decided to attack, and in the attack,

Mother was kidnapped because she was Princess Annita Eirdon back then." Brandi's hair bounced along with her movements.

Renna rubbed her thumb along the leather reins. Lord Alistair would've been about Shadrach's age, Lady Alistair about Jolene's. Somehow, she couldn't picture them as anything other than the adults they were now.

"Your mother was quite the lady, she was." Walter shook his head, steering his horse around an outcropping. "From that very first day, we realized we'd stolen more than we could handle."

Brandi grinned. "That's when Father volunteered to rescue her."

"So I heard later. I was the Rover in charge of keeping your mother from escaping, and we were too busy doing that to even pay attention to who was tracking us."

"Uncle Leon wanted to set out after Mother himself, but Lord Alistair and Father convinced him that it'd be foolish for him." Renna trotted her horse closer to Brandi's. "And Lord Alistair had just gotten married and couldn't go. So Father, being Lord Alistair's best friend, set out instead."

"We got a ways into the Hills, but those tracking us kept getting closer. When they were only a day behind us, your mother convinced us that it'd go better for us if we left her behind. She could convince those following us to stop and turn around. Since it was either that or get captured and executed by the king, we dumped her on a rock and left." Walter patted his horse's neck. "Last time I saw her, she was perched on that rock as pretty as you please and wearing a smirk like that had been her plan all along."

Brandi smirked, her nose wrinkling. "And that's how

Father found her. He was disappointed that she'd rescued herself before he'd gotten the chance."

"So how did you go from being a Rover to a trusted man in the Resistance?" Renna leaned against her saddlehorn and stretched her legs.

"I got to thinking about some of the things your mother had said. She'd never stopped chattering. Never. Got some of the others a might bothered." Walter shrugged. The arrows in his quiver tapped against each other. "I left the Rovers a couple of months later. Showed up at Nalgar Castle and your mother got me a job in the army. When Respen took over, I joined the Resistance."

Renna wiggled in the saddle. And now he was taking them to the far-off safety of Eagle Heights. Would they truly be safe? Would Respen believe that Leith had killed them?

Or would Respen track them down even there?

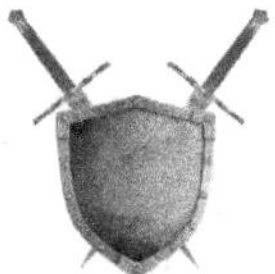

25

Blizzard's hooves tapped against the yellow-brown stone as Leith, Shad, and Jamie wound their way through the scrub pines and junipers. Leith opened his mouth but couldn't think of anything to say. A problem he'd had ever since he'd watched Renna and Brandi leave yesterday.

Somewhere to their right, something clacked on the rocks. A hoof. Too loud to be a deer. It had to be a horse. Some wild horses roamed the Sheered Rock Hills, but usually in herds.

Leith held up a hand and halted Blizzard. "Stay here. Don't move until I say it's safe."

Shad nodded and eased his horse deeper into the shadows provided by a pine growing next to a boulder. A mass of junipers screened them from the other set of hoofbeats.

"Jamie, you'd better come with me." Leith hardened his

features and urged Blizzard around the blue-green bushes. Jamie's horse followed.

A few yards away, another horse and rider scrambled up the slope. Knives glinted against the rider's black clothes. From this distance, Leith could make out the Blade's slim build and mass of wavy, brown hair. Eleventh Blade Ranson Harding.

He allowed himself to relax a fraction. Of all the Blades patrolling the Hills, Harding was the best one to run into. Nudging Blizzard, Leith met Harding at the top of the slope. Harding thumped his right fist on his chest. "First Blade."

"Eleventh Blade." Leith returned the salute. "We buried the girls' bodies deep in the Hills where no one will find them. Where are the others?"

Harding pointed north. "The Seventh Blade is north of me somewhere. I don't know where the Third Blade is. He disappeared our second day out."

Leith clenched his fist against his thigh. Where had Martyn gone? Had he decided to do some scouting on his own regardless of Leith's orders? Harding had wandered farther east than Leith would've liked. What if Martyn did the same?

Nothing Leith could do about it but pray. He forced a hard glint into his voice. "If you see the others, tell them to work their way towards Walden. Keep an eye on Walden in case Vane makes an appearance as Respen believes he will."

"Where will you be?" Harding's forehead creased.

An impertinent question, one Vane would've punished, but Leith just nodded. "I'm returning to Walden with the trainee to keep up my disguise. Lord Alistair has been preparing defenses, and he will most likely put every able-bodied man to work. We'll be able to observe his defenses and sabatoge them if we can. If Vane does come, I'll be hard-pressed to avoid him and might not be able to inform you."

Harding nodded. "Yes, First Blade." He pointed his horse northwest, angling away from where Shad hid.

Leith remained where he was until the sounds of clattering hooves faded into the rustle of the breeze in the junipers. He waited a few minutes more to be positive Harding hadn't circled back before he and Jamie returned to Shad. "One of the Blades on his patrol. They've stuck closer east than I would've liked."

Shad's square jaw tightened. "Will they endanger Renna and Brandi?"

Jamie gripped his knife as he stared in the direction Harding had gone.

"I don't know." And that was the scary part. Leith was the First Blade, and even he couldn't predict the Blades' movements.

They crested the hill overlooking Walden at dusk. Leith and Jamie had changed back into peasant clothes, though this time they had their knives and black clothes bundled into saddlebags to bring into Walden with them.

Below, most of the town remained dark. Only the main street had a few people hurrying along it. Around Walden Manor, figures labored in the ditch and hacked at logs.

As they drew closer, Leith noticed the odd silence first. Not silence, exactly. The shushing shovels and thwacking axes made plenty of noise. The people were silent. No one spoke as they stabbed their shovels into the ground or swung their axes. Lines creased their foreheads and furrowed their cheeks. Only a few women remained scattered between the men, and everyone, even the women, carried some form of weapon strapped to their waists or backs.

How much harm had they done to Walden by faking Renna's and Brandi's deaths right before the coming battle? Renna and Brandi were the last of the Eirdon line. Without them, who did the Resistance fight for? That mysterious Leader no one outside a select few even knew about?

Shad greeted the guards and led the way towards the manor. Several thick planks spanned the ditch in a temporary bridge. When Respen's army arrived, the planks would be withdrawn.

As they dismounted in front of the manor, Leith glanced northwards one last time. Were Renna and Brandi all right? Were they safe deep in the Hills? Or had they run across trouble where even Leith couldn't rescue them?

26

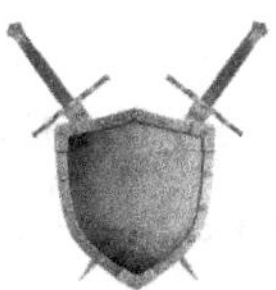

Renna curled into her blanket on one side of their fire. Her back and legs throbbed, but her stomach swelled contentedly with the rabbit Walter had roasted for their supper.

One of the pine boughs beneath her dug into her hip. She shifted but the pine needles prickled through the blanket. After sleeping on pine branches in the lean-to for two nights and on the trail last night, she should've been used to it by now.

She forced her body to relax and her breathing to slow. No point in shifting around and keeping Walter and Brandi awake.

Walter's slow breaths told her he slept. Next to her, Brandi's breathing deepened until raspy hisses poured from her mouth. Renna sighed. Now she'd have to move and nudge Brandi until she rolled over and closed her mouth.

Renna opened her eyes, but before she moved, one of the

horses picketed on the other side of Walter lifted its head. Its ears pricked. It gave a low huffing sound.

Walter's eyes snapped open, though his breathing remained slow and even. His gaze flicked towards her, and his brow lowered as if he were trying to warn her without moving or making a sound.

She slitted her eyes and struggled to keep her breathing steady and silent. What was it? A wild animal? Another mountain lion? Or, worst of all, a Blade?

Behind Walter, all three horses had their heads up, but their ears remained upright and curious, not low and panicked. Wouldn't they be more scared if it was a wild animal?

A black shape rose out of the darkness behind Walter. The light cast from the fire's coals glinted along his blond curls and raised knife.

A Blade. Renna's heart thumped high in her chest. A shriek built in her throat, so strong she couldn't stop the squeak that escaped.

The Blade's head snapped up and his gaze focused on her.

Walter lunged, grabbed the Blade's knife hand, and yanked him down. The Blade tumbled forward, flipped, and landed on his back inches from the fire. Walter pinned the Blade to the ground. "Run!"

Renna scrambled to her feet and gripped Brandi's arm. Brandi's eyes blinked open. "What's going—"

No time. Renna hauled Brandi to her feet. Across the fire, the Blade had twisted away from Walter's grasp. They couldn't wait around to see who won. Renna dragged Brandi into the trees. "Run."

They barreled through a stand of firs. The branches scratched their faces and tore at their hair. Renna clamped her mouth shut against the scream that built in her throat. She mustn't scream. She needed all her breath to keep running.

Brandi tugged her arm, guiding her around an outcropping of rock. Renna stumbled as Brandi sprinted down jagged steps formed of rocks sticking from an embankment.

Shapes loomed in the darkness, lit only by the far-off stars. Run. Her heart beat the word into her chest. Run.

The earth ended in front of them. Renna dug in her heels. They skidded to a stop at the edge of a fifteen-foot drop off. The forest continued below them, stretching out in crags and lumps, the tops tinged with starlight.

Renna glanced over her shoulder, but she couldn't tell if the Blade had followed them. His black clothes blended in with all the other black shapes that created the nighttime forest. Was Walter all right? Maybe he'd killed the Blade?

Somewhere along this cliff was the path they'd climbed to get here, but Renna couldn't find it. They were trapped by the edge. No matter what way they ran, the Blade could head them off if he was chasing.

Renna leaned forward, staring at the ground below. Should she and Brandi attempt to climb down? It wasn't that far. How much time did they have?

Something crashed in the forest behind them. Twigs snapped. Branches skittered across each other as they were shoved aside. Chills shot through Renna's stomach. If Walter had won, he would've called to them. The noise had to be the Blade.

Pebbles ground beneath boots. Footsteps crunched

closer. They didn't have time to hide. They didn't have time to run.

She did the only thing she could do. She grabbed Brandi around the waist and jumped.

27

Renna didn't have time to scream as they plummeted downwards. Her left leg punched the ground first, pain flaring into her body.

Her momentum catapulted her forward, slamming her back and side into the ground, Brandi's weight on top of her. She skidded several feet, rocks tearing into her back, before her left hip crashed into a tree and stopped their movement.

She couldn't breathe. Her mouth hung open. She tried to drag in air, but her body refused to move even that much. Black spots danced across her eyes.

Brandi's face swirled above her. Her mouth was moving, but Renna couldn't understand the words.

Something thumped against her back. Hard. Renna hauled in a breath, the air rushing through her body. She gulped in several deep breaths and winced. Her back and side ached. She pushed herself straighter. Agony jolted through her left leg. She sucked in a breath and blinked at the hot prickle in her eyes.

Brandi knelt, her eyes wide. "Renna, are you all right? Can you move? Please say you're all right. Renna?"

"I'm all right. I think." Renna leaned forward and felt along her leg. Her hands connected with a growing lump along the bone in her lower leg. She whimpered and squeezed her eyes shut. "Brandi, I think my leg is fractured."

At least it wasn't a bad break. It wouldn't need to be set, and she didn't have any shards of bone sticking through her skin. Small comfort. Either way, she wouldn't be able to run any farther.

"What do you need me to do?" Brandi's voice strained in a tone Renna had never heard before.

"You can..." Renna paused and waved Brandi into silence. They froze. Something crackled and scuffled on the cliff's edge above them. Peering into the darkness, Renna spotted the black form of the Blade prowling the cliff top. She held herself still. In the shadows under the tree, they'd be nearly invisible.

Her heart pounded in time with the throbbing in her leg. Would the Blade guess where they'd gone? Brandi's hand slipped into Renna's. Renna squeezed her sister's fingers.

Gravel clattered down the rock face. Brandi gave a small squeal in the back of her throat. Renna squeezed her sister's hand tighter.

The scrabbling at the top of the cliff moved farther away. Hopefully he'd believe they'd run along the cliff's rim and neglect to look down below.

The sounds kept moving farther away until they vanished into the distance. Renna released a sigh and relaxed her grip on Brandi's hand. "We have to keep moving.

It won't take him long to realize we didn't go that way. Help me up."

Brandi tugged Renna to her feet. "What about Walter?"

"If the Blade is after us, then Walter must be dead." Renna's throat hurt. Walter must've died to protect them. Just like their parents had four years ago. Why? Why did everyone who protected them have to die?

Brandi's jaw set, though tears shone in her eyes. She wrapped an arm around Renna's waist. Renna laid her arm over Brandi's shoulders. Brandi stood a few inches shorter than her so Renna could lean against her easily. With Brandi's help, she hopped forward.

They pushed deeper into the trees. Renna's chest constricted tighter and tighter with each hobbling step forward. Too slow. They were going too slow.

Her leg shot pain all the way through her body into her head. The darkness swirled and tilted.

She lay on the ground. How had she gotten there? Brandi's face hovered in the hazy blackness above her. Her mouth moved, but the words didn't penetrate the pain buzzing in Renna's head.

Renna gripped her left knee as if squeezing there would cut off the pain spasming through her leg. "I can't go any farther."

"You can't give up." Brandi tugged on her arm. "If you stay here, the Blade will find you."

Renna managed to push herself upright. Even that much movement churned her stomach. Perhaps if she had something to numb the pain or they had the time to make a proper splint, she could make it. But, they had neither time nor painkiller.

A shiver tore down her back. She should tell Brandi to go on without her. By herself, maybe Brandi could find her way out of the Sheered Rock Hills and back to Walden.

Or maybe Brandi would get lost and die out there by herself. Perhaps they'd both die alone, and what would be the sense in that?

Renna pulled her arm from Brandi's grasp. "You should—"

"Don't tell me to leave you here." Brandi crossed her arms. "Do you remember what you told me the night Father and Mother died? As long as we're together, everything's going to be all right. So I'm not leaving you."

"Actually, I was going to say that you should go find somewhere we can hide." Renna clutched her leg as another lance of pain travelled through her bones. "Not all of the Blades are expert trackers. Maybe this one isn't, and if we hide for a while, he won't find us."

A slim chance, but the best one they had.

"All right." Brandi clambered to her feet. "I'll be right back."

Renna squeezed a section of her divided skirt. What if Brandi fell off another cliff in the dark? Or stumbled across a mountain lion?

Best not to think about it. Brandi could take care of herself.

Would they be able to hide from the Blade? What would happen if he found them? Would he kill them right away?

But what if he didn't find them? What then? She had no idea where they were or how to get to Eagle Heights. She didn't even know where Walden lay. How would they even go anywhere on foot and Renna hobbling on a broken leg?

They'd die either way. Her hands shook. If the Blade found them, he'd kill them. Or he'd bring them to King Respen, and King Respen would kill them. If they got away from the Blade, they'd die while wandering around the Sheered Rock Hills.

Renna touched the silver cross dangling from the chain around her neck. After all they'd survived, why did God bring them out here to die?

Was it because she hadn't done what she was supposed to? She'd tried to stop hiding and start doing her duty, but that had messed up everything. Why didn't God show her what to do?

A black shape crunched towards her. She drew the knife from its sheath.

"It's me." Brandi bounced to Renna's side. "I found a place. Come on."

Renna gritted her teeth as Brandi hauled her to her feet. Together, they hop-skipped down the slope. Partway down, Brandi turned left and shoved into a thick stand of junipers. Their prickles nipped through Renna's clothes into her skin. The green, earthy smell of the shrub filled her throat.

Somewhere in the tangle, Brandi stopped. She plopped onto the sandy soil. "Here it is. Let's hope there's no snakes."

Renna collapsed next to Brandi. "Thanks. Now I'm going to worry about snakes as well as Blades."

She gripped her leg. She couldn't help rocking at the pain. "I need to make a splint. Help me get my boot off."

Brandi shuffled to Renna's leg and unlaced the boot. Together, they pushed and pulled on the boot until it popped from her foot. Renna wiggled her toes and waved her foot. At least she could move it. That was a good sign.

She inspected her leg, gritting her teeth at the knives stabbing through her bone. The bone in her leg felt straight, though a tender lump formed over the place it had fractured.

"I'm going to need two straight sticks and lots of strips of cloth." Renna shoved the words between her teeth. She couldn't let herself cry out no matter how much pain she suffered. Too much noise would call the Blade to them.

Brandi scurried off. In the darkness, Renna couldn't see Brandi, only hear scratching, rattling sounds. She drew in and breathed out several deep breaths. She had to remain calm.

Tugging on her bodice, she tried to rip a section from the bottom, but the tough fabric of her travelling clothes refused to tear.

Why was she trying to tear them? She had a knife. She drew it and sawed at the bottom of her blouse and the ends of her divided skirt. Once both of those were as short as she dared, she set to work on her boot.

Working by feel, she sliced the top part of the boot off, turning it into a low-cut shoe that she could slip over her foot once she had the splint in place. She sliced the remaining leather lengthwise so that she could widen it to accommodate her swollen leg.

Brandi scrambled back to her, carrying two sticks. She plopped to the ground and held them out. "These were the straightest sticks I could find."

"Thanks." Renna wrapped the sticks with the strips of cloth in order to add a layer of padding. She placed them on either side of her leg. "Hold these in place."

While Brandi held the sticks still, Renna wrapped the

leather top of her boot around her leg and laced it snuggly. The leather and laces kept the sticks tight against her leg. With the last few strips of cloth, she tied the bottom and top of the sticks in place so that her leg and ankle were immobilized. She slipped the remnant of her shoe over her foot and the end of the splint, protecting her foot from the cool, night air that nipped at their exposed skin.

Brandi snuggled next to Renna. "Don't worry. God will protect us."

Renna wrapped her arm around her. Would He? Why couldn't she find the same assurance Brandi did?

In a few minutes, Brandi's snore whuffled into the night. What would they do in the morning? Would they be able to move fast enough with Renna's injured leg? Would they be able to find their way to Walden?

She prayed for God to keep them safe, but the darkness wrapped around them so completely Renna could't be sure of anything.

Her hand drifted from Brandi's shoulder to touch the knife she'd placed beside them. They were safe for tonight. At the moment, that would have to be enough.

28

Pain pulsed through Renna's leg. She bit back a groan and curled tighter in their hollow under the junipers. If only she had a bit of willow bark tea or a spoonful of laudanum. Anything to stop the grinding ache in her bone.

Something crunched outside the shrub. Renna held her breath and slowly twisted her head. Through the tangle of trunks and branches, she could see the graveled slope outside. In a flat section a few yards away, four sets of hooves stomped and shifted in a picket line. The saddles lay in a neat row, the saddlebags and bedrolls placed beside them.

The crunching sound came again, and a pair of black boots strode into her limited view.

Black boots. The Blade.

Renna nudged Brandi. Brandi's breathing hitched and her body jolted awake. Renna waved her to stay quiet. Still, Brandi's movements rustled the dead, spiky juniper twigs that coated the ground.

The boots froze. "I know you're in there."

Of course he did. He simply hadn't bothered dragging them from the juniper in the dark when he knew he had them trapped.

"And I know you're the ladies Rennelda and Brandiline."

Brandi's eyes widened. She pushed into a sitting position.

What were they going to do? Renna scrunched her fingers into the ragged end of her blouse. If they tried to make a break for it, the Blade would catch them.

"Now why don't you come out and save us all a bit of hassle." The Blade's voice was closer now. His boots ground against the pebbles a few feet from the junipers.

Brandi leaned close to Renna's ear. "He doesn't want to go into here."

Renna nodded. Her own hands and face prickled with the juniper's sharp needles. She swallowed her pounding heartbeat.

"We need to convince him to come into here after us." Brandi hissed. Her breath tickled the inside of Renna's ear. "While he's busy shoving his way in, we dash out the other side and run for the horses."

Renna's gaze flicked toward the row of saddles on the ground. "We'd have to ride bareback."

"We'll manage."

Maybe Brandi could, but Renna couldn't. She wasn't the best horsewoman with a saddle. She'd fall off at the first jump without one. But she wasn't going to tell Brandi. They had one chance, and they had to take it.

Brandi straightened her shoulders. "We aren't coming out. You're going to have to come in after us."

"Or I could wait until thirst drives you out." The Blade's voice flattened as if he couldn't care less.

Renna grimaced. He could do it. All he'd have to do is sit there until she and Brandi grew desperate enough that turning themselves in to a Blade sounded like a good idea.

Brandi's nose wrinkled. Apparently that hadn't been part of her plan. She rose to a crouch and tugged Renna with her. "Get ready."

Renna tightened her grip on the knife in her free hand. She'd go along with whatever Brandi was planning.

Brandi shoved at the juniper on the opposite side of the Blade. Renna hopped to keep up as they pushed through the first few branches.

The Blade outside their hideout cursed. His footsteps thumped in a wide circle around the juniper stand. When he was nearly to the far side, Brandi halted, whirled, and shoved into Renna. Renna stumbled. Brandi jerked her back the way they'd come.

A warmth curled and burst in Renna's stomach. Her sneaky sister. She'd tricked the Blade into running to the far side, leaving their way clear to the horses.

Brandi broke from the bush, and Renna fell out after her. Scrambling back to her feet, she hopped as quickly as she could. Not fast enough. She tried to put weight on her leg, but the bolt of pain collapsed her leg beneath her. Only Brandi's grip under her shoulders kept her upright.

Two yards to go. One yard.

Renna grabbed the lead rope for the nearest horse. Her hands shook so much she struggled to untie the knot that held the horse to the picket line. Her heart roared in her ears. Faster. Faster.

Brandi had Sunshine untied. She gripped the leadrope. "Hurry."

Renna glanced over her shoulder. The Blade dashed around the junipers.

They weren't going to make it. She didn't have time to untie the rope for both her horse and the other two horses, nor did she have time to have Brandi help her onto her horse's back.

Both of them couldn't escape. Renna slowed Brandi down too much. She shoved Brandi towards Sunshine. "Go. I'll catch up. Go."

Perhaps if Renna delayed the Blade long enough, he wouldn't be able to catch Brandi. She choked on a sob. She'd have to face the Blade alone, but at least Brandi would be safe.

Brandi shook her head. Her jaw thrust forward. "Not without you."

Couldn't Brandi see both of them couldn't escape? "Leave me here. Go. You have to escape."

Brandi crossed her arms. "No."

"Please, Brandi!" Tears seared the corners of her eyes.

Brandi's eyes flicked to something behind Renna. She dropped Sunshine's leadrope and swatted the horse's rump. Sunshine jumped and bolted down the gravel slope.

A twig snapped. Renna whirled and stabbed at the black figure reaching for her. The Blade jumped out of the knife's path. He grabbed her wrist and twisted, hard. Her wrist burned. Pain shot to her shoulder.

Her fingers opened. The knife fell, slowly spinning, and clunked hilt-first to the ground.

Drawing his own knife, he placed it against Renna's

throat. The metal rested on the tender skin below her chin, cold as an unwanted touch.

She shivered. She was going to die. The Blade would slit her throat and drop her dying body to do the same to Brandi. Her pulse pummeled her ears in a painful roar.

"Come here, girl." The Blade beckoned to Brandi.

Renna met Brandi's eyes. She squirmed away from the knife and scratched at the Blade's arm. "Don't listen to him. Run."

Her voice choked as he pressed the flat of his knife against her throat. The pressure built. Yellow and black spots burst across her eyes. She clawed at his arm, but he wouldn't release her. Wouldn't budge.

Breathe. She needed to breathe. A gag spasmed in her chest but couldn't release past her throat.

"Come here or I'll kill your sister." The Blade's harsh voice cut through the tumult in her ears.

No. Renna couldn't force the word out. Blackness chomped at her vision. *Run.*

The Blade released her. She crumpled, gagging and sobbing. Her cheek pressed against the dirt. She dragged in a breath and choked on her tears.

She cracked her eyes open. Brandi trembled but didn't run as the Blade tied her hands together. Her eyes focused on Renna.

The Blade tied Brandi's hands to the picket line and approached Renna. He knelt and picked up her knife. His eyes widened, then hardened. He gripped her upper arm and dragged her towards him. "Where'd you get this?"

His fingers squeezed her muscles against her bone.

Renna sucked in a sob and squirmed. She spotted the initials LT carved into the hilt of the knife Leith had given her.

Leith's initials. She'd forgotten that detail. She met the Blade's cold, brown eyes. He knew this was Leith's knife. Her stomach dropped into her toes. She'd given Leith away, and he didn't even know it. What would happen when he returned to Nalgar Castle? Would he ride into a trap?

Could she make something up? Was there some way she could explain the knife away?

The Blade shook her so hard her teeth clacked. He held the knife a few inches from her face. "Where did you get this?"

She hesitated, and the Blade's face tightened. She bit her lip. Another mistake. If she had nothing to hide, she would've answered him by now.

"The First Blade gave it to Renna." Brandi tugged on the picket line. The horses' heads shot up and swiveled towards her.

The Blade's gaze snapped to Brandi. "The former First Blade?"

What was Brandi doing? Renna held her breath.

"I don't know his name." Brandi somehow managed a huff and eyeroll. "I don't even know your name."

"When?" The Blade's eyes narrowed.

"Over a month ago."

The Blade released Renna's arm. She collapsed on the sand. Her upper arm throbbed in time with her leg.

He raked a hand through his hair and stared at the knife. But at least he didn't look so suspicious. Even though Brandi had told the truth, she'd implied that former First Blade

Vane had given it to Renna. They'd let the Blade figure out how that came about. The less they said, the better.

But the knife wasn't the only problem. She and Brandi weren't supposed to be here. They were supposed to be dead. How were they going to explain why Leith hadn't killed them?

"So what's your name?" Brandi's gaze flicked to Renna. "And what do you plan to do to us?"

Renna nodded back. If they distracted the Blade, maybe he'd forget to ask why they were alive. A faint hope, but they had to try.

The Blade weighed Leith's knife for several more minutes before he drew one of the knives from his boot. He stabbed the knife into the sand and put Leith's knife in his sheath instead. He turned to Renna. "I'm Third Blade Martyn Hamish."

Martyn. Renna sucked in a breath. The Blade that used to be Leith's best friend. But Renna wasn't supposed to know that. She shouldn't even recognize his name.

He grabbed her arms and dragged her to her feet. She cried out and sagged in his grip. He huffed and dropped Renna next to the saddles. "I'm taking you to King Respen. I'm sure he'll be very interested in why you're both still alive."

29

Leith stabbed his shovel into the ground once again. The blister on the inside of his thumb rubbed and broke. Pain flared across his skin. Sweat trickled between his shoulder blades. Pausing, he swiped his forehead against his sleeve, leaving a greasy splotch on the cloth.

Behind him, Shad directed the men razing the back flower garden. All the carefully arranged plants were being cleared, though some of the hedges remained in place. Stacks of wood and stone lay beneath each of Walden Manor's first-story windows. In a few weeks, they'd board up the windows to slits.

Men stacked more wood and stone into a makeshift barrier running a few yards inside the dirt mound and ditch. Once Respen's army breached the ditch and the dirt wall, the defenders could fall back to this second line of defenses before retreating into the manor itself. It wouldn't hold off an army the size of Respen's, but these defenses would make Respen's army pay for every yard.

Lydia trudged towards him, a bucket of water in each of her hands. Dirt streaked her skirt and blouse, and sweat dampened the hair wisping from the braid coiled on her head. She set the buckets down and held out a tin cup. "Water?"

He gulped three cupfuls. "Thank-you." He handed the cup back to her.

She took it but didn't move on to the next man. Instead, she cocked her head and eyed him.

He shifted and tugged at his sleeves, checking that the rolled ends hadn't ridden up his elbows and exposed the marks on his right arm. "Was there something you wanted?"

"Did you like Renna?" Lydia frowned at him. "Because if you did, you're taking her death really well."

Leith glanced around to make sure no one was in earshot. "I know she's not dead."

"Shad told you." Lydia snapped her fingers as if that explained everything.

Leith let her go on thinking it. He'd stood in the shadows that night, so she didn't recognize him as the Blade who'd helped fake Renna's and Brandi's deaths.

"So did you like her?"

What would it matter if he admitted the truth to Lydia now? Though, Lydia would probably tell Renna exactly what he said when they saw each other at Eagle Heights. He opened his mouth but couldn't get out anything more intelligent than an empty hiss of air.

Lydia's eyes gleamed. She grinned. "I see." Picking up the buckets, she tromped down the ditch towards the next man.

Leith grabbed his shovel. Great. That could've gone better.

As he stomped his shovel into the dirt, a commotion outside the circle of sharpened logs drew Leith's attention. He straightened and raised his hand to block the sunlight.

A man walked from the direction of the Sheered Rock Hills, leading a horse. A palomino.

Sunshine. Brandi's horse.

He dashed to the stables as the man reached the knot of people. Everyone babbled at once. As Leith shouldered his way through, Lord Alistair and Shad joined the crowd. Shad halted next to the palomino and ran his hand over its back.

Leith stumbled and fell against the stable wall. Renna. Brandi. What had happened? Were they hurt? Or—he pressed his arm across his stomach—dead.

No. He wouldn't believe that. He couldn't believe that.

He pushed his way into the stables. He didn't need to hear what had happened. He could already guess most of it, and, in the end, it didn't matter. He grabbed his saddle from its rack and headed for the stall that held Blizzard.

He'd failed. And now he had to fix it.

Shad stepped into the stable and leaned against the post next to Leith. "What do you think you're doing?"

"Going after them." Leith slung the saddle blanket, then the saddle onto Blizzard's back. "They're in trouble."

"You don't know that for sure. The horse might've simply run off."

Leith shook his head and tightened the saddle's girth. "This is Brandi we're talking about. She wouldn't let Sunshine out of her sight unless something bad happened."

Shad frowned. "There wasn't any blood. That's a good thing."

"No, it's not." Leith eased the bridle into Blizzard's

mouth. His chest tightened. "If Brandi had been knocked off her horse due to a wild animal or because the horse spooked or something accidental like that, the horse would still be wearing its bridle and saddle. Sunshine is unsaddled. They were attacked at night, after they'd stopped."

"So they were probably attacked by a Blade."

Leith blew out a breath. "Yes."

Shad rested a hand on his shoulder. "I'm going with you."

Jamie stepped from the shadows, his horse's bridle slung over his shoulder. "Me too."

Leith nodded. Whatever they'd find in the Hills, he'd be able to face it with Shad and Jamie at his side.

30

Renna curled on the ground and rested her head against the seat of a saddle. Her hands remained bound to the horn. If she wanted to escape, she'd have to drag the saddle along with her. An impossible task even without her broken leg shooting agony into her chest.

She curled tighter, as if that could cure the pain. Two days of hard travel hadn't helped her leg any.

A breeze whispered across her skin with the chill of descending night. She shivered and pressed her arms against her body to stay warm. Frogs burbled and chirped around the nearby creek, and somewhere in the distance, an owl cooed a haunting note.

A few feet away, Brandi tugged on her hands, tied in a similar fashion to her saddle. Beyond her, the three horses grazed on a small stretch of grass next to the creek. Renna pressed her face against her arms. Had Sunshine run back to Walden like Brandi believed? How long would it take the horse to find its way home? Would Leith be able to track them?

Her chest ached. Would Leith get here in time? He had to. They didn't have any other option. Either he rescued them, or they died at Nalgar Castle. King Respen had no reason to leave them alive and many to want them dead.

Worse, Martyn would show him Leith's knife. King Respen would know Leith neglected to kill Renna and Brandi. And if King Respen guessed Leith was the traitor, he'd be as dead as they were.

She prayed for rescue. Prayed for it so hard her stomach clenched with the force of her silent words. If God loved them, surely He wouldn't let them be taken to Nalgar Castle.

Martyn crouched next to her and untied her hands. She scooched upright and rubbed her wrists. Her leg throbbed with the movement.

He held out a steaming tin cup. "Here."

She grabbed the cup. Willow bark tea. He'd made some for her each morning and evening. Small kindness. It hardly made up for the hours jolting in the saddle, especially the afternoons once the painkiller wore off. Still, she wasn't going to refuse when he offered it to her.

He returned to the fire and placed a few strips of dried meat into the rest of the boiling water. Brandi wrinkled her nose. "More boiled meat? Don't you Blades ever eat anything else?"

Martyn glanced at her. The firelight shone against his blond hair in the gathering dusk. "If I didn't have to make tea for your sister, you'd be eating dried meat instead."

Brandi's grimace deepened. "It's still chewy and icky."

"We'll reach Nalgar Castle tomorrow." Martyn poked at the meat in the pot. "You might be grateful for it then."

Tomorrow. Renna sipped at her tea to hide her intake of breath. So soon. Would Leith have time to rescue them?

She studied the set of Martyn's jaw. "Why are you doing this? You could've let us escape. You could still turn us loose. King Respen wouldn't know the difference."

Martyn's eyes met hers across the fire. A hard gaze, but was that a hint of something else buried in his deep, brown eyes? "I'm the King's Third Blade. It's my duty."

"You know he's going to kill us. He might even order you to do it." Renna gripped the tin cup tighter. Its warmth seeped into her fingers as the night chilled around them. "Surely you don't want to do that."

Martyn shrugged and speared a piece of meat with his knife. "Doesn't matter what I want. I'm loyal. I follow orders." He placed the meat on a plate, then pointed at her with the knife. "Don't mistake my kindness for sympathy. I give you painkiller and food because I need you alive and well enough to answer the king's questions. Nothing more. If he gives the order, I will kill you without hesitation."

She dropped her gaze back to the cup in her hands and took another sip. He was so hopeless, so hard. The same way Leith had been when she'd first met him. She drew in a deep breath and tried the same words she'd told Leith. "You're a slave to him."

"So? What difference does that make?" Martyn stood and handed her a plate. "You're a slave to your faith. You have to obey or face punishment, same as me."

"It's not like that." Renna bit her lip and glanced at Brandi.

Brandi struggled to sit up. "We obey because God loves us, and we love God. Not because we're forced or anything. He doesn't punish us."

Martyn raised his eyebrows at her. "Really? Then what do you call this?" He waved at Brandi's bound hands and Renna's broken leg. "I might be a slave to King Respen, but at least if I obey him, I'm not punished. You're hurt, captured, and might be killed even when you serve your God faithfully. You tell me whose slavery is worse."

Renna bit her lip. She should quote a few Bible passages that said otherwise. She could give all the right answers.

But did she believe them? She'd thought she did. But sitting here, captured and facing Martyn's hard gaze, she couldn't be sure. The words wouldn't come.

Brandi launched to her feet. Her shoulders hunched, probably with the saddle's weight dragging against her wrists. "God is good, and this is good even if we can't see how. It's like Daniel's three friends in the Bible. They couldn't see how it could be good to be thrown into a burning furnace, but they refused to deny God. When they were thrown into the furnace, God rescued them. They weren't burned."

"You still hope for rescue?" Martyn snorted. "Faith and hope. I don't believe they exist any more than your God does. I believe only in things I can see."

"You can't see loyalty." Brandi shifted her hands, like she wanted to plant them on her hips.

"You can see the evidence of duty and loyalty in actions."

"And you can see the evidence of faith and hope in actions too." Brandi's jaw thrust forward.

Renna would've hugged her sister if she could get up. If

only she had an ounce of her sister's faith and bravery. Then she'd be the one standing up and debating with Martyn instead of sitting in silence.

Martyn dragged a hand through his hair. "Sit down. Eat."

Brandi plopped back to the ground, chin held high. She tugged on her hands. "You're going to have to untie me."

He huffed and untied her. Brandi clenched her fists but didn't try attacking the Blade. The knot in Renna's stomach eased. At least Brandi had learned after attacking Martyn the first night they'd stopped.

They ate and curled up in their blankets in silence. All through that dark night, Renna counted the hours. Each noise woke her. Every sound set her heart to pounding.

But Leith didn't come.

31

Leith pushed Blizzard upward into the Sheered Rock Hills, ever higher and higher. Shad and Jamie drove their horses alongside Leith. They didn't complain at Leith's pace, though they had to be tiring.

He should be cautious. They could run into one of the Blades watching the Hills. But Leith didn't care. He might even welcome it. A fight would release the tension grinding deeper into his chest with every hoofbeat.

They'd barely paused for a few hours sleep in the meadow where they'd last seen Renna and Brandi. From there, Leith followed the faint trail left by their horses. They'd had to slow for Leith to find the days-old tracks. Walter had taken a winding route, hiding their tracks as best he could. Leith ground his teeth. Renna and Brandi could be hurt, and he couldn't go any faster.

Blizzard snorted. His nostrils flared wide. Leith patted his horse's neck. His hand came away drenched. If they didn't find the girls soon, they'd have to stop for the horses' sakes, if not for their own.

Leith leaned forward as Blizzard lurched up another rough slope. Gravel slid beneath Blizzard's hooves, but the horse scrabbled up. Behind him, Shad's and Jamie's horses lunged up the slope. Reaching the top, Leith urged Blizzard forward.

A few yards into the trees, Blizzard crow-hopped sideways. He blew out another uneasy snort. Leith halted the horse and patted his neck. He scanned the woods. He didn't see anything. The trees remained still. A breeze rustled the branches and swept toward them.

As Blizzard snorted again, Leith smelled what Blizzard had already sensed. A sickly scent drifted on the air. His stomach churned. No. Please no. Anything but that.

Leith dismounted and dropped Blizzard's reins. Shad swung from his horse and joined Leith. "What is it?"

Jamie sniffed. His eyes widened as he turned toward Leith.

Swallowing, Leith pointed toward the stand of trees in front of them. "Something's dead over there."

Shad paled. Pushing the screen of branches aside, Leith stepped through. The smell hung in the small clearing. The rock face to the north side blocked the breeze.

Leith's heart dropped as he spotted the blood coating the grass on the other side of an old fire. Leith strode around the ring of stones. The smell smacked his nose. In the long grass, Leith found the torn flesh and scattered bones of a body.

Shad peered around him. He made a sound in the back of his throat and backed away, his face a pale gray. Jamie stood back, his fists clenched and shaking.

Even though Leith's stomach churned, he crouched and sifted through the torn carcass. "Looks like animals got to the body." Leith tugged on a scrap of fabric. It looked like the grey leather vest that Walter Esroy had worn when they'd last seen him. The boots on the stumps of the legs had belonged to Walter as well. "It's Walter Esroy."

"How can you stand it?" Shad's voice sounded muffled as if he had his hands over his face.

Leith gave a bitter huff. "I'm a Blade." While this sight was bad, Walter had been dead before the animals had torn his body apart. The torture King Respen did to living human beings was much worse than this.

Leith stood and glanced around the clearing. He didn't see any other bodies, nor did he see their packs and blankets.

Had the girls escaped? If they had, why hadn't they taken Sunshine? Leith scanned the ground. It hadn't rained in the last month. Coyote tracks pressed into the ground overlaid with the scuffs from him, Shad, and Jamie.

He followed faint marks from the camp, through the trees, and toward the cliff edge. He climbed down the rock face. At the bottom, a large mark carved into the sand and gravel. He followed the trail down the mountainside to a place where another larger mark displaced the gravel. Too much time had passed to give him an exact shape.

A few yards ahead, a flat spot opened next to a thick stand of juniper. He circled the spot and found another set of prints. Three horses and a man wearing the same, soft-soled boots Leith wore.

In the center of the flat spot, a knife stabbed into the ground. Leith pulled it out. It was identical to the knife he'd given Renna, except for the hilt. Instead of the initials *LT* that marked his blades, this knife wore the initials *MH*.

Martyn Hamish.

Leith collapsed to the sand, staring at the knife in his hands. Martyn knew. How much would he guess? And how much would he force Renna and Brandi to tell him?

Would Martyn show the knife to Respen? Would he choose loyalty to Leith or to the king? If he chose the king, then Respen knew by now that Leith had turned traitor. Leith couldn't return to the castle. He couldn't continue helping the Resistance.

He'd failed. He pounded the sand with his fists. He'd promised Abel Lachlan. He'd promised Renna. He'd promised himself. And he'd failed.

He should've gone with them. He would've been able to protect them from Martyn. What good had he done by staying? He was the First Blade, and he hadn't even been able to control the Blades. He'd failed to bring Lord Alistair any news from Nalgar Castle that he didn't already know. He'd done nothing worth getting Renna and Brandi captured to protect his cover.

A scrambling, sliding sound came from the cliff. He tucked the knife into his belt by his other knives. Jamie skidded to a halt and stared at the scene. Shad dropped to his knees beside Leith. "What did you find?"

Leith waved at the footprints. "Renna and Brandi were taken by a Blade."

He'd keep the Blade's identity to himself for now. He'd know soon enough if Martyn showed the knife to Respen.

Shad leapt to his feet. "Let's get moving. We have to rescue them."

Leith shook his head. "It's too late. The Blade was here days ago. If they haven't already reached Nalgar Castle, they will before we have a chance to catch up."

Jamie blinked and wrapped his arms over his stomach. Shad kicked at a tree. "We should've gone straight to Nalgar Castle."

Leith's shoulders hunched. "It was too late by the time we knew something was wrong. They would've reached Nalgar before we were half-way there. We never had a chance."

That was the worst of it. He'd failed, but he'd never had a chance to succeed this time. Not without failing in his duty to the Resistance.

Shad rested a hand on the tree he'd been kicking. "What will Respen do to them?"

"He might've had the Blade kill them right away." The words lashed across his tongue. Respen had spent years waiting to kill them. Vane's failure only made it worse. Why would Respen spare their lives when he held them in his grasp?

Shad pounded the tree, turning his face away from Leith. He muttered something under his breath that Leith couldn't hear. Jamie sagged to the ground. His shoulders shook.

Leith might've cried too if Respen hadn't beaten that weakness out of him long ago.

Perhaps he should pray for their safety. It'd be a futile request at this point. Respen might've ordered Martyn to slit the girls' throats. A prayer now would do little good.

Leith corralled his grief into that cold corner in his chest and stood. "We should bury Walter Esroy's body."

They returned to the abandoned campsite at the top of the cliff. At the sight of Walter's carcass, Shad paled even further. Leith swallowed at his roiling stomach. "Start digging a grave. Jamie, help Shad. I'll gather the body."

Shad nodded. They headed for their horses on the other side of the trees. Shad retrieved a dagger to use as a shovel, and Leith took out his blanket. Slicing a strip from the end, he cut the strip into three pieces. He tied one section around his face over his mouth and wrapped the other two sections around his hands so he wouldn't have to touch the corpse.

Returning to the body, he laid the blanket on the ground. He worked quickly, not allowing himself to dwell on the sight or stench of the body he dragged onto the blanket.

When he'd gathered the last of the remains onto the blanket, he stripped the soiled cloth from his hands and dropped it on top of the body, along with the cloth from his mouth. He folded the blanket over so the result looked more like a body wrapped in a blanket than the leftovers of a coyote's meal.

Shad joined him a few minutes later, and together they carried the blanket-wrapped bundle to the shallow grave hacked into a crevice of the mountain side. Placing the body inside, they shoved the dirt over it and piled a mound of rocks on top to prevent the wild animals from digging up the remains.

Shad carved Walter's name into a wooden board and jabbed it between two of the rocks. He rested his hand on one of the rocks for a moment. "God will redeem my soul from the power of the grave: for he shall receive me."

Leith bowed his head at the quote from Scripture. This pile of rocks was a lonely grave deep in the mountains. When the wood wore away, no one would even know this haphazard pile had even been a grave at one time. But God knew. That's all that really mattered.

Would Leith's grave be like this? A lonely grave somewhere on the prairie or deep in the mountains? Or perhaps he'd be thrown into an unmarked grave after Respen had finished whatever torture he'd inflict.

Leith washed his hands as best he could with water from his canteen. He scrubbed at his fingers for several minutes, but the prickle of death still tainted his skin.

Jamie swiped at his face and straightened his shoulders. Leith rested a hand on his shoulder.

Shad dabbed at the sweat running from his dark brown hair. "What now?"

"We head back to Walden." A shudder iced Leith's spine. "Let's find somewhere else to camp for the night. I have no wish to linger here."

Shad glanced at the bloody grass on the other side of the old campfire. "Agreed."

As they took their horses' reins and led them the way they'd come, Leith gripped the hilt of Martyn's knife. At least one person had died because of his failure to predict the Blades' movements. How many more would die because of his failures?

32

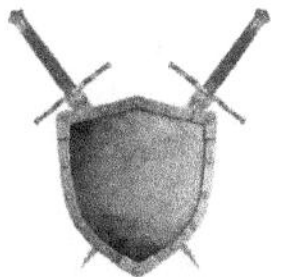

Renna's clothes stuck to her skin with sweat that never got a chance to dry. Her scalp itched with the dirt clinging to her hair. She turned her face and tried to wipe her forehead on her sleeve.

A dark smudge rose on the horizon to their south. As they drew closer, the smudge sharpened into a grey wall with round, crenulated towers at the corners. Her heart flipped in her chest. Nalgar Castle. She shivered despite the heat.

Martyn led their horses to the twin towers guarding the main gate. At his hail, the guards swung open the gates. Renna closed her eyes as they passed through the wall's shadow.

The horses' hooves echoed on the cobbles. Martyn halted them in front of a stable. Several thin, pale-faced boys ghosted to their horses and grabbed the bridles. They kept their eyes on the ground, as if they didn't dare meet the gaze of the Blade or his victims.

She glanced around the courtyard. Across the way, servants bustled around the kitchen tower, their heads lowered, eyes dull, as if the hopelessness of this place had seeped into their bones. Soldiers clanked along the ramparts and trotted across the courtyard. Renna and Brandi weren't going to find help in this place.

Martyn swung off his horse and approached Brandi's. In a few deft tugs, he untied Brandi, dragged her from the horse, and placed her next to him. He repeated the motions with Renna, his hands firm and cold on her waist. She swayed on her good leg.

Brandi hurried to her side. Renna looped her arms over her sister's shoulders. For a moment, their gaze met. Renna squeezed Brandi's shoulders. "As long as we're together, we'll be all right."

Brandi touched her bound hands to her chest, over the spot where her silver cross necklace tucked beneath her shirt. "God is our strength."

Renna nodded. Her own necklace shifted against her skin. She'd try to remember that.

With his hands pressed against their backs, Martyn shoved them forward. Renna stumbled, nearly taking both her and Brandi to the cobbles. Brandi stretched her hands up and clasped Renna's fingers.

Martyn directed them into an arched passageway that connected the cobblestone courtyard with the Queen's Court, a grass courtyard on the other side of the Great Hall.

Midway through the passage, an opening cut into the stone wall to their left. A wooden bridge spanned what was a dry ditch at this time of summer. The massive, five-story Blades' Tower loomed above the moat, standing taller than the rest of the castle as if to emphasize the king's might.

Across the passage, stairs curled upward. The Blade pushed them that direction. Renna grimaced. Hopping on flat ground was difficult enough with her broken leg. How were they going to manage stairs?

Brandi walked up the first stair and paused. With a deep breath, Renna bounced onto the stair, planting her arms on Brandi's shoulders to steady herself. Brandi moved up the next stair, and they repeated their movements.

Each stair became harder since Renna had to balance on the thin stair before hopping up the next one. Still, Martyn never offered to untie them or help. He stalked up the stairs behind them, a stone-faced shadow.

As they ascended, the stairs darkened, only partially lit from candles recessed into the stone walls. Renna nearly ran into the thick door that barred the way at the top. Martyn reached past them and knocked.

"Enter," a deep voice boomed from the other side of the door. Martyn lifted the latch, nudged the door open, and pushed Renna and Brandi inside.

The plush carpeting caressed Renna's boots. Paintings hung on the wall over dark paneling. A broad window streamed light into the room.

King Respen lounged behind his large desk. His dark hair waved above a tanned face. At the end of his chin, his trimmed beard sharpened into a knife's point underneath a razor-thin mustache. He would've been a handsome man, except for his eyes. Renna had never seen eyes so cold, not even on Harrison Vane.

Martyn clicked the door shut and brushed past them. He

knelt before King Respen, bowed his head, and thumped a fisted right hand over his heart. "My king."

"My Blade." King Respen repeated the fist over heart gesture, though his head remained unbowed. "You are the Third Blade. Why do you dare to report directly to me?"

Martyn waved a hand in their direction. "I captured these two girls deep in the Sheered Rock Hills and killed their guide. They are the ladies Rennelda and Brandiline."

"Have you interrogated them?"

"I waited for your instruction, my king." Martyn bowed his head once again. Was this the slavery Leith experienced? Did he bow and scrape before King Respen like this Blade did?

"Very wise."

Renna choked on a breath when King Respen's eyes fixed on her, scouring across her as if to sift her every secret.

Martyn pulled Brandi's Bible from his saddlebag. He presented it to King Respen. "They had this with them."

King Respen took it and flipped through the pages. He met Renna's gaze, turned, and tossed the book onto the embers of the fire in the fireplace.

Renna gasped while Brandi shrieked. She charged forward, dragging Renna with her. Renna hopped as fast as she could. Before they could reach the fireplace, tongues of flames shot up from the book.

"No." Brandi dropped to her knees, her whole body shaking.

Renna hugged her and watched the pages curl and blacken. The fire ate at the cover, consuming the front page with the words *Love Mother and Father* written across it. The last gift from their parents to Brandi.

Renna pressed her face against Brandi's hair. Another memento lost. Renna's Bible, with the same message in it, had been stolen by Vane months ago. Only Renna's silver cross remained.

King Respen bent over them. His hand closed around Renna's face and yanked her head up. "You claim your God is powerful. Where is that power now? Do you think you will be saved from me? I am the power over your lives now."

Shivers quaked down Renna's spine. His fingers dug into her cheeks and under her chin. Her skin crawled at his touch. She tried to pull away, but his grip tightened. Any tighter and he'd choke her.

"Is this your God's love?" King Respen pulled out a knife and placed its tip below Renna's left eye. She whimpered. The flash of steel filled her sight.

Brandi's voice pleaded with King Respen. Renna didn't dare move.

He shoved Renna away. She tumbled and dragged Brandi to the floor along with her. He kicked her broken leg. Pain blasted through her body. She sobbed and curled into a ball.

He stalked back to his desk. "By the time I'm done with you, you will deny your God."

Renna cringed. She wasn't brave. She wasn't strong enough for this. Already, her body begged to tell him anything he wanted to stop the pain.

Beside her, Brandi pulled both of them upright. Her eyes blazed. "We'll never deny our faith."

King Respen laughed, a sound like the booming of ice as it shifted on a springtime lake. "You do not understand my power. Not yet. But you will." He waved to Martyn. "Take them to the dungeons."

Martyn hesitated for a fraction of a second. Renna held her breath. Would he give King Respen Leith's knife?

King Respen's fingers tapped on the desktop. "They will be interrogated. I am as interested as you to find out how they escaped death at the hands of my Blades yet again. But nothing will be gained while they retain their defiance." His lips turned upward, but it wasn't a smile. "Better they get a taste of my hospitality first."

"Yes, my king." Martyn thumped his fist on his chest and reached for Renna and Brandi. He dragged them to their feet and yanked them from the room.

At the top of the stairs, Martyn gave a sigh and heaved Renna over his shoulder. She squealed but forced herself not to struggle. She'd fall if she hopped down the stairs on her own.

Martyn didn't set her down at the bottom of the stairs. Renna twisted, trying to see where they were going, as he carried her and dragged Brandi across the cobblestone courtyard. He entered a huge, squat tower at the northeast side of the courtyard. Two sets of stairs led away from the doorway, one headed up and the other down. He took the stairs down into a clammy darkness.

At the bottom of the stairs, two guards stood in front of a huge, iron door. She felt Martyn stand straighter. "King Respen ordered me to bring these prisoners down here."

Renna grimaced. The guards were getting a great view of her rear end sticking in the air over Martyn's shoulder.

One of the guards grunted and pulled out a set of keys. Unlocking the door, the guard led them into a tight, circular space. Renna counted six doors set into the stone wall.

The guard paused and unlocked a door. "This one's empty."

Martyn shoved Brandi forward. She stumbled into the dark cell. Renna didn't even have time to shriek as he tossed her from his shoulder and into the cell. She careened into Brandi. Both of them landed hard on the stone floor.

Renna pushed herself onto her elbows, gasping for breath. She met Martyn's gaze and pointed at the hilt of Leith's knife in his boot sheath. "You didn't—"

Martyn grasped her arm and shook her. "Don't mention it. Ever. Got that?"

She nodded. Why was Martyn protecting Leith? Had he decided to honor their friendship? Or was he waiting until Leith returned to set a trap for him?

Martyn dropped her arm and slammed the door behind him. Renna lay still for a moment. Her leg ached while the skin under her eye throbbed. But they were alive for now.

She pushed herself into a sitting position and glanced around. The cell was six feet wide, six feet tall, and five feet deep. Not even a pile of old straw or a tattered blanket filled the empty space. A thin shaft of light filtered down from a small opening set near the ceiling.

Brandi scrambled to her feet and tiptoed to the wall. Gripping the ledge, she pulled herself up to peer out the opening. After a moment, she dropped back to the ground. "There's a barred window at the top of this long shaft that goes up to the ground level. I can see a bit of the courtyard. The shaft and window are too small. Even I can't squeeze through."

"I bet water runs down it when it rains." Renna grimaced. As bad as this cell was now, it'd be worse if they were forced to sit in a puddle of cold water.

Brandi plopped to the ground. "It's summer. It isn't going to rain."

Renna leaned against the wall and stretched her injured leg. As long as she didn't move, her leg didn't hurt. She held out her bound hands to Brandi. "Now that we're alone, do you think you can untie this?"

"Maybe." Brandi bent over Renna's hands, her face scrunched. She tugged on the knots, her own hands still tied. After several minutes, the rope slackened. Brandi grinned and ripped it off. "Got it!"

"Good job. Here, let me do yours." Renna reached for Brandi's hands. She clawed at the rope. The sisal jammed underneath her fingernails and slivered into her fingers.

The rope eased and fell away. Renna tossed the rope away. They were free, or at least as free as they could be in a dungeon cell. She rubbed her wrists, wincing at the prickle of rope slivers stuck in her skin.

Brandi curled up against Renna's side and rested her head on Renna's shoulder. "What's he going to do to us?"

A lump gathered in Renna's throat. What could she tell her? King Respen would torture them until they denied their faith. Then he'd kill them. But Renna couldn't tell Brandi that.

Renna leaned her cheek against Brandi's hair. She should tell Brandi that God was with them. As a Christian, the words should flow from her mouth. But she couldn't do it.

Maybe Martyn was right. Surely love didn't look like this,

sitting in a dungeon wondering what day King Respen would decide they'd die.

Brandi's question still hung in the air. Renna hugged her tighter. "I don't know what King Respen plans to do with us. But whatever happens, I'm going to be here."

Brandi nodded and hugged Renna back. Renna's stomach clenched at her empty promise. If God couldn't keep His promise to be with His people, then Renna didn't have a prayer of keeping her promise to Brandi.

33

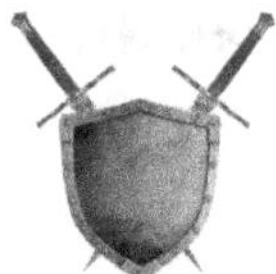

Leith slumped into one of the chairs in front of Lord Alistair's desk. Shad leaned against the wall, legs sagging, as if he might crumble at any moment. Leith had ordered Jamie to tend to the horses. At least he wouldn't have to re-live the last few days.

Lord Alistair bowed his head. Gray flecked his brown hair at his temples. "Are they dead?"

"Walter Esroy is dead. We buried his body." Shad's voice wobbled.

"Renna and Brandi were captured by a Blade." Leith stared at the floor.

"Is there any chance King Respen would've spared their lives?" Lord Alistair steepled his fingers. "Is there a chance he'd use them to bargain with the Resistance?"

Leith shook his head. "Respen won't bargain. What would he have to gain? The Resistance's surrender? He'd be better off killing Renna and Brandi and getting the Resistance to surrender afterwards.

"So they're already dead." Shad pounded his fist into the bookcase.

Leith tried to think of a reason—any reason—why Respen would've decided to keep them alive. He couldn't accept that Renna was dead. Not yet. Not until he'd seen her body himself.

Power. That was the driving force behind Respen's decisions. He'd created the Blades to gain power. He'd taken the kingdom for the power he would wield. Every time he met with his Blades, his every move was calculated to remind his Blades that he was the one in power.

Leith straightened. "Renna and Brandi might be alive." He glanced between the two sets of brown eyes staring at him. "When a Blade fails three times, Respen has them killed. If they try to run, Respen has them hunted down."

"What does that have to do with Renna and Brandi?" Shad cocked his head. His hands remained clenched.

"A failed Blade is always killed at a Meeting of the Blades in front of all the Blades. It's a reminder of Respen's power." Leith's mind whirled. "Brandi and Renna have escaped him three times. Respen has to prove to the Blades that Renna and Brandi aren't invincible. He'll wait to kill them until the next Meeting of the Blades two weeks from now."

Shad clenched his sword's hilt. "What will he do to them in the meantime?"

"He'll want them to admit that he controls their lives. He'll do what it takes to make that happen." Leith pressed his shaking hands against his knees. If he closed his eyes, he could see the torture. Renna chained in the meeting room at the top of the Blades' Tower, blood flowing from cuts across her face. Brandi curled in a ball, screaming, as a Blade raised a whip again.

No. Surely not. God wouldn't let torture like that happen to them, would He?

"I'm going to return to Nalgar Castle to try to rescue them." A cold steel flashed through Leith. Whatever it took, he would rescue them.

Lord Alistair shook his head. "Even if Respen hasn't already guessed you're working for us, if you return before your assigned mission length is over, he'll grow suspicious."

"I can't just sit here." Thanks to Martyn, Respen probably knew about Leith's treachery. But that didn't matter. Only rescuing Renna and Brandi did.

"I know. And I know I can't stop you from going if it comes down to that." Lord Alistair leaned his elbows on the desk. "Charging in there without a proper plan won't help anyone. If you get yourself killed, you won't be able to help them."

Leith crossed his arms. "We can't just leave them in Respen's hands."

"I know." Lord Alistair tugged on his beard. "But what can we do? We don't have the numbers to rescue them. You might be able to sneak in, but getting out would be difficult. With your cover blown, you can't return to Nalgar Castle."

"Possibly." Leith drew on the well of cold in his chest. Time to think this through as logically as possible. "Based on the evidence, Respen might not know I'm a traitor. A failure as a Blade, yes, but not a traitor."

That all depended on whether or not Martyn gave Leith's knife to Respen. For now, Leith had to trust his friend would protect him. His chest ached too much to contemplate anything else.

Shad rubbed his sword's hilt. "That's true. Unless he forces Renna and Brandi to tell him, he can't know how they got out of Walden Manor."

"I'll have to claim that Vane got them out before I arrived, and that Jamie and I killed decoys you'd placed in their beds." Leith scuffed the rugs with the toe of his boot, first one way, then the other, forming patterns in the weave. "But I'll have to continue on as if everything's normal. I can't go to Nalgar Castle early."

The words hurt so much Leith had to close his eyes for a moment. How could he possibly leave Renna and Brandi in Respen's power even for a day, much less two weeks?

But he couldn't do anything else. As a Blade, he'd be able to walk freely into Nalgar Castle and straight into the dungeons. He could free them without the guards daring to question him. It was the only way to rescue them.

"Even then, you could ride straight into a trap. Respen might arrest you the moment you return to Nalgar Castle." Shad crossed his arms.

"No, he won't wait to arrest me until I return. It's a power thing. He'd want me brought back in chains." Leith shoved the shiver at those words deep into his chest. "The moment Respen realizes I'm a spy, he'd send someone to alert the Blades searching for Vane to arrest me instead. If that doesn't happen, then I'll know it's safe to return."

"I see. So the more we convince him that Vane is still alive, the more he'll believe that Vane rescued Renna and Brandi, not treachery on your part." Lord Alistair tapped his fingers against his chin. For the first time since Leith and

Shad had reported the girls' capture, the glint returned to Lord Alistair's eyes. "We'd planned to have you make your first appearance as Vane shortly. We'll stick to that plan. Tomorrow Shad will announce to the men that there's a Blade helping us, and you can make your first appearance as Vane."

Despite the knot in his stomach, Leith nodded. "Once that's done, I'll slip out of Walden as myself and report to Eleventh Blade Harding, who'll have seen Vane's appearance. I'll send him to Nalgar Castle to report both Vane's reappearance and my failure to kill Renna and Brandi. Hopefully that'll head off any doubts Respen might have about me."

"Good." Lord Alistair nodded once. "For the next two weeks, it seems all we can do for Renna and Brandi is pray and place them in God's hands."

Leith swallowed. Abel Lachlan had said something similar before he'd returned to Stetterly. "The Lachlans will have to be informed."

"Yes. I'll send a rider, though he might have some difficulty getting through." Lord Alistair's jaw tightened. "Uster is under siege."

A war lay between Walden and Stetterly. And a castle stood between Leith and rescuing Renna and Brandi.

Two weeks. How were Renna and Brandi going to survive two weeks?

Leith bowed his head but couldn't find the words. How could he ask God to grant Renna courage for torture that even Leith feared to face?

34

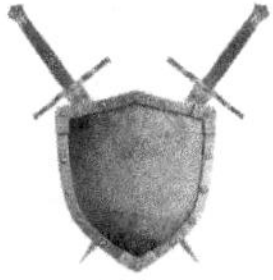

Renna pried at a stone in the dungeon floor, but her fingers slipped and scraped against the stone. She slumped against the wall. "It's no use, Brandi. None of the stones are loose. Not even in the floor."

Brandi kicked at the wall and slumped next to Renna. "We can't just sit here. We have to do something."

Renna bit her lip. If only she could think of something. But what could they do? The walls, floor, and ceiling were solid layers of stone. Martyn had taken Renna's knife, and they didn't even have a hair pin between them. Even if they could get out of the dungeon, what good would it do? Renna couldn't walk without assistance. How far would they get hobbling?

Several pairs of boots thumped down the stairs. Renna tensed. It wasn't time for one of their meals. "Brandi, help me up."

Brandi tugged Renna to her good foot and tucked underneath one of Renna's arms. Renna wrapped her arm around Brandi's shoulder.

Their door rattled and swung open. Several guards and Martyn stood in front of their cell. Martyn drew one of his knives and stepped into their cell. Renna tightened her grip on Brandi's shoulders. Shivers tore down her spine and into her legs.

Martyn grabbed Brandi's wrist and dragged her forward. "Come with me."

Renna hopped forward, using Brandi as balance. Martyn shoved her shoulder. She tumbled backwards, striking her back against the stone.

"Not you." He hauled Brandi away from her.

Brandi twisted her arm and beat at him with her free hand. "Let me go! I'm not going without my sister." She kicked him in the shins and leaned forward, her teeth bared to bite his arm.

Martyn pressed the knife to her throat, halting her. "If you bite me, I will kill you."

Renna's heart stuttered at the sight of a knife pressed to Brandi's neck. "It's all right, Brandi. Go with him."

For a moment, their eyes locked. It wasn't all right. For all they knew, King Respen was taking Brandi away to kill her.

Brandi managed one last whimper before Martyn dragged her from the cell. The guards slammed the door closed.

Renna slid to the floor, gasping at the force of the tears shuddering through her body. She pressed her fingers into her palms. The bite of her fingernails focused her onto that narrow point of pain.

She couldn't panic. Not yet. Brandi would be all right. King Respen would most likely only question her. If he'd planned to kill her, he would've made Renna watch.

She curled on the floor of the cell, waiting, waiting, waiting.

What was taking so long? What was King Respen doing to Brandi?

Let her be all right. Protect her from King Respen. The prayer clustered against the ceiling by all the other unheard prayers Renna had muttered for the past few days. She rested her face against the floor. God felt as cold and hard as that stone.

When the door finally clanked open, Renna shoved herself upright. Martyn shoved Brandi inside.

Brandi stumbled and fell against Renna. She pressed her mouth against Renna's ear. "The First Blade rescued us."

Renna opened her mouth to ask what she meant when Martyn grabbed her elbow and yanked her to her feet. Renna only had time to glance over her shoulder at Brandi before Martyn hauled her from the cell. The door clanged shut between them.

Martyn hefted Renna to his shoulder and strode up the stairs. She bounced against his shoulder as he strolled across the cobblestone courtyard, through the dark passageway, and up the stairs to King Respen's chambers.

Chills spiked through Renna's body as Martyn opened the door and stepped into the king's study. As before, King Respen sat behind his desk. His pen scratched against what appeared to be some important document.

Martyn dropped Renna on the floor. The thick burgundy carpet cushioned her fall. She rolled into a sitting position and drew her good leg up to her chest, stretching her injured leg out in front of her. Whatever they planned to do to her, she'd be helpless to resist.

King Respen swiveled in his chair and fixed his dark eyes on her. His fingers stroked the ends of the armrests. "How did you and your sister evade the death I decreed for you?"

Ice froze Renna's bones. What could she say? One wrong word, and she'd get Leith killed. That's why Respen had decided to question her and Brandi separately. She didn't know what Brandi had told him. He'd see through their lies in an instant if they didn't match up. What had Brandi been trying to tell her?

The First Blade rescued us. It was the truth. Leith was the current First Blade. He'd rescued them by not killing them and taking them away from Walden. But surely Brandi hadn't confessed Leith's spying activities to the king?

The First Blade. Leith had framed the former First Blade, making it appear that he was the spy, not a Leith. Renna clenched her fists. If she said that the First Blade had rescued them, would King Respen assume that the First Blade she was talking about was Harrison Vane? Was that what Brandi had done? Told the truth and let King Respen assume a lie?

Renna took a deep breath. "The First Blade knew you were going to try to kill us. He got us out of Walden so you couldn't hurt us."

He slapped his hands flat against the armrests. "Harrison Vane thought he could outsmart me again, did he? He didn't succeed this time."

Renna trembled. King Respen could do whatever he wanted to them. No one even knew they'd been captured.

Leith probably believed they were safe in the Resistance hideout by now.

What would happen when Leith returned to Nalgar Castle at the end of his mission? He wouldn't know what they'd told King Respen. He might not even know that King Respen had them at his castle. Leith would walk into a trap, and he wouldn't even know it. She dug her nails into her palms. She didn't have any way to warn him.

King Respen leaned forward, his eyes fixed on her. "I can read your fear. You are right to fear me. I hold your life in my hands."

She should deny his words. She ought to tell him that her life rested in God's hands, not his. But Renna's mouth glued shut.

He was right. He did hold their lives in his hands.

King Respen slouched into his chair, a smirk twisting his slim beard. "Take her back to the dungeon."

Martyn picked her up and slung her over his shoulder once again. She didn't struggle. She was too empty to resist. She hung limply as the Blade headed back down the stairs, across the courtyard, and into the dungeon tower once again. He deposited her in the cell next to Brandi and left without another word.

Brandi's eyes searched Renna's face. "Did he hurt you?"

Renna shook her head and studied Brandi. She opened her mouth to ask the same question but stopped. A red splotch marked Brandi's cheek. "What did he do to you?"

Brandi touched her cheek. She grinned, but it didn't sparkle in her eyes. "I told him that he only had the power that God gave him. He didn't like that very much."

Renna wrapped her arms around Brandi and hugged her

tightly. Of course Brandi wouldn't remain as silent as Renna had.

If only Brandi had a little less courage. One of these days, her bravery would get her killed.

35

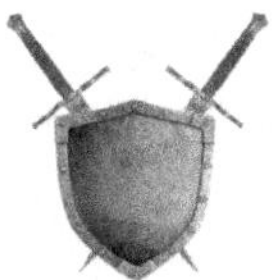

Leith crouched in a tree in front of the flat area to the north of the manor. Walden's soldiers stood at attention, every eye following Shad as he paced in front of them, directly below the tree where Leith hid.

He held himself still, resisting the urge to swipe his hands on his black trousers. Even with Shad preparing them, the men assembled below him wouldn't react well to having a Blade step into their midst. They might decide to kill him and ask for answers from Shad later.

Shad's voice rose in a steady, commanding tone, silencing the men's hushed whispers. "Less than two months ago an assassination plot against my father was stopped."

From his spot in the tree, Leith could see a few of the men shift in the ranks.

"As some of you know, that assassination attempt was carried out by a Blade. We were able to stop him because another Blade warned us and helped us that night."

Those words caused a louder stir. Shad had to hold up his hands for silence and shout to be heard when the men were too shocked to fall silent. "As another Blade's incursion into Walden less than a week ago shows, you aren't ready to face the Blades. In light of this, our Blade has agreed to come out of hiding to help train you."

The murmuring rose to a roar of babbling voices.

Leith inched his hand upward and checked that the hood and cowl Shad had found for him were in place. The hood covered his head and hung down over his eyes while the cowl covered his mouth and nose. Even when he spoke, no one would match his muffled commands with the soft-spoken peasant Daniel.

Too bad the hood and cowl were so hot and scratchy. Leith's breath pooled, hot and wet, inside the cowl. He hadn't even begun the training, and sweat already beaded along his forehead and neck.

Shad shouted for silence. He had to wait several minutes, arms crossed, eyes glaring, for the soldiers to quiet. When they did, he swept the ranks with a hard stare. "My father and I trust this Blade. He's proven he's on our side. Listen to him. What he has to say may not only save your life, but it could also save the lives of your families. You're not to try to kill him. The attempt will be punished by my father, if you survive it."

The men were stone silent now. Leith drew in a deep breath. The cloth pressed against his mouth and nose. He jumped from the thick limb and landed lightly on his feet beside Shad.

The men panicked. Some stumbled backwards and half-turned as if to run. Others grabbed for their swords and started forward. The rest froze, too scared to move. Leith ignored all of them, even the ones drawing their swords. They, at least, had the right reflexes.

He stepped closer, pretending he didn't see the row of swords pointing at his chest. "Thanks to your lack of observance, your lord's heir is now dead."

The soldiers halted, glancing between him and Shad. Leith didn't need to turn around to know that Shad leaned against the tree, arms crossed, a smirk playing across his face.

"If I hadn't sneaked the ladies Rennelda and Brandiline out of Walden, they would be dead." Leith let all the cold steel he'd developed during his years as a Blade flood into his voice. "You need to be observant. In the past months, I've slipped in and out of Walden Manor many, many times. I've never been stopped. Had I wanted to kill your lord, he would've been dead long ago. That's why I am here. Because not all of the Blades have the conscience I have."

He could see by their stunned expressions that his words had hit home. Even the bravest of the soldiers, the ones who'd drawn their swords, shrank back from him.

He stepped forward, coming within feet of the first ranks. "You fear the Blades. You think we aren't human or that we can't be killed. I'm telling you right now. I am human. The other Blades are human. So far this year, common soldiers like yourselves have killed several Blades. Lady Lorraine killed the Second Blade by herself. If they have the courage to stand against a Blade, then you do too."

The ranks of soldiers blinked at him. Leith suppressed a

sigh. It had been so much easier when he was training only Shad. He pointed at a soldier. "Step forward."

With a glance at the soldiers around him, the man slid his feet forward. His sword remained loosely gripped in his hand. His Adam's apple bobbed.

"Attack me." Leith stood on the balls of his feet, his hands resting at his sides.

The soldier glanced between Leith and Shad, eyes wide with fright. Leith could almost hear the man's brain sizzling as he tried to decide if he should disobey an order given by his commanding officer or if he should disobey a Blade.

After letting the man dither for several minutes, Shad barked a new order. "Don't attempt to attack the Blade unless he orders you to."

By the time the soldier turned his attention back to him, Leith had pulled two knives from his belt and pressed one knife under the man's chin and the other to the man's ribs. "You're now dead. Why?"

The man shook. "I...I didn't pay attention."

"Correct. You took your attention off me." Leith kept his knives pressed against the man's stomach and throat. He had to get his point across. The next time a Blade got his knife to the man's throat, he'd die. "You also hesitated. You cannot hesitate with a Blade."

When the man nodded, Leith stepped back and sheathed his knives. The soldier stumbled to his place in line, rubbing his neck and trembling like he'd seen death itself. Leith squashed any sympathy he might have for him. By the time he was done with these men, they'd be able to stare death in the face and keep on fighting. They'd have to, or they'd die.

By the time the afternoon ended, Leith had worked with all of the small groups of soldiers he'd had them form. Sweat plastered his black clothes to his skin. His muscles ached after the unaccustomed amount of fighting. Stifling a groan, he managed to slip into the manor while Shad distracted the soldiers by calling them to attention.

When no one was looking, Leith ducked into the room in the servant's wing that he'd been given as Daniel the peasant. He peeled his shirt from his skin, grimacing. The black clothing the Blades wore had been designed for assassinations in the dead of night. Not the middle of an Acktarian summer day.

Changing into his homespun shirt and trousers, Leith placed his weapons and black clothes in a hiding place in the ceiling of his room.

As he turned to leave, Jamie slipped into the room, his mouth pressed into a solemn line. "I know why you dared to stand up to King Respen. You're really good." He ducked his head. "I snuck over and watched."

Leith crossed his arms, not sure what to say. "Yes, I'm good at fighting. But skills with weapons don't give me my courage. You can have all the skills in the world and still be afraid to do what's right."

"But you're the First Blade. You aren't scared of anything."

"I'm still shaking in my boots every time I report to Respen." Leith swallowed at the bitter taste in his mouth. He met Jamie's gaze. "True courage comes from knowing that you belong to God both body and soul so completely that the evil men in this world don't own you."

The right words to say but so hard to live by.

Jamie chewed on his bottom lip and nodded.

Leith patted Jamie's shoulders. "Come on. We need to rejoin the work on the fortifications."

Exiting the room, they strode down the hallway towards the kitchen. As soon as they stepped into the kitchen, the cook pounced on them. "Did you see the Blade training the lord's soldiers?"

Leith nodded. The less he said the better. Double identities had been bad enough. Triple identities were downright confusing. He was going to start running into himself.

One of the kitchen maids gave a loud sigh. "I wonder what he looks like under that hood and cowl. I bet he's handsome."

Leith resisted the urge to roll his eyes. Not that he wasn't flattered, but the girl wasn't giving him a second glance at the moment. What was it about a change of clothes, a mysterious hood, and weapons that made a girl look twice?

Jamie gave him a side-long glance, and Leith shrugged. He couldn't explain girls. He was too confused himself.

LEITH TRUDGED AROUND A BOULDER AND ENTERED A HOLLOW created by a cliff face, the boulder, and a stand of pine trees. As he approached, Eleventh Blade Harding shot to his feet. "Did you see him?"

"Couldn't see much under that hood and cowl he was wearing, but it's Vane." Leith rubbed at the peasant's shirt he still wore. It had taken him a few hours to find an opportunity to slip away without being seen and hike into the Hills to find Harding. "Are the others spread out north of here?"

Harding waved back toward the Hills. "The Seventh Blade is north of us. I still haven't seen the Third Blade. Seems Vane slipped past us."

"Yes, but we mustn't let it happen again." Leith crossed his arms and eyed Harding with all the steel he could muster. "Contact the Seventh Blade and the Third Blade if you see him, then ride to Nalgar Castle to report to the king. Turns out the girls Jamie and I killed were only servant girls Lord Alistair had placed as decoys. Vane sneaked the real ladies Rennelda and Brandiline out of Walden before I arrived. So far, I've managed to stay out of Vane's way. I'll try to learn where he's hiding inside the manor so we can flush him out."

"Where do you want the rest of us?"

"Stick to this section of Hills for now. Be ready to cut Vane off if he tries to flee into the Hills again. I don't want any of you trying to sneak into Walden, understand?" Leith sliced Harding with a look until he nodded.

After they saluted each other, Leith hiked back the way he'd come. After he was well out of sight and sound of Harding, he leaned against a boulder and rested his head in his hands.

So many lies. When was it going to end? Each plot spiraled more and more out of control. Every lie needed another to keep up the pretense.

If only he could stop it all. But if he did, Renna and Brandi would have no hope of rescue. Lord Alistair would face Respen's Blades without knowledge of their plans.

Leith pushed up his right sleeve. Thirty-seven scars marred his skin from his shoulder down to his elbow. He'd gained thirty-five of those while following Respen's orders to the letter. All that bloodshed. All those lives taken.

No, he couldn't run from this. No matter how many lies it took, he couldn't be responsible for more bloodshed and more lives lost.

36

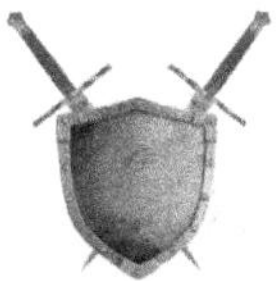

Renna clung to Brandi as Martyn dragged them across the cobblestone courtyard, through the now familiar passageway, and up the winding stairs to King Respen's chambers.

When they were called to enter, Renna and Brandi tottered onto the rugs. Instead of lounging in the chair next to his desk, King Respen stood next to the wide window overlooking the courtyard below, his hands clasped behind his back. Renna shuddered at the power that rolled from his shoulders.

"Bring them here." King Respen didn't bother to turn around.

At Martyn's shove against her back, Renna hopped forward. Brandi kept pace with her. They stopped near the far side of the window. Renna leaned against the wall, her stomach twisting. She didn't like being this close to King Respen. He stood a good eight inches taller than her. The sun outside cast a shadow across his hatchet-sharp face.

"I received word from my Blades in the Hills. For all his claims to moral righteousness, it turns out Lord Alistair is not opposed to sacrificing a few servant girls when it serves his purposes."

Renna twisted the ragged end of her blouse in her fingers. "What do you mean?"

"My First Blade killed the servant girls posing as you." King Respen's gaze swept over them, as if searching for some kind of reaction.

What reaction was he expecting? What servant girls?

Brandi stilled, her head cocked to the side. After a moment, her mouth tilted briefly upward before curving into a frown. She doubled over as if in pain. "They're dead? They volunteered to take our place." Her voice quavered.

Renna let herself slump against the wall. Hopefully her relief looked like shock. Leith had figured out they'd been captured. He'd come up with a false story, and thankfully the little they'd said matched it.

When she raised her head, she spotted Martyn standing by the door. Martyn met her gaze, bent, and touched the hilt of Leith's knife. They might've convinced King Respen, but Martyn knew the hole in their story. He knew something wasn't right. Would he betray Leith?

With his back to the Blade, King Respen hadn't seen the movement. He waved at the courtyard spread below them. "Did you notice the rider waiting by the stables?"

Renna peered at the courtyard. From here, she could only see the edge of the stable roof set directly below them. Next to it, a teenager dressed all in black held the reins of a mouse-brown horse. Another Blade.

Brandi poked her head next to Renna. Her eyes widened. "Where's he going?"

King Respen's mouth curved into a thin smile. "The Twelfth Blade will carry a message to a company of soldiers detached from the divisions surrounding Uster. This company is stationed a day north of Stetterly."

Brandi snapped her head around so fast she banged the top of her head into Renna's chin. "No!"

Renna reared back. She opened her mouth, but she couldn't force any words out. King Respen was going to attack their home. He'd kill Uncle Abel, Aunt Mara, all the people who attended their hidden church. She blinked at a rush of tears. "Please. Please don't."

He faced them, one hand stroking the windowsill. "Why not? Stetterly has defied my edicts for too long."

She swallowed and hugged Brandi tighter. Brandi clenched her fists and glared at the king. "You leave them alone."

His eyebrows shot up. He stroked his pointed beard and the windowsill, as if he considered Brandi's words. "I might spare them. But that all depends on you."

"What do you want us to do?" Renna's chest crumbled. His demands wouldn't be good.

The slick smile returned to his face. "All you have to do is admit that your God is worthless, and that I have the ultimate power over your life. Nothing much, since it is already true."

Renna licked her dry lips. Could she say the words, but not really mean them? All Respen wanted was a verbal denial. If it'd save Uncle Abel and Aunt Mara, then surely the lie was all right. She'd be saving lives. She took a deep breath and cracked her mouth open to speak.

Before she could, Brandi stepped forward. One fist shook at her sides, the other touched the lump of her silver cross necklace under her bodice. Her eyes flared like the coals of a white-blue fire. "Never! We'll never deny Christ!"

Renna snapped her mouth shut. Wrapping her arms around Brandi, Renna gripped Brandi tight to prevent her from doing anything rash. Like punching the king.

"Then their blood will be on your heads." King Respen waved Martyn forward. "Return them to their cell and tell the Twelfth Blade to depart."

As Martyn grabbed her arm, Renna met King Respen's eyes. He smirked at her, his eyes dancing. A bitter pain flooded into her toes.

He'd seen the truth written her eyes. He knew what she'd nearly done.

37

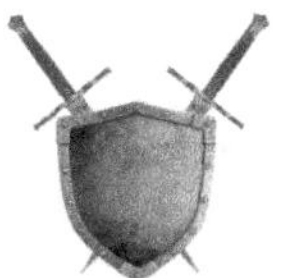

Leith stepped into the manor after yet another training session. The cool shadows inside washed over him.

So far so good. The Seventh Blade watching from the Hills hadn't noticed that Vane's movements and fighting style resembled Leith's, and the distance prevented him from realizing Vane stood several inches shorter than he used to. When Harding returned from Nalgar Castle last night, he hadn't been carrying orders to kill Leith. Instead, he'd brought word that Martyn had captured Renna and Brandi, and Respen wanted Vane caught at all costs.

Leith reached to unwrap the cowl from his face and froze. A face peeked from one of the rooms along the hallway. Leith reacted even before his brain recognized the face belonged to Seventh Blade Daas. He bolted down the hallway, kicking the door as he passed. The door slammed into Daas's face, smashing his head between the door and its frame.

While Daas fell to the floor, stunned, Leith sprinted up the stairs, using the newel post at the top to swing to his right without slowing his momentum. Daas thumped up the stairs after him.

Slowing, Leith ducked into the room that had been Renna's when she'd first moved to Walden several months ago. He shut the door and clicked the lock shut. The door wouldn't stop Daas for long, but hopefully it'd be enough.

Leith dashed across the room and swung out the window. His feet landed on the stone ledge that ran around the manor at the base of the second floor.

Leith had nearly fallen to his death trying to get on this ledge last time. Only his knife's firm grip on the stone had saved his life.

Dropping to his hands and knees, Leith felt under the ledge. His hand encountered a metal object still sticking from the brick wall. He tested it. After all this time, the dagger remained imbedded in the crack between the bricks. Taking a deep breath, he extended his feet over the edge and felt for toeholds. Above him, something clicked as Daas picked the lock.

His feet found a crack between bricks. He wiggled his toes into the crack, gripped the dagger with one hand, and dropped below the edge. Heart pounding, he scrambled down the wall and swung into the open window to Lord Alistair's study. Lord Alistair glanced up from his desk as Leith slammed the windows closed and bolted the locks.

No time to explain. He raced across the room, down the hallway, and skidded into his room. Locking the door behind him, he shucked his black clothes and yanked his homespun on.

After stuffing his Blade outfit and weapons into their hiding place, he leaned against the wall and gasped several deep breaths. His heart pounded in his ears. He swiped at the sweat coating his face.

When his breathing steadied, he opened the door and stepped from the room as the Seventh Blade slid down the stairs.

Leith met Daas at the bottom, collared him, and dragged him into one of the linen closets lining the hallway. Leith slammed him against the wall. "What do you think you're doing?"

Daas squirmed in Leith's grip. "I was following Vane. I nearly had him."

"Fool! He knows this manor far better than you do. You weren't about to catch him." Leith sharpened his words with a growl. He had to convince Daas not to try again. "Your stunt might've ruined everything. If everyone hadn't been outside working on the fortifications, you might've been caught by Lord Alistair's soldiers."

"I didn't see you trying to catch him."

Leith pressed his face closer, lowering his voice. "Harrison Vane has a secret hiding place somewhere in this manor. We won't find it by chasing him, only by being sneakier than he is. I've been watching him every day from inside the manor, tracking his movements from the moment he enters. I've been getting close to finding his hiding spot, but I won't find it if you chase him off."

Daas hung his head. "I see."

"Do you?" Leith stared at the Blade until he met Leith's gaze. "If we fail to catch Harrison Vane, the king will count it my failure. I don't like to fail."

Daas flinched. When Vane had said things like that when he'd been the First Blade, it had been a threat. The others might not suffer Respen's wrath, but Vane's beatings had been as just as bad.

Leith let go of the Blade's collar and stepped back. "Now get out of Walden before you draw any more attention to yourself."

Daas nodded and hurried towards the back kitchen door. Leith sighed. The Blade had had the sense to wear a tan shirt and trousers smeared with dirt, but he still stuck out. Hopefully he didn't cause too much chaos sneaking in and out.

After he was sure Daas had left, Leith strode toward Lord Alistair's study. He stepped into a milling crowd of soldiers, all jabbering about the Blade they'd seen climb down the manor wall. Leith winced. So much for not causing chaos.

Lord Alistair's gaze snagged on Leith. "Everybody out. As Shadrach has explained, it was only our ally. I thank you for your alertness. Now please return to your posts."

The men shuffled from the study until only Leith, Shad, and Lord Alistair remained in the room.

Lord Alistair waved Leith farther into the room. "I wondered how long it would take you to report. What happened?"

Leith sagged into one of the chairs. "Sorry about the lack of explanations earlier. The Seventh Blade decided to ignore orders and explore Walden on his own. He never came close to catching me, but I won't have it so easy next time."

"There'll be a next time?" Lord Alistair steepled his fingers and leaned back in his chair. The sunlight peeking through the curtains glinted on the strands of silver at his temple.

Leith crossed his arms. "The Seventh Blade had the nerve to question me about my whereabouts, even hinting I wasn't doing my best to find Vane. I threatened him, but I'm not sure it'll be enough. If it had been Eleventh Blade Harding, maybe, but Daas has been prickly ever since I became First Blade."

Shad flexed his fingers on his sword's hilt. "You can't keep this up. We'll have to stop this ruse."

The lines on Lord Alistair's face deepened. "More than that, we're running out of time. I received word this morning that Uster has fallen. The survivors are falling back to here. Respen's army isn't far behind them. They'll be here before the week is out."

Leith leaned his head into his hands. Only a week until the war arrived on Walden's doorstep.

Shad's whole body sagged. "We have to get Mother, Jolene, and Lydia out of here. They can't stay any longer."

"I would if I could." Lord Alistair rubbed his temples. "But there are two Blades watching this manor. If anyone tries to leave, they'll be attacked. Respen's army will arrive before the Blades leave for the next Meeting."

Their own ruse had turned on them. Leith closed his eyes and let his head hang. They'd trapped Lady Lorraine, Lady Alistair, Lydia, Jolene, and everyone else who'd decided to remain at Walden to help build the fortifications.

"What if we kept the Blades occupied one night so everyone can slip past them?"

Leith raised his head and stared at Shad. "What could possibly keep both Blades busy that long?"

A grin broke the grim lines around Shad's mouth. "We kill Harrison Vane. Well, we let all of you Blades kill him. It won't matter if we kill him off now, because after you rescue Renna and Brandi, Respen will know the truth anyway."

Leith gaped at him. "How am I going to kill myself while the Blades are watching without actually dying?"

Shad's grin widened. "I'll be Harrison Vane for a night. We make the other Blades think you killed me. That way, you can return to Nalgar Castle looking successful, and we can get everyone out of Walden who wants to leave without the Blades noticing."

"You look nothing like Vane." Leith toyed with the hilt of Martyn's knife stuck in his belt. "You're several inches taller, and much broader."

"It's only two Blades we have to fool." Shad crossed his arms. "How well did they really know Vane? Enough to see those differences at night after they haven't seen Vane up close for nearly two months? Especially if their First Blade, who they have no reason to distrust, tells them it's Vane?"

Leith leaned his head back against the chair. Vane had mostly avoided the younger Blades except to berate them. Would that make Vane seem bigger to them than he really was? Leith had trained Harding himself, so Vane hadn't spent a lot of time close to him. And Daas? He so desperately wanted the glory of capturing Vane himself that he'd disobeyed his current First Blade's orders to enter Walden. Would his eagerness deceive him into thinking he was seeing Vane?

"It's possible it might work. The mind has a way of seeing what it wants to see." Leith stood. "It's complicated. A lot of things can go wrong."

Lord Alistair steepled his fingers. "Our situation is

complicated." He glanced at Shad. "You'll be facing two Blades. You could be killed."

"Three Blades. And one Blade trainee. I won't be able to help him much without giving myself away."

Shad shrugged. "It won't be for long. I'll just have to die before they have a chance to kill me."

Leith shook his head. When had life gotten so muddled? It used to be that when people were dead, they were dead. Now, Leith could barely remember who was actually dead but supposedly alive and who was actually alive but supposedly dead. "I still don't like it. Our plan to pretend Renna and Brandi were killed didn't turn out."

Shad shook his head. "That wasn't a problem with our plan. The problem happened afterwards."

"I wish I could take your place."

Shad fingered the knives belted to his waist. "You need to be with the Blades tracking Vane. And I'm the only one who can throw knives well enough to pass as Vane. We all know you can't throw a knife to save your life."

Shad was right. Leith ground his teeth. If only there was another way. But they'd backed themselves into a box canyon, and the only way out was more deception.

38

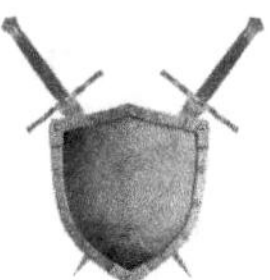

Renna leaned against the stone wall, breathing shallow breathes. Brandi rested her head on her shoulder. They'd barely moved, rarely spoken, for the past few days.

King Respen's soldiers would've attacked Stetterly by now. No matter how hard Renna tried, she couldn't banish the image of a horde of soldiers descending on Stetterly. She heard the screams of the townspeople, echoing her mother's screams from four years ago. If she closed her eyes, she could see Aunt Mara falling to the floor exactly like Renna's mother had, blood running down the front of her dress.

Renna pressed a kiss into the top of her sister's head, but Brandi didn't stir. The fire in Brandi's eyes had flickered out. How could Renna restore Brandi's hope when she had no hope of her own?

Her stomach churned. She'd nearly denied her faith. If Brandi hadn't interrupted, she would've done it. She'd tried to tell herself that it would've only been a lie to appease King

Respen, but that wasn't the truth. She'd denied her faith in so many ways already. The words would've only made it official.

Blinking at tears, she curled her legs tighter to her body, wincing as she jarred her injured leg. Her faith had been as tenuous as the first blossoms of spring, ready to shrivel up and die at the first sign of frost. Renna had survived by letting Brandi's faith, and eventually Leith's faith, be strong for her.

But Brandi's faith had been shaken. Leith wasn't here. How did Renna reverse the roles now? How could she be the strong one? She touched the silver cross dangling from her necklace. *Do not be afraid, only believe.* Her mother's favorite verse. How could Renna face fear when she couldn't even believe?

Renna couldn't let Brandi stay like this. She had to do something. Stroking Brandi's hair, she leaned her head against the stone.

Brandi had touched Leith's heart with stories. Perhaps Renna could reach Brandi the same way. She touched Brandi's forehead. "There are a lot of Bible stories about people in prison. Daniel was captured as a young boy. Joseph spent years in prison. The apostle Peter was locked in jail."

"He was let out by an angel." Brandi didn't move.

"And we don't want to forget Paul and Silas. They sang while locked in prison." She bit her lip. Brandi had better pay attention soon. Renna was running out of Bibles stories.

"As they sang, there was a big earthquake, and all the prison doors opened, and all their chains fell off." Brandi heaved a big sigh but didn't raise her head.

"Do you want to try it? Singing, I mean." Renna held her

breath. If Brandi didn't respond to that, she didn't know what else to try.

Brandi inched upright and shoved her hair out of her face. "I guess. What song do you want to sing?"

Renna frowned. What song? Why hadn't she thought of a song before starting this? She couldn't remember the words to a single psalm. Closing her eyes, she pictured her songbook and tried to flip through the pages. The words of one song stuck out to her. She hummed the tune, then sang the words. "In God will I trust, though my counselors say, O flee as a bird to your mountain away."

Renna faltered. Her counselors had advised her to flee to the mountains to escape King Respen. Had she ever trusted God with her safety? Or had she placed her trust in Leith's strength and Lord Alistair's cunning?

Brandi drew in a breath and sang the next line. "The wicked are strong and the righteous are weak."

"Foundations are shaken, yet God will I seek." Renna touched the silver cross again. Her faith's foundations had been shaken. Instead of seeking God, she'd given in to despair. How did she even begin to change that?

Brandi slumped against Renna. "Nothing happened."

Renna hugged her. Perhaps the walls hadn't come tumbling down and the bars hadn't broken, but at least Brandi was talking.

39

Leith unwrapped the cowl after his final appearance as Vane. Jamie eyed him, his back pressed to the door to listen for anyone loitering on the other side in case the other Blades should have any more ideas about tracking Vane inside Walden.

Leith dropped the cowl onto his cot and sat next to it. "Jamie, when I return to Nalgar, you don't have—"

"No, don't say it." Jamie crossed his arms, his blue eyes narrowed. "I'm going back to Nalgar Castle with you."

When had Jamie become so determined? "It'll be dangerous."

"I know." Jamie pointed at Leith's belt. "Third Blade Hamish left one of his knives behind when he took Brandi. He knows you were the one to get them out of Walden, doesn't he?"

Trust Jamie to notice the initials when no one else had. "Yes, he must know some of it. I don't know why he hasn't turned me in yet. That's why you shouldn't come with me."

"No, that's exactly why I have to go with you." Jamie faced him with a boldness Leith had never seen in the trainee before. "I can help you get Renna and Brandi out, and we can't leave the other trainees there."

If Leith had had half of Jamie's courage when he'd been thirteen, he never would've become a Blade. "All right. The rescue will be easier with two of us inside the castle." He eyed Jamie. "I reported to Respen that you killed a servant girl. Do you understand what that means?"

The muscles at the corners of Jamie's jaw knotted. "It means that in Respen's eyes, I've done my first kill."

"He'll give you your first mark and make you a Blade at the Meeting." Leith pressed his hand against his leg to stop himself from rubbing his own first mark. "We should be able to rescue the girls and leave the castle before the Meeting, but if something goes wrong, you're going to become a Blade. You'll carry that mark the rest of your life."

Jamie touched his right shoulder. "I know. But it's not like I actually killed for it, and one scar isn't going to look like a Blade mark if someone else sees it. It'll be worth it to rescue Brandi and her sister."

Leith rested a hand on Jamie's shoulder. Hopefully when this was all over, he could get Jamie to safety at Eagle Heights. Until then, Jamie would have to step up and do a man's job.

After he changed, Leith stepped into the hallway. Before he'd gone a few steps, Shad caught his arm. "Lord Segon from Uster arrived while we were drilling the men. The news isn't good."

"What happened?" Leith's stomach knotted at the white tinge to Shad's face.

"Respen's army attacked Stetterly."

"What?" Leith sagged against the wall. "When?"

"When he retreated from Uster, Lord Segon and his men ran into a few survivors from Stetterly. They said Stetterly Manor was attacked last Sunday while almost everyone was gathered for the church service." Shad's voice lowered. "Both the town and the manor were burned to the ground."

Leith jerked at the words. Stetterly burned? The kitchen where Renna had tended him, the blue room with the chipped paint at the end of the hall where he'd recovered, the ballroom-turned-church with its balcony where God's Word had so stabbed at his heart...all gone. Burned to ashes. "The people? Renna's aunt and uncle?"

"Most of the people in the town managed to hide in the Spires Canyon along with a few from the manor. The rest were either captured or killed." Shad pressed a hand to the wall. "The Lachlans weren't among the survivors that arrived here with Lord Segon."

Leith closed his eyes and leaned his head against the wall. Those words ached more than he'd expected. Abel and Mara Lachlan were the closest thing he'd had to family, and they'd known his mother. They couldn't be dead. "What happened to those who were captured?"

"Last the survivors saw, they were being marched towards Nalgar Castle."

Leith pushed himself upright. "Looks like I'll have to rescue all of them too."

Shad raised his eyebrows, but he thankfully didn't tell Leith how impossible that was.

Leith didn't care. Somehow, he had to get all of them out. He couldn't let his family die again.

LEITH DROPPED ONTO A LOG NEXT TO THE SMALL CAMPFIRE THE other Blades had built in the hollow. Eleventh Blade Harding took one look at him and shifted farther away from him. Even Seventh Blade Daas eyed him warily. Leith could only imagine how grim his face looked. "I learned today that Vane plans to return to Eagle Heights tomorrow night."

Seventh Blade Daas pulled out one of his knives and inspected it. "We can catch him on the prairie."

That was the last thing Leith could let happen. "We can't attack him while he's crossing the prairie. Have you forgotten his skill with knives? He'd see us coming and either bolt for Walden or make a stand and take us out with his knives before we got close enough to harm him."

Harding gulped and rubbed his chest like he could feel a knife penetrating his skin. Daas crossed his arms. "You're scared to face Vane."

Leith glared back. "You forget. I've faced him before. I've taken his knife in my shoulder. I know how he fights. You will obey my plan or you will fail. Understand?"

Daas lowered his eyes and nodded. Leith could see a spark still tightening his stance, but at least he listened.

Leith layered a hint of steel in his voice. "We'll corner him as he enters the Hills. The trees will give us cover and make throwing knives difficult for him."

Harding nodded vigorously. Daas shrugged. "Sounds like it will work."

Leith drew a map in the dirt. "There's a high cliff here. I just scouted the area, and it will be the ideal place to corner him. I want you to be stationed here and here where we can all herd Vane toward the cliff. Any questions?"

Neither of them spoke.

The knot in Leith's stomach tangled tighter. Plans normally went wrong because no one could predict their enemy's plan. But in this case, he was the enemy. This should be as simple as playing Raiders against himself.

If the Blades didn't realize Shad looked and acted nothing like Vane.

If...the enemy of the best-laid plans.

40

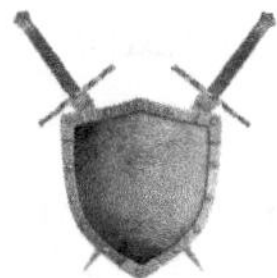

Leith leaned against the wall and watched Shad wrap the black cowl and hood around his head. They'd scrounged a black shirt and trousers for Shad and modified the belt and sheathes taken from Vane's body to fit him. He wore the former First Blade's knives strapped in the same places.

Perhaps this would work. Except for Shad's four inches of extra height, bulkier muscles, and several additional pounds, he looked somewhat like Vane.

"Are you sure you're ready?" Leith searched for any detail he might have missed, but he couldn't see any.

Shad turned to him. His eyes, the only part of his face visible, squinched with a grin. "Sure. I've always wanted to be hunted by a bunch of Blades."

"I'm sure after the first few minutes, the excitement will wear off." Leith crossed his arms.

Running his hands over the knives strapped to his waist and chest one last time, Shad nodded. Together, they strode to the back kitchen door. Jamie appeared at Leith's side, dressed in his black clothes once again.

Shad slipped out the back door and sneaked through the remains of the flower garden. The guards had been alerted that he'd be sneaking out tonight. No reason to keep that secret from them. After all, Vane was supposedly on their side.

Shad exited the flower gardens, glided around the hedge, and disappeared into the trees and barricades on the other side. Except for the fact that his sneaking resembled a pleasant stroll through the garden, he didn't pause in every shadow to take stock of his surroundings, and he didn't glance over his shoulder to check for someone following him, Shad might've passed as a Blade.

Leith prayed that the other Blades remained blind tonight.

When he deemed Shad had a reasonable head start, Leith slipped out the back door. Jamie followed as if tied to Leith's heels. When they broke through the tree line and crossed the ditch, Leith spotted Shad's black silhouette cresting the hill. He motioned Jamie forward.

They wove through the long grasses. The lopsided, almost full moon rose in the distance. Steel grey clouds scudded across the sky and dappled the grass. Leith breathed easier when Shad stuck to the shadows provided by the clouds. If he hadn't, his black clothes would've stuck out midst the silver grass. A trainee mistake the real Vane would never make.

A mile from Walden, Leith spotted the scurrying form of the Seventh Blade shadowing Shad's movements four hundred yards to Shad's left. As they continued onward,

Leith kept an eye on Daas in case he got any ideas about attacking Shad early.

Half a mile from the foothills, Leith slipped towards Shad's right, leaving Jamie as rearguard. After a few minutes, Shad froze as if he'd finally noticed he was being stalked by two Blades and a trainee. He broke into a fast lope, headed for the foothills.

Daas broke into a run as well and closed to within two hundred yards. Leith kept pace with him on the right. So far, everything had gone according to plan.

Shad scrambled into the Sheered Rock Hills. Harding appeared in front of Shad. Shad wheeled and angled toward his right as if seeking escape.

As Leith and Jamie entered the foothills, only a few tendrils of moonlight wiggled through the pines to touch the ground. Leith picked up his pace, following the sounds of rocks clunking and branches rasping.

Ahead, Shad stumbled and slipped. Daas drew his knives and crept closer. Leith waved to Jamie and gave a small flick of his hand toward Daas.

Jamie nodded and dashed forward. He stumbled into Daas, throwing both of them off balance. Daas shoved Jamie away. "Watch where you're going, boy."

By the time Daas looked up, Shad had regained his footing and disappeared around the boulder above them.

Leith hurried to their side. He swiped his hand at the side of Jamie's head in a move that in the dark would look like he'd hit Jamie. "Follow orders."

Jamie bowed his head and nodded. When Daas resumed following Shad, Leith patted Jamie's back. Jamie glanced up at him and grinned.

At the base of the boulder, Leith gave a low whistle. Daas, about to round the boulder, glared at him, but he turned around and headed back to Leith. He crossed his arms while they waited for Harding.

Harding broke through the tree cover. Leith glared at each of them. He needed to give Shad a few moments alone, but he couldn't dally too long here without the other Blades growing impatient. "The cliff's up ahead. He's cornered. Harding, head to the right and come up this ridge from that direction. Daas, circle to the left. The boy and I will work our way in from the center. Don't try to engage Vane by yourself. Wait until you see the rest of us closing in."

Leith met the gaze of each Blade in turn. They nodded that they understood the plan. With a flick of his hand, he sent them scurrying to their positions.

Leith pulled two knives from his belt and crept forward. Hopefully he'd given Shad enough time. He crested the ridge and eased around the boulder. Shad crouched with his back to the cliff. The knives in his hands sliced the shafts of moonlight.

Daas stepped from the trees to Shad's right. Shad's hand blurred. A knife thunked into a tree six inches from the Blade's stomach. Daas dove behind a tree.

Leith slid into cover behind a large rock. As Harding emerged from the trees to Shad's left, Shad threw another knife. It thunked into the ground by Harding's feet.

Shad's knives were going too wide from their supposed targets. Daas and Harding would be dead now if they'd been facing the real Harrison Vane.

A cloud piled across the moon, plunging this corner of

ridge in darkness. Brandishing his knives, Daas leapt forward. Harding jumped out of hiding a moment later.

Leith threw himself forward. Somehow, he needed to make sure that Shad didn't get killed in the next few minutes.

Shad parried two of the Blades' knives and sidestepped a third. Leith nudged Harding to the side with his shoulder and pressed forward. Shad stepped backwards out of their reach. With another step forward, Leith crowded Shad towards the cliff edge. The narrowing ledge prevented all but him and Daas from attacking Shad.

Leith swept his knife towards Shad's head in a move Shad parried easily. Shad backed up, his heels grinding against the edge. Daas sliced at Shad's leg. Shad knocked the knife away, its tip tearing through the fabric of his trousers.

Daas plowed forward and stabbed at Shad's ribs. Leith saw the knife, saw Shad's stance, and caught his breath. Shad wouldn't be able to block in time. Leith lunged, but he wasn't fast enough.

Shad twisted, but the knife sliced through his shirt and into his skin. He cried out, stumbled backwards, and fell over the edge. He shouted as he plummeted down. Less than a second later, the air cracked with the sound of a body slamming into stone.

41

Leith and the other Blades remained motionless on the top of the cliff for a heartbeat, listening to the still night.

Inching forward, Daas peered over the edge. Leith leaned forward as well. A ledge jutted from the cliff a few yards down. The ravine was too deep and the night too dark to see the bottom.

Daas backed away from the edge. "He's dead. No one could survive a fall like that."

Nodding, Leith turned back to the Blades gathered on the cliff top. He crossed his arms to hide the sick feeling in his stomach. "Vane is dead. I'll camp here tonight and climb down in the daylight. The rest of you return to the hollow. Leave for Nalgar at first light. The king will want a report as quickly as possible, and you don't want to arrive late."

Leith was counting on the Blades' fear of returning to Nalgar late. He couldn't have them sticking around this cliff tonight.

Harding nodded and headed towards the woods. Daas crossed his arms. "I'd like to see the body too."

Leith glared back. "And risk both of us returning late? Do you want another mark on your left arm?"

Daas grimaced, spun on his heels, and marched after the other Blade.

When Leith could no longer hear the sounds of their boots on gravel, he whistled, and Jamie popped out from his position behind the boulder. "Watch to see if any of them decide to come back."

Jamie nodded and slunk back into the woods.

Leith knelt on the edge of the cliff. If he glanced to the right, he could just make out the rope running from under a nearby spruce and down the cliff's side, hidden in the tree's shadow. "Shad, are you all right?"

Shad's voice grunted from the darkness twenty feet below the rim, concealed by the ledge. "Well enough. That last one got me pretty good though."

"How bad?" If only Renna were here. Leith wasn't sure he had the skills to tend Shad if he were hurt badly.

"Hurts like fire and it's bleeding a lot, but it's not too deep. Just grazed my ribs." A note of pain glinted in his voice. "Nothing's broken."

"I'm going to pull you up." Gripping the rope tightly, Leith hauled the rope upward. His muscles strained to pull Shad's weight.

Finally, Shad's head, then shoulders crested the rim. With one last heave, Shad rolled onto the cliff top. Sprawled on his back, he pressed a hand to his side. "Hitting the cliff face hurt just as much as I thought it would."

"Thankfully none of them noticed your body hit the

rocks a few seconds earlier than it should've." Leith knelt and felt along Shad's shirt. His hand came away wet, but the splotch hadn't spread too far.

The moon ripped away its veil of clouds, splashing the landscape silver once again. As their clearing beside the cliff brightened, Leith helped Shad untie and remove the rope looped around his waist. Leith pulled out a knife to cut the shirt away from Shad's wound.

An owl hooted in the trees. Leith froze. That was no owl. Jamie's signal. "Someone's coming. Get under the spruce."

Shad rolled under the spruce's spreading branches. Jumping to his feet, Leith kicked the rope out of sight under the branches, rubbed his bloody hand against his trouser, turned, and strode away from the edge.

Daas sauntered into the open space. His eyes darted around, as if looking for something suspicious. Leith prayed he wouldn't notice the slight swaying of the spruce's lower branches.

Leith crossed his arms. "What are you doing back here? I gave you orders to head for Nalgar."

"I came to fetch a few of Vane's knives. If we can't return with the body, we'll need something to convince the king that we killed the traitor." Daas eyed Leith as if he wanted Leith to give him a reason to keep arguing.

Leith waved at the knife sticking out of a tree several yards away. "Go ahead. Take them. You're right. You'll need to show them to the king."

Daas blinked at him. He strode over to the tree and yanked the knife out.

Leith strolled over to another tree and jerked the knife free. He handed it to Daas. Daas took it wordlessly. Leith suppressed a smile. His easy agreement had taken the fire from the Blade's argument.

Tucking the knives into his belt, Daas nodded at Leith and headed back the way he'd come. Leith held his breath and didn't move for several minutes. Even after all sound had faded, he continued to wait.

After ten minutes had passed, he relaxed. "It's safe to come out now."

Shad rolled out from the spruce and blew out a long breath. "That was close."

Leith knelt at Shad's side once again. "I should've given him the knives in the first place." A small detail, but it'd nearly cost them. If he made a mistake like that at Nalgar, none of them would get out alive.

Drawing one of his own knives, Leith cut Shad's shirt away from his wound. With water from his canteen, he cleaned it as best he could. It ran for six inches along his ribs, but not deep. Slicing another section of Shad's shirt, Leith pressed the fabric to the wound. "Hold this."

Shad did as ordered. "You Blades must go through a lot of shirts. I was a Blade for only a few hours, and I've already ruined one."

"Trust a lord's son to be worried about his fancy clothes." Leith picked up a scrap of fabric and headed into the trees. Thankfully, Shad's wound wasn't deep enough to warrant stitches or cauterizing, but it'd need something to keep it sealed.

Leith halted at the base of a white pine. Hacking into the trunk with his knife, he collected the sap that spilled from the tree's wound with the scrap of fabric. When he judged he had enough, he returned to Shad's side.

Shad raised an eyebrow at him. "What's that?"

"Pine pitch. It'll close the wound." Leith nudged Shad's hand aside, pulled off the bloody cloth, and spread the pine pitch over the wound.

"Better than cauterizing it, I guess." Shad grimaced and clenched his fists. "Can you at least try to be gentle?"

"If you want gentle, you'll have to ask Renna to look at the wound after we rescue her." Leith tried to keep his tone light as he placed a bandage over the pine pitch. They would rescue her.

He couldn't fail this time.

LEITH ROUSED THEM SHORTLY AFTER FIRST LIGHT. AS THEY made their way out of the Hills, he checked the hollow. Thankfully, the Blades had followed his orders and already left for Nalgar Castle.

Walden bustled with a grim focus. No more drilling. No more preparations. Only one aisle through the sharpened stakes and tangled rope remained open and only one set of planks, propped up by supports in the center, spanned the ditch, now so deep and wide it formed a dry moat.

All of the women and most of the men had left last night. Only a few volunteers remained behind for what would probably be a last stand to buy the others time to get away.

When Leith watered Blizzard in the trough outside the stables, he spotted only empty stalls through the open doorway. Those left behind would have no means of escape except by foot. A few yards away, Lord Segon paced behind the barricade, a sword buckled at his side.

When Blizzard had his fill, Lord Alistair met Leith by the front step and clapped him on the shoulder. "In the past few months, I've asked a lot from you, more than I've asked even of my own son."

"Nothing I wasn't willing to do." Leith bowed his head. He couldn't deny his own part in the tangle he'd lived for the past weeks.

Lord Alistair scrubbed a hand across his beard. "I know you understand duty. You understand better than anyone else here why I'm staying behind."

Leith nodded. He did understand. Lord Alistair knew that anyone who stayed behind in Walden would most likely die. He wouldn't watch his children grow into adults. He would miss his daughters' weddings, his sons' courtships. He wouldn't be there to hold his grandchildren.

The heart might demand that Lord Alistair leave Walden with his family, but duty demanded he stay. Someone had to stay behind, and Lord Alistair couldn't ask the others to make such a sacrifice without sacrificing along with them.

Leith met Lord Alistair's gaze. "If I could, I'd stay also."

"And your help would be greatly appreciated. But you know you can't. Renna and Brandi need you alive." Lord Alistair shot a glance toward the stable where Shad let his horse drink. "And my son will need you. He's never experienced loss like you have. He's still unprepared for the burden he'll now have to carry. He's going to need you at his side."

"I'll be there." Leith let the weight settle onto his shoulders.

"I'm thankful he has you for a friend." Lord Alistair clasped Leith's shoulder again. "Protect my family."

Leith straightened his shoulders and widened his stance. "As much as in my power, they will be safe."

Lord Alistair's grip relaxed. He slapped Leith on the shoulder one last time. "God go with you."

As Lord Alistair strode towards Shad, Leith bowed his head. How many more would die in this war?

Lord Alistair gripped both of Shad's shoulders and said something too softly for Leith to hear. Shad hugged his father tightly.

Leith turned away and swung onto Blizzard, his throat tightening until he could barely breathe. Jamie nudged his horse next to Leith's.

A few minutes later, Shad joined him. His eyes gleamed with an extra brightness, but his jaw set. They rode across the wooden planks and past the sharpened logs. Behind them, ropes shooshed as soldiers tied off the last opening. The planks thunked as they were pulled back.

They headed north, back the way they'd come that morning, to avoid running into the approaching army.

After climbing through the foothills and into the Sheered Rock Hills, Leith halted Blizzard at the top of a tall promontory that overlooked the valley where Walden lay. To the south, a line of black smudged the horizon, growing larger and more distinct with every moment. The black line expanded, circling to engulf Walden Manor in its arms.

Shad's horse tossed its head. Leith glanced at Shad's white-knuckled, shaking grip on the reins. Nothing Leith could say would make this moment any better.

42

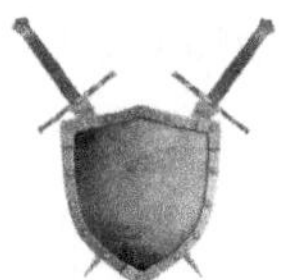

Their cell door slammed open. Four guards, Martyn, and another Blade she didn't recognize pounded inside. A guard tied her hands, shoved a black hood over her head, and threw her over his shoulder.

"Renna?"

Renna squirmed, but she couldn't see Brandi past the hood shrouding her face. "It'll be all right."

Something was different. Wrong. The guards never bound them like this. Was this it? Was King Respen going to execute them?

Her stomach bounced against the guard's shoulder as he trudged up the stairs. As his stride leveled, voices babbled around her. Feet scuffled against stone. She twisted her head. Where were the sounds coming from? It sounded like a mass of people bustled around the courtyard.

The coldness of the stone passageway engulfed her. Renna squeezed her eyes shut. She had this passageway, these stairs, memorized by now. Martyn's knock sounded on the door to the king's chambers. King Respen's voice slithered through the wood and fabric, bidding them enter.

Renna shrieked as the guard dumped her on the floor. She curled her body as she fell and landed on her back and shoulder, sparing her already injured leg. Her own hot breath swirled around her face.

"Untie them."

The black bag jerked off her head along with a handful of her hair. While the guard ripped the bindings from her wrists, she gulped in the cool air. Brandi tore away from her guard and flung herself toward Renna. Renna wrapped her in a hug. As long they were together, they'd survive.

Martyn dragged them to their feet by their elbows and shoved them forward. King Respen stood alongside the window overlooking the cobblestone courtyard, his hands clasped behind his back.

He turned toward them. A smile creased his face. "My soldiers informed me that Stetterly was burned to the ground."

Renna staggered with the force of those words. Her home was gone? The white outer walls, the tall chimneys, the gilt ballroom. Gone. Burned. Nothing but black, bitter ashes.

She could taste the ash on her tongue, feel the gritty coating of dust billowing in the air. If she ever returned to Stetterly, the prairie wind would've carried off the piles of cinders. Not even the hint of smoke would remain to grate in her lungs.

Brandi turned wide eyes toward Renna, the vibrant color leaching from her face, burned away with Stetterly. Renna tightened her grip as grief melted Brandi's spine one bone at a time.

Renna cleared her throat. "What about the people?"

King Respen's smile spread like rot on an apple. He stepped back and motioned to the window as if he presented them with a gift. "See for yourself."

Martyn's fingers dug into her arm as he hauled Renna forward. Brandi stumbled with her, refusing to let go even if it made walking difficult.

As the view of the courtyard spread out before them, Renna caught her breath. Soldiers shoved thirteen men and women into a line.

A group of soldiers blocked Renna's view of the center of the courtyard. One soldier had his arms crossed. Another soldier, apparently an officer, snapped an order, and the protesting soldier was hauled to the side.

Renna gasped. A wooden block hunkered on the cobblestones. A black-garbed man stepped forward, an ax in his hands. Renna clapped a hand over her mouth as her stomach heaved.

King Respen was going to execute them all.

Her eyes scanned the captives, skipping from one familiar face to the next. They all belonged to their underground church at Stetterly. The baker and his wife. A farmer whose leg she'd stitched after he'd cut it plowing. Two of the men who herded Stetterly's cattle. Several women she'd talked with after church services. A boy whose arm she'd once bandaged.

She latched onto two faces at the end of the line. Uncle Abel and Aunt Mara held hands, their mouths moving in words she couldn't hear this far away. As she watched, Aunt

Mara glanced upward. Their eyes locked. Aunt Mara nudged Uncle Abel, and he met Renna's gaze also.

"No." The word tore from Renna's throat. She crumbled to the floor. "Please don't do this."

"Your God cannot stop death. I am the master of life and death here." King Respen twitched his hand. Screams pierced morning sky. A dull thud rang out.

Renna flinched. If only she could cover her ears and pretend she didn't know what was happening outside that window.

But she couldn't abandon her people through ignorance. Her duty lay with Stetterly.

"Admit your God's weakness." King Respen loomed over her, as invincible as the walls of the Blades' Tower.

His words curled slick fingers around her heart. Did he speak the truth? He held the power of life and death over her, Brandi, Aunt Mara, Uncle Abel, and the eleven—no, ten —other captives of Stetterly.

Thunk. Her stomach twisted.

Brandi fell to her knees beside her, her face white. Her body shook.

Thunk. Renna choked on a sob. Another life taken.

"I will spare them. All you have to do is acknowledge my power." King Respen gazed out the window. A smile lingered on his face, framed by his thin mustache and pointed, black beard.

Thunk. The curve of his lips grew.

Bile scraped at the back of her throat. He enjoyed this. How could a human being enjoy watching the execution of thirteen people?

She should give him what he wanted. They were empty

words. She wouldn't mean them. Leith lied to save lives. Surely she could do the same. It'd be a meaningless denial. Right?

In the Bible, Peter had denied Jesus three times. Meaningless denials given out of fear. It was wrong, but Peter hadn't done it to save lives.

Thunk. Renna pressed her hand over Brandi's ear and held Brandi's head to her shoulder. A weak effort. Nothing could block the sound of that relentless ax.

It was her duty to sacrifice for Stetterly. She should offer to trade her life for her people. Her back quivered. Who was she fooling? She didn't have the courage to even open her mouth.

Thunk.

"Lives are wasting." King's Respen's voice pounded her fragile strength.

Jagged edges splintered through her soul. Resolve, courage, strength bled through the cracks, dumping her spirit onto the carpet at King Respen's feet. She had nothing left.

Her mouth creaked open. What did she have to lose anyway? Hadn't she all but denied her faith earlier?

A voice—one Renna had listened to every Sunday for the past nine years—rose above the sobs and ax, singing clear and strong. "Jehovah is my light, and my salvation near."

Renna blinked. As Uncle Abel's baritone joined Aunt Mara's soprano, tears trickled down her face. They were singing a song based on Psalm 27, Renna's favorite psalm.

"Who shall my soul affright, or cause my heart to fear?" Slowly at first, then swelling into a chorus, the other captives joined in the singing. They might believe their minister and his wife were singing for them, but they sang for Renna.

The wails and screams died away. The ax thunks muted. The captives of Stetterly sang with one voice, one heart, for one Lord. "While God my strength, my life sustains, secure from fear my soul remains."

How could they sing as they watched their loved ones succumb to the ax? They should be shaking their fists at stone-hearted Heaven. God could stop this. He had the power to create the world in a word. Saving them from King Respen was paltry compared to that. Yet, God remained silent.

"When evildoers came to make my life their prey, they stumbled in their shame and fell in sore dismay."

Renna couldn't understand their courage. The words seemed to make them fearless, but she wasn't fearless. She cowered at King Respen's feet, flinching every time the ax came down. The Lord should be her Light. He should be her Courage. But all she saw was darkness. All she felt was fear. Her enemies weren't stumbling. They were powerful.

Thunk.

In her arms, Brandi squirmed. Turning her face to the window, her voice wobbled into song as well. "Though hosts make war on every side, still fearless I in God confide."

Even Brandi had hope. Renna shook. What was wrong with her? Why did everyone else find such hope in God while she felt such emptiness?

The stones of the castle hummed as the remnant of Stetterly's congregation sang the next verse. "My one request has been, and still this prayer I raise, that I may dwell within God's house through all my days."

One request. Her one request of God was safety. She'd prayed for it over and over until it had become a constant chant.

But, her focus was wrong.

In all her prayers for safety, she'd focused solely on her earthly life around her, the power of her enemies, and her pitiful strength.

Her sight should be on Heaven. She tipped her face upward. Everything that happened on this earth prepared God's people for the moment He brought them into the glory of Heaven. Her parents were there now, basking in the beauty of God.

Thunk. Another soul lifted to Heaven.

How many times had Renna placed Leith's life in God's hands? She hadn't understood what that meant until this moment. God's hands wrapped around her, around Brandi, around Aunt Mara and Uncle Abel in the courtyard below. He never let them go. Not even here.

Renna tottered to her feet. She faced the window but kept her eyes shut. With a deep breath, she added her voice to the dwindling number of singers below. "When troubles round me swell, when fears and dangers throng."

Brandi slipped her hand into Renna's. Renna squeezed Brandi's fingers and kept singing.

"Stop that!" Respen snapped.

Renna ignored him. "Securely I will dwell—"

A blow struck her cheek. She stumbled backwards and clenched her fingers to resist rubbing her throbbing cheek. With a glare at Respen, Renna faced the window and kept singing.

Thunk. Only two voices sang in the courtyard below.

Renna risked a peek. Her aunt and uncle stood all alone in front of the red-coated block. She focused on them rather than the bodies stacked in a wagon by the gate. They turned to each other. Uncle Abel swept a lock of Aunt Mara's hair from her face and kissed her.

As a soldier strode towards them, Aunt Mara stepped back. They held hands as long as possible, their fingers sliding against each other until they fell free. Aunt Mara faced the block, her posture perfect, and sang once again.

Renna hugged Brandi and turned her sister's face from the window. She shouldn't witness this. Squeezing her eyes shut, Renna sang as loudly as she could. "Uplifted on a rock above my foes around…"

Thunk. Aunt Mara's voice cut off mid-word. Uncle Abel's voice wobbled, but he continued singing. "Amid the battle shock my song shall still resound."

Brandi shuddered and pressed her face against Renna's shoulder. Her singing, though muffled, didn't stop. Renna took a deep breath. Hopefully Uncle Abel heard her. "Then joyful offerings I will bring…"

Thunk.

Brandi broke down into tears and stopped singing. Tears gathered in her throat, but Renna forced herself to finish the last line even though she now sang alone. "Jehovah's praise my heart will sing."

The last word clung to the air like a drop of dew, perfect and innocent. She'd grieve later. Right now, she turned her eyes towards Heaven and felt…joy.

"Do you acknowledge my power now?"

Renna snapped her gaze to Respen. He glared at her, arms crossed, eyes on fire. A shiver slipped down her spine.

She was not going to fear. Focus on Heaven. Focus on the joy of being with Jesus.

"No." The word squeaked across her tongue. She drew in a deep breath. "No."

The members of their church had died rather than deny Jesus. By herself, Renna didn't have the courage to do the same. But she wasn't alone. God was with her. He'd been with her this whole time, even when her fear had imprisoned her.

Brandi straightened and swiped at her wet face. "Like Daniel's three friends."

Of course Brandi would see the resemblance to that story. Renna squeezed her shoulders and found the words she needed to tell Respen.

"Our God is more powerful than you. He can deliver us out of your hand if He wills. If He doesn't, He will bring us home to the deliverance of Heaven. Don't you see? You can't harm God's people." She waved at the window. "God is in control. No matter what you do, you can't shorten my life a fraction of what God has already planned for me."

"You're a fool!"

As her gaze collided with Respen's burning eyes, Renna caught her breath. She saw the anger there, but also something else. Pain. A wounded heart. The question slid from her tongue before she thought better of it. "What happened to you?"

Respen reared back from her. "Silence!"

A long forgotten memory sparked in her mind. She was five. Her parents missed her birthday. Something about a funeral in Blathe.

"You lost your wife and son years ago. You blame God for taking them. You—"

Respen backhanded her across her face, harder than before. She crashed to the floor. Dark spots lurched across her eyes. Before she could recover, he grabbed her shoulders and yanked her off her feet. Renna kicked and squirmed, but she couldn't loosen his grasp.

"Your God didn't save them. Didn't save her." Respen shook her. "The healer couldn't help her. The preacher said it'd be all right, but it wasn't. Of course it wasn't."

She stilled. Where had Uncle Abel and Aunt Mara lived before they moved to Stetterly? A knot in her stomach told her it was Blathe.

Brandi squealed and tugged at King Respen's arms. "Let her go!"

King Respen flung Renna to the ground and backhanded Brandi. Brandi tumbled to the floor next to Renna.

Renna trembled and clenched her icy fingers. She'd probed too deeply. Now Respen would kill them.

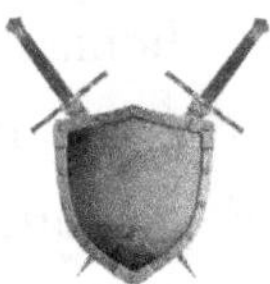

43

Leith neared the hill overlooking Nalgar Castle. He turned back to his companions. Shadrach leaned his forearms on top of his saddlehorn. His bow and quiver rode across his back. Jamie sneaked glances at the hill in front of them, his face pale beneath his tousled hair.

Leith met Shad's gaze. "Wait here. If I'm not back in three days, assume I'm dead and head into the Hills as quickly as possible."

Shad nodded. No words were needed. Leith understood. Shad had his back.

Facing forward, Leith nudged Blizzard into a walk. As they crested the hill and started towards the castle silhouetted against the sunset, something on the far hill caught Leith's eye. A wagon heaped with indistinct lumps parked next to a large pit. Shovels stood in a dirt pile next to it. Whoever had been ordered to dig that pit had probably returned to the castle to eat their supper before they continued their work.

Leith turned Blizzard's head to investigate. As they neared, Blizzard snorted and shied away. A faint breeze carried the musty stench of blood and death.

Stomach churning, Leith dismounted and dropped Blizzard's reins to the ground. "Jamie, stay here with the horses."

Eyes wide, Jamie gripped his horse's reins and nodded. Leaving Blizzard in Jamie's care, Leith trudged through the thigh-high grass until he stood at the edge of the pit.

Not a pit. A mass grave. Headless bodies stacked on top of each other in a tangle of stiff arms and strangely angled legs. Blood spattered the ground, the dirt, the bodies' clothing. The heads belonging to the corpses lay tossed in the pit with no concern for dignity. A few bodies remained on the wagon, waiting for the grave diggers to return from supper.

Leith collapsed to his knees, teeth clenched to keep his stomach from heaving up his throat. In all his years as a Blade, he'd never seen such death. Men and women heaped like hay after a grotesque harvest. The odor of death—a sour scent of human body, metallic tang of fresh blood, and a sweet smell of fear—bruised the air. He'd smelled all of the reeks of death before, but never on this scale, never to the point he might never exhale another breath that didn't carry the taint of death.

He wobbled to his feet and forced himself to glance at the faces. Near the edge of the grave partially covered by the layer above them, Leith discovered the remains of Abel and Mara Lachlan.

He'd arrived too late to save them.

Heat pounded through his chest. He'd failed to save his mother. Now he'd failed to save the Lachlans. Why did he always fail to protect those he cared about? Would he fail to save Renna and Brandi too?

Something trickled across his face. He swiped at it. A hot, wet smear spread across his fingers and cheek.

No, he wasn't going to give in to that weakness. Not here. He scrabbled for the cold that numbed his heart so many times before this.

He'd once promised Lachlan that he'd protect Renna and Brandi, a promise he'd failed to keep so many times already. Lachlan was beyond hearing him now, but Leith clasped his hand over his heart anyway. "I promise I will get them out of here. With the last breath in my body, I will rescue them."

Leith returned to Blizzard but couldn't find the strength to haul himself into the saddle. He gripped the saddlehorn and leaned against his horse's warm neck.

"Who is it?" Jamie's voice wavered.

"The people of Stetterly. Respen executed them." Leith swallowed and swung into the saddle. "Renna and Brandi weren't there."

"Good." Jamie eyed Leith and chewed on his bottom lip. "You might want to wait a few more minutes."

How much of what he'd seen still showed on his face? Leith leaned his arms on his saddlehorn and fought to banish the images to the same place he buried all the memories he'd rather forget.

Might as well use the time to go over last minute instructions. "Remember to watch the door to the Tower. If I can, we'll sneak out tonight."

"I know." Jamie's eyes focused on Nalgar Castle below them. "If you can't get away tonight, we'll rescue them after the Meeting. I'll be the Thirteenth Blade then, and I'll watch for you from my new room. When I see you leave the Tower, I'll go to the trainee rooms and get whoever will come with me. We'll go to the stables and saddle the horses so we can ride out of there as fast as possible."

"Exactly." Leith straightened and gripped Blizzard's reins again. "Let's go."

He nudged Blizzard into a lope down the hill, up the cobbled road, and through Nalgar Castle's gates. His stomach churned at the sight of the courtyard. Blood trickled along the cracks in the cobblestones. The block remained, the ax leaning against it. Blizzard's hooves clopped and splashed as they crossed the courtyard to the stables.

By the time they reached the stables, Blizzard's hooves stained red. Red droplets speckled his legs. Swinging down from their horses, Leith and Jamie handed the reins to the stable boys and headed for the wooden bridge that connected the Blades' Tower with the rest of the castle.

Jamie slipped away to the trainee quarters in the stone wall surrounding the Tower along the moat. Leith didn't look or wave goodbye. A Blade didn't bond with a trainee.

The cool air of the Tower closed around him as he stepped through the door. He drew in a deep breath. This was the last time he'd step into this tower as a Blade. When he left Nalgar Castle, Respen would know the truth. Leith would be a hunted man, hunted even more than Vane had been.

It was past time. Only a few more hours. Then he'd be free.

He climbed the long, winding stairs to the fourth floor.

This late at night, he could neglect to report to King Respen without rousing suspicion. Respen would hear his report in the Meeting of the Blades the next morning. Not that Leith planned to be here by morning.

After cleaning up from his travels in his room, Leith waited for full darkness to fall around Nalgar Castle. When the arrow slit in the stairway showed winking stars, Leith slipped from his room and headed for the stairs.

"Where are you going?"

Leith froze at Martyn's voice. He turned to find the Blade he'd once considered his best friend leaning in the doorjamb of his room, a room that up until a few months ago had been Leith's.

Martyn didn't wait for Leith to answer. He stepped forward and spoke in a lowered tone. "What're you up to, Leith? What's going on?"

"Nothing." Even in his own ears, his tone sounded too hurried.

Martyn pulled a knife from his boot and held it out to Leith. Even in the semi-darkness, Leith spotted the initials *LT* on the hilt. "Please tell me this is a mistake. Tell me that Vane got a hold of your knife that night you fought him in Walden. I'll believe you and never mention this again."

Leith didn't have an answer for him. Even lying to save a life had consequences. And right here, right now, this was the price Leith would pay. Not his life. Not just his integrity. But the slow fracturing of a friendship.

Martyn raked a hand through his blond curls. When he spoke, his voice held a biting pain. "So you did sneak those girls out of Walden."

Leith drew the knife he'd stashed in his belt, the one

with *MH* on the hilt, and handed it to Martyn. "What did the girls tell Respen?" He reached for the knife Martyn held.

"Only that the First Blade rescued them." Martyn didn't let go. "The king assumed they were talking about Vane. But they meant you, didn't they?"

Leith couldn't deny it. "Are you going to tell Respen?"

Martyn swore under his breath and let go of the knife. "Come on, Leith! This isn't like you. What did those girls do to you? I understand that you don't want to hurt them. I don't either. But an order's an order."

"Are they alive?" Leith pressed a hand to the wall. What if they were already dead? Buried in another grave?

"Yes. The king plans to have them killed during the Meeting of the Blades tomorrow morning." Martyn's dark brown eyes searched Leith's face. "What could they possibly have done to get you to turn on King Respen? Don't you remember everything he's given us? The food. The clothes. The family. Surely you haven't forgotten all that?"

Leith hadn't forgotten. For years, he'd followed Respen willingly because he'd given him more than his own father ever had. He, like Martyn, hadn't realized the poison that came with the gifts. "Goodness isn't found in gifts. It's in the thought behind it. Respen doesn't give us food and shelter because he cares about us."

Martyn gaped at him. "They got to you with all their God talk."

A chill swirled in Leith's stomach. If he was arrested now, he wouldn't be able to save the girls. But he couldn't lie to Martyn. Not when the conversation had come this far. "Yes."

Martyn shoved a hand through his hair and swore again. Leith crossed his arms and waited. Martyn paced in front of his door. He turned back to Leith. "Do you remember my first day at Blathe Manor?"

Leith nodded. "You'd nearly starved on the streets."

"Vane would've beaten me to a bloody mess if you hadn't stepped in." Martyn met Leith's gaze. "We promised we'd watch each other's backs."

"I'm your friend." Another lie. Leith had broken that promise several times over. He could've gotten Martyn killed when he'd foiled that assassination attempt. He hadn't shared the hope of Scripture with him. What kind of friend did that?

"And for that, I didn't tell the king about finding your knife." Martyn's eyes hardened. He leaned closer. "But know this, if you try anything, I will stop you. I don't know what's come over you, but this has to stop. You're a Blade. You don't go soft-hearted. Not for anyone. I don't want you turning traitor like Vane."

Martyn didn't know the full truth yet. Leith pressed his hand harder against the wall to stop his body from sagging. Martyn believed Leith had been taken in like Vane had. He didn't realize the treachery was all Leith's. Would he keep his promise when he learned Leith had already broken his?

"I wouldn't expect anything else." Leith turned and strode to his room. His back prickled with the sensation of Martyn's eyes following him until his door shut between them.

He leaned against the door. He wouldn't be able to sneak out tonight. Martyn would watch him too closely. Somehow, he'd have to prevent Respen from killing Renna and Brandi during the Meeting of the Blades.

Most likely, they'd all die in the attempt.

44

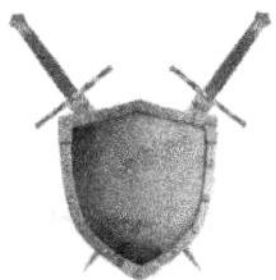

Renna rocked Brandi gently. Brandi's shoulders still quaked with sobs, but they were quieting. Renna held her own tears back, waiting to pour them out later. Perhaps she'd never have a chance. Her time was short.

They were going to die tomorrow morning. A shiver racked her body. Her chest squeezed until she couldn't breathe. She shook her head. Best not to think about it.

She drew in a deep breath to steady herself and coughed at the stench. A dark pool formed beneath their window as blood from the courtyard ran through the opening and down the wall. Gagging, she tore her eyes away. As a healer, she should be used to blood. But she'd never seen blood like this, so separated from the body it was supposed to fill.

Brandi stirred and tipped her face towards Renna. Tears streaked her face and pooled in her blue eyes. "Does dying hurt?"

Renna's throat seized. What could she tell her sister? If

only she could protect her, but Brandi should be prepared. As much as anyone could be prepared for their execution. "It might hurt for a moment, but we'll be in Heaven after that."

Brandi nodded, but she still shivered. Renna understood. Death was closer than Heaven. It leered over her, tearing at her soul while she waited for it to pounce. With that monster clawing at them, the idea of Heaven wisped through her fingers. Renna needed a solid picture for them to cling to during their last hours on this earth.

"Nothing will hurt anymore. Aunt Mara and Uncle Abel will be there. Uncle Leon and Aunt Deirdre. Our cousins Aengus, Keevan, Rorin, and Duncan. You probably don't remember them very well."

Brandi cocked her head. "I remember Duncan. We used to visit the horses together when they came to Stetterly."

"And we'll see Mother and Father again." Tears gathered behind Renna's eyes. She blinked them away. She mustn't dwell on the sorrow now. They needed hope tonight.

"What did Mother look like?"

Five years was a long time to spend with nothing but an old portrait to refresh Renna's memories. Now even that portrait was gone, burned along with Stetterly Manor. At least she still had her memories. Brandi had far fewer of those.

Renna leaned her head against the wall. "Mother used to smile like you do when she got an idea. Sometimes she'd drag us out to the Spires Canyon for a picnic or decide she wanted to take us jumping in mud puddles. Father would roll his eyes at her crazy ideas, but he'd always go along with them."

"I like jumping in mud puddles."

Renna touched Brandi's hair. "She had long, wavy hair like yours. She wore it down all the time because Father liked it that way."

Brandi tugged on the end of Renna's braid. "But her hair was light blond like yours. I remember that."

"And Father's was darker like yours." As Renna ran her fingers through Brandi's hair, she drew in the sense of warmth the memories brought. Parts of her parents remained in Brandi's smile, Renna's hair, the colors of their eyes. Soon they'd be reunited in Heavenly glory.

Renna pulled her silver cross necklace from under her blouse. *Don't be afraid, only believe.* "God will give us strength tomorrow."

Brandi gripped her cross necklace and rested her head on Renna's shoulder again. "Can we sing?"

Renna nodded. She suggested a song, and together she and Brandi sang that one and as many songs as they could remember. Sometime late that night, Brandi fell asleep. Renna hugged her tightly, thankful that Brandi could have one last night of peaceful sleep.

Renna couldn't sleep. Not with their deaths so close. Would they kill her or Brandi first? Would it hurt? Tingles curled in her stomach.

Would Leith be there? Her heart throbbed. Would he try to rescue them? What good would it even do? He'd end up dead along with them if he tried.

She leaned her cheek against Brandi's head. A tear slid down her cheek and splashed into Brandi's hair. She couldn't pray for safety. Right now, it looked like it was God's will that she watch her sister die tomorrow. But perhaps He could make it hurt less? Or less scary? Surely

He'd at least make Brandi's death gentle as He carried her home.

A stillness settled into Renna's chest. Did she dare call it peace? Was this how Uncle Abel and Aunt Mara felt as they stood in that line waiting to die?

Her fears didn't matter anymore. God cradled her and Brandi in His arms, and He'd continue to hold them through whatever death Respen had planned for them.

45

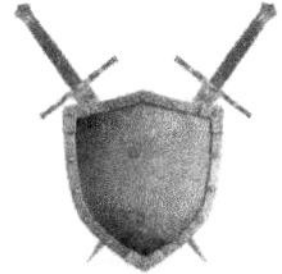

Leith woke well before dawn. Lighting his candle, he sat cross-legged on his cot. How was he going to prevent Respen from killing Renna and Brandi during the Meeting of the Blades in a few hours? Would Martyn speak up if he noticed Leith was trying to spare them?

Tension squeezed him until his bones might crack one by one. What if he failed? What if he had to watch Renna and Brandi die?

Renna and Brandi's lives depended on him. He couldn't fail them now. He picked up his weapons and strapped them on one by one. He glanced toward the bed. Should he take the knife he'd hidden against the bedpost?

No, better to leave it there. Respen usually locked failed Blades in their rooms in the Tower. If something went wrong or if he were ever captured and brought back to Nalgar Castle, hopefully that knife would survive a search of the room.

A few minutes before eight, he climbed the stairs towards the large meeting room on the fifth floor of the Blades' Tower. Several of the Blades glided up the stairs in front of him, the lower Blades breathing hard from the sets of stairs they'd had to climb from their rooms.

Leith slipped into the dark meeting room. Shadows danced along the walls and pressed low along the ceiling. He hung his weapons on the peg next to the door and strode toward his seat.

As he pulled his chair out, a noise from the doorway drew his gaze. He caught his breath. Martyn carried Renna over his shoulder, one of her legs wrapped in a splint. Twelfth Blade Altin dragged Brandi into the room. Both of the girls had black hoods shoved over their heads.

Martyn dropped Renna at the far end of the room, but his grip on her bound hands prevented her from tumbling to the floor. Leith gripped the back of his chair. He couldn't intervene now. His only hope—and the girls' only chance— was for him to remain hard as his knives.

Altin shoved Brandi against the wall next to Renna. He clamped one of two manacles that dangled from a ring in the stone around her wrist. Martyn snapped the other manacle around one of Renna's wrists. He and Altin yanked the hoods off but left the girls' hands tied.

Renna's eyes swept around the room, latched on Leith, and widened.

He turned away and plopped into his seat. Hopefully Martyn hadn't noticed Renna's reaction.

Jamie slipped into the thirteenth seat at the table, hunched low as if hoping the Blades wouldn't notice him. His eyes flicked toward Renna and Brandi. His mouth pressed into a thin line for only a moment before his expression relaxed. Good. He was doing his part to appear the uncaring soon-to-be Blade.

At eight, Respen swept into the room. Leith surged to his feet with the rest of the Blades and pounded his fist over his heart. The words of the Blade salute burned his mouth.

Leith crossed his arms as each Blade knelt in front of Respen and gave their report.

Seventh Blade Daas presented Respen with Vane's weapons. "I never saw the body, my king, but the First Blade assured us that Vane is dead."

Daas was clever. If he'd been the Second Blade, Leith might've worried about getting a knife in the ribs on a dark night. But Daas had to go through a few Blades before he ever got a chance to take Leith's spot as First Blade. Not that Leith cared about the job. Daas would be more than welcome to it.

When Martyn knelt to make his report, Leith held his breath. Martyn knew some of Leith's secrets. One word from him and Respen would have him arrested. Surrounded by eleven Blades, Leith wouldn't be able to escape.

Martyn described how he'd found the girls' tracks and followed them to their campsite. He fought and killed their guide. The girls ran and jumped over the small cliff to get away from him.

Leith resisted the urge to glance at Renna and Brandi. If only he could've protected them from what must have been a terrifying night. How bad was Renna's broken leg? Should he change his plans with Jamie? But if he did that, they'd be slowed down when they reached the stables and had to saddle their horses.

"I tracked them down, captured them in the morning, and brought them back here." Martyn's gaze didn't waver from King Respen.

No mention of Leith's knife. Leith exhaled.

As Martyn walked back to his seat, he gave Leith a piercing stare. He'd be watching Leith's every move. How were Leith and Jamie going to sneak out past him?

When the Second Blade finished, Leith stood to make his report. He knelt at Respen's feet, clasped his fist over his heart, and forced his mouth to say "My king" yet again. His report was as straightforward as he could make it. No need to make up any more details than he had to.

Respen scowled at Leith. "I expected more out of you, my First Blade."

Leith flinched. He deserved that. When Vane had been the First Blade, he'd been able to capture traitors and kill his victims all in the same mission without failure. Renna and Brandi were his only failures.

"Your orders were to kill the ladies Rennelda and Brandiline. You failed. Another Blade brought in your quarries for you after you killed the wrong girls." Respen's voice reverberated off the walls even though he never raised it above a measured tone. "Barring that, you were to kill the traitor. You may have succeeded in cornering him, but only on the last day with the help of two other Blades. Even then, it was not you but the Seventh Blade that killed him. You failed."

Leith bowed his head. He had many failures to regret, but not the ones Respen listed. He rolled up his left sleeve and turned his shoulder towards the king. Respen picked up one of Vane's knives and sliced across the top of Leith's arm below the white scar he'd received only a few months ago. Blood slithered down his arm and pounded in his shoulder.

Respen leaned closer. "Do not fail me again, my First Blade."

Leith met his gaze. "I won't."

As Leith returned to his seat, Respen turned to Jamie. "Blade Trainee Jamie Cavendish."

Jamie stood and strode toward the end of the table. He knelt and pounded a shaking fist across his chest.

Leith clenched his own fists beneath the tabletop where Respen couldn't see them. Somehow, Jamie becoming a Blade hurt like another failure, even if Jamie's kill was another lie.

"Blade Trainee Cavendish, I have been informed that you performed your first kill while on your mission with the First Blade. Well done."

Jamie swallowed and rolled his right sleeve to his shoulder.

Respen leaned forward and slashed the first mark. Jamie bit his lip but didn't flinch.

"Return to your seat, my new Thirteenth Blade."

Jamie scrambled to his feet and all but bolted back to his chair.

Before he'd even sat down, Respen turned back to Leith. "My First Blade, you have failed me twice. Do not fail me in this." He held the knife out to Leith point-first and nodded toward Renna and Brandi. "Kill them."

Leith took the knife. It warmed in his hand as if eager to taste flesh once again. The edge still dripped with Jamie's blood. He stalked along the length of the table. All eyes in the room focused on him.

He latched his eyes on Renna. Her face scrunched, her eyes wide. If only he could reassure her that he wasn't going to hurt her. Instead he kept his Blade mask in place.

He must've succeeded too well. Renna shrank against the wall. Brandi opened her mouth. Leith sent her a glare that caused her to snap her jaw shut.

He stalked closer to Brandi and growled in a low voice. "You should be afraid."

Brandi cocked her head. Leith relaxed his hard expression and winked. Brandi's face contorted into the roundest scared eyes he'd ever seen.

Renna gaped at him. Leith took a deep breath, stepped closer, and pressed the knife against Renna's throat. She swallowed and blinked. Her eyes brightened. A wrinkle formed across her forehead, as if she couldn't figure out why Leith had a knife to her neck. Did she really think he would hurt her?

Brandi screamed and squirmed against her chains. "No! Don't you dare hurt my sister!"

"I'm getting you both out today." With Brandi's screams, the other Blades couldn't hear what Leith said. They'd assume he was gloating.

The lines on her face smoothed.

He tightened the grip on his knife. If only he didn't have to do this. "I'm sorry, Renna." He drew on every scrap of the hard darkness he'd carried as a Blade and swiped his knife as lightly as he could across her throat.

Blood dribbled down her neck. Not goat's blood this time. Her blood. Spilled by his hand.

Her mouth dropped open. If Leith lived to be a thousand, he'd never forget the shock flashing across her eyes.

He turned away. Lies had their consequences. He'd had to deny the light in his heart to stay in the darkness. And now he'd had to hurt Renna. For years, he'd despised his father for raising a hand to his mother. But now, he'd done the same thing to Renna. Perhaps he'd turned into his father after all.

But to save her life, he had no choice. He had to hurt her to prove to Respen he wasn't afraid to spill her blood.

Leith swaggered toward the table. "They shouldn't be killed yet."

"You dare question my order?" Respen stiffened. His fingers clenched the end of the armrests.

Leith bowed his head. "My king, Vane convinced most of Acktar that these girls were dead. It destroyed hope. But now the towns have moved on from the tragedy. If the people were to find out that these girls were alive, only to have them publically executed, then the tragedy would be doubled and their hope broken."

He waited. If Respen didn't go for this, then Leith and Jamie would have a single knife to hold off twelve people for as long as possible before they were killed, Renna and Brandi after them.

Leith's heart drummed the seconds in his chest. Would Respen listen to the counsel of his First Blade? Would Martyn speak up?

Respen's fingers tapped the arms of his throne. The rhythm echoed in the silent room. Two taps. Pause. Two more taps. Pause. Over and over again until Leith's skin crawled.

The tapping stopped. Respen nodded. "Your words are

wise. A public execution would be more fitting for these two."

If he wasn't standing in front of Respen and his Blades, Leith might've sagged into the nearest chair. Instead, he saluted Respen, returned the knife, and slid into his chair. Next to him, Martyn had his arms crossed. Leith ignored him, even though the back of his neck prickled with the force of Martyn's stare.

Leith struggled to concentrate as Respen gave the Blades their new assignments. Most were the same as before, though the Seventh and Eleventh Blades had been sent to reinforce the two army divisions attacking Walden and Twelfth Blade Altin ordered to join the Blades stationed with the western division of the army attacking Arroway.

"The Third and Thirteenth Blades will remain here." Respen fixed Leith with a glare. "The First Blade will take charge of the Blades at Walden. You spent a month studying their defenses. You can get my army past them."

No chance of that, but Leith saluted anyway.

His stomach knotted. How was he going to sneak Renna and Brandi past Martyn? One thing was certain. This time when he rode away, he wasn't coming back.

46

After Martyn returned them to their cell, Renna waited until his footsteps disappeared up the stairs before she hugged Brandi. "Leith's going to rescue us."

Brandi grinned. "I knew he'd have a plan. Did he say when?"

"Just that it would be sometime today." Warmth flooded through her. They weren't going to die after all.

Brandi's grin faded. She pointed at Renna's neck. "Does it hurt?"

Renna touched her neck. Her fingers came away with flakes of dried blood. "I'd forgotten about it. No, it doesn't."

Brandi's nose wrinkled. "Leith...he..."

Renna touched the dried blood again. It had shocked her too when Leith had skimmed his knife across her neck. When she'd looked into his eyes, she hadn't seen Leith. She'd seen a Blade. A killer.

Was that how he'd managed to kill as a Blade? Block out his own heart?

But then he'd turned away and presented his fake plan to King Respen, and she'd understood. "It's all right, Brandi. Leith had no choice. If he didn't cut me, Respen would've thought his plan was a ploy to get out of killing us."

That's exactly what it was. A ploy. A diversion. While Respen planned their public execution, Leith would sneak them out of Nalgar Castle and out of Respen's reach.

She was beyond ready to leave this place. Brandi needed some place safe to properly grieve for Uncle Abel and Aunt Mara. As did she.

This time, they'd head to Eagle Heights with Leith. Perhaps she'd finally spill those tears leaning against Leith's shoulder while he held her close. And after she was done crying, they'd figure out where to go from there. Together.

Time lumbered by. If Renna's leg hadn't been in a splint, she would've paced across their cell. Brandi did her own kind of pacing, skipping back and forth.

After an agonizing hour, the door to their cell rattled. Brandi froze, and Renna squeezed her hands together. A guard? Martyn? Had Leith been arrested?

The door creaked open. Leith stood framed in the doorway. "Time to go."

Renna couldn't help herself. She hopped across the few feet and hugged him as tightly as she could. He smelled of open sky and campfires. Leith's arms wrapped around her and pulled her close. She tucked her head against his shoulder.

He pulled back and traced his finger along the throbbing line left by his knife. His touch sent a new sort of throbbing into her chest. His eyes had shed their hard look and now shone a bright green. "I'm so sorry. For this. For not protecting you. For not saving your aunt and uncle."

"You can finish apologizing later." Brandi tugged one of Renna's arms over her shoulder. "Let's get out of here first."

Heartfelt reunions could wait. Renna let Leith pull her other arm over his shoulder. With both of them supporting her, they maneuvered out of the cell and into the main room of the dungeon.

"Where do you think you're going?"

The voice chilled the shadows around them. A dark figure leaned against the door to the stairs. Martyn stepped forward. The torchlight glinted up and down the blades he carried.

Leith let go of Renna and stepped in front of her and Brandi. Renna fisted her hands. Leith was prepared to fight for them. What if he got hurt? They'd never be able to get away on their own, nor would she want to leave him behind.

Leith held out his hands, palm up. "I don't want to fight you."

"You knew I'd stop you, yet you did it anyway." Martyn shifted his grip on his knives. "Why? What's so important about these girls?"

"God saved me, Martyn. He redeemed me from the years of bloodshed. I'm sure Brandi told you stories from the Bible. You've heard about God's power. He is powerful enough to save us from Respen."

Martyn shook his head and tightened his grip on his knives. "I don't know what they've done to you, but the friend I knew didn't believe in fanciful tales."

Renna glanced between the two of them. Martyn's disbelief was the price Leith paid for playing his role too well. Would things have been different if Martyn had glimpsed the change in Leith's heart?

Leith's shoulders sagged. Renna squeezed his shoulder. He glanced at her, a smile softening the pain in his green eyes. If only she could heal this hurt as she healed other wounds, but her skills only extended so far. Leith faced Martyn again. "Let me get them out of here."

Renna clasped her hands together. Her nails bit into her palms. She prayed that God would soften Martyn's heart and open his eyes to the truth.

Martyn shook his head. His curls swept over his forehead. "I can't. They're my prisoners. If they escape, the king will deem it my fault. You know the punishment I'd face."

"Then come with us." Leith stepped forward. "We have friends who can protect you from Respen. You won't have to follow orders. You can be free."

Martyn shook his head. "My duty is here. As is yours. Now put those girls back in their cell, and we'll forget this ever happened."

"I can't." Leith gripped the hilts of his knives. Whatever softening she'd seen on his face a few minutes ago had vanished now, replaced with that same, cold mask. "If you want to stop me, you're going to have to fight me."

Martyn's head bowed. His shoulders rose and fell once. When he straightened, his face had hardened. He raised his weapons and lunged forward.

Leith drew his knives and shoved Renna with his shoulder. She stumbled backwards and crashed into Brandi. Both of them slammed into the wall, but Brandi regained her balance and steadied Renna before they both tumbled to the ground.

Steel rang in the tiny room as Leith blocked Martyn's knife. Renna hugged Brandi and pressed them against the wall. Both men moved quickly, their knives and hands darting too fast for her to follow.

Footsteps pounded down the stairs. Three of the guards from the entrance burst into the room and skidded to a halt. Their drawn swords wavered as they stared at the two Blades fighting in the center of the dungeon.

Renna searched around her. Not even a rock or a spare chain to use as a weapon. Not that she would've been able to wield a weapon against three guards. She tucked Brandi behind her and squeezed her fingers into fists. If they came any closer, she'd hit them. Maybe.

Leith tumbled to the ground and rolled to his feet a yard away from Renna and Brandi. Martyn pointed at him. "The First Blade is a traitor. He's helping the prisoners escape."

The guards hesitated. Their eyes focused on Leith as if waiting for him to contradict the other Blade's accusation. Leith didn't try. He gripped his knives, glared at the guards, and stepped closer to Renna.

His glare must've convinced the guards he was the threat Martyn claimed. They raised their swords but stood back, as if waiting for Leith to make the first move. The guards apparently weren't eager to attack a First Blade, not even when they outnumbered him.

Still, they weren't going to make it. Leith couldn't fight four men by himself, not while one of those men was a fellow Blade. She glanced down at her injured leg. Her injury slowed them down.

They were going to die. If not now, then after they were captured and Respen executed them. She glanced over her shoulder at Brandi. Brandi's hair frizzed around her head, her eyes wide, her fists clenched.

Someone shouted outside. Boots clumped on the cobblestones. Reinforcements.

Tears heated Renna's eyes. She couldn't prevent their deaths. She couldn't run. She couldn't even walk.

Unless...her mouth filled with a sour taste. Did she have the courage? Her hands trembled. If she went through with this, she'd stay here in the darkness of Nalgar Castle. She'd have to face Respen alone.

But Brandi would be safe. Renna dragged in a shaky breath. Brandi's safety was worth any sacrifice on her part. The sense of peace she'd gained the night before washed through her once again. Her life was in God's hands.

She touched Leith's arm, leaned forward, and pressed her mouth close to his ear. "You have to get Brandi out."

Leith cocked his head towards her. His mouth barely moved. "I'm not leaving you."

"I can't run. Not with my injured leg." Renna drew herself straight. This was the right thing to do. "Leave me. Get Brandi out of here."

Martyn flexed his fingers on his knife's hilt. "Surrender, Leith. I don't want to kill you."

Leith glanced back at her. His green eyes bled pain. She couldn't let Leith see she was shaking inside. If he saw her fear, he'd refuse to leave.

She couldn't let that happen. Brandi's life depended on it.

They had no choice.

47

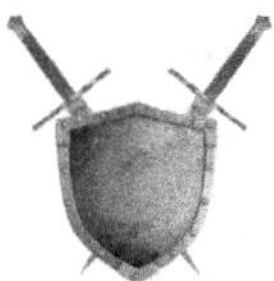

His chest ached. Leave Renna? She'd be at Respen's mercy.

He couldn't leave her. He had to find another way. Perhaps if he picked Renna up, shoved the guards out of the way, dashed up the stairs, and...Martyn or the guards would snatch Brandi. If he sacrificed himself to get the girls out of the dungeon, Renna's injury would slow them down. They'd be caught before they managed to cross the courtyard.

He couldn't save them both. A pain cracked deep in his chest. Renna had already chosen which life he had to save.

If only Jamie had come with him. But if they wanted to rescue the trainees and the girls, they'd had to separate. Doing both together would've taken too long, and Martyn probably would've stopped them on the bridge to the Blades' Tower instead.

Martyn shifted. The guards' eyes darted between Martyn and Leith, waiting for the signal to attack. Leith fixed his attention on Martyn. The guards wouldn't dare attack the First Blade without Martyn going first.

He'd failed to protect the girls yet again. That was his purpose. Their lives depended on him.

A chill doused him from head to toe. What was he thinking? When had he begun to believe their lives depended on his success and him alone? Their lives were God's to save or take. God had used Leith to protect them before, but perhaps that wasn't God's will this time.

How quickly he forgot the lessons he'd learned only months ago. He needed to trust God with Renna's life.

No more hesitation. He had to leave.

"I'll return for you." He laced his fingers through hers and squeezed her hand. He didn't dare take his eyes off Martyn and the guards. "Tell Respen the truth."

She hopped forward, using his grip on her hand to steady herself. As she turned to face Martyn and the guards, her hand slid out of his.

Martyn's eyebrows scrunched. Before he had a chance to puzzle out their plan, Renna flung herself at him. He toppled over and slammed into one of the other guards. All three landed in a heap on the floor.

Sheathing one of his knives, Leith wrapped an arm around Brandi's waist and lifted her off her feet. She screamed as he dashed across the room and rammed his shoulder into one of the guards who remained on his feet. The guards stumbled out of his way as he charged up the stairs.

Brandi shoved at his arm, her legs flailing. "Renna!"

Two more guards hurried down the stairs toward him. He didn't stop. "Get out of my way!"

As far as they knew, he was still the First Blade. They plastered themselves against the wall and let him pass. He burst from the dungeon, blinking at the sunlight. A squad of guards milled in front of him. He pointed back the way he'd come. "Assist the other guards. I'm taking this girl to the king."

The guards obeyed him without question. They pressed into the doorway to the dungeons, blocking the guards scrambling up the stairs.

In his arm, Brandi squirmed. "We can't leave Renna."

Leith tightened his grip as he sprinted across the courtyard. Behind him, the guards shouted at each other. In another moment, they'd turn and give chase. "I'm sorry."

Brandi kicked at him and shoved at his arm to free herself. "Let me go!"

Leith sheathed his knife and wrapped his other arm over both her arms, trapping her. He couldn't run quickly, but he didn't have far to go.

A tide of horses galloped from the stable. Four Blade trainees clung to saddles, their eyes wide as their horses charged toward the gate.

Jamie guided his horse towards Leith, leading Blizzard. Leith threw Brandi onto Blizzard and swung into the saddle before she had a chance to scramble off. He wrapped both arms around her as she bucked and twisted. He kicked Blizzard in the ribs. "Go!"

Jamie nudged his horse and both horses burst into a gallop. All around them, riderless horses tossed their heads and dashed toward the freedom of the open gate.

Brandi reared back and smashed her head into Leith's

chin. He gritted his teeth and gripped her tighter. No matter how much she fought him, he wouldn't let her go.

Soldiers strained to close the massive gates. Blizzard stretched out, his ears flat against his skull. Even Brandi froze, her eyes focused on the shrinking opening between the two iron-wrapped gates.

Leith flattened himself and Brandi against Blizzard's neck and back. The gates screeched as they gained momentum inward.

Blizzard streaked through. Leith's boots scraped on the wood. The gates crashed closed behind them. Blizzard snorted as he thundered down the cobbled causeway and onto the prairie.

Brandi flailed again, screaming when Leith wouldn't release her. She twisted and sunk her teeth into his shoulder. He sucked in a breath at the pain and yanked his shoulder out of her reach.

"Let me go! I won't leave Renna! Let go!" Tears streaked Brandi's red face. She screamed again, yanked an arm from his grasp, and struck at him with her fist.

One wild swing connected with his cheekbone. Pain flashed across his face as black dots danced in his vision. He managed to recapture her hand and pin her against him. If only this wasn't necessary. She didn't understand that if he could, he'd punch someone too. Preferably Respen. Probably Martyn as well.

As Blizzard hurtled up the hills surrounding Nalgar Castle, a rider crested the ridge above them and charged down. Shad reined in his horse and lifted his bow. Leith craned his head to see behind him as Blizzard continued galloping.

With their prisoners outside the castle, the guards now struggled to open the gates. Soldiers dashed onto the causeway, a few mounted on horses they must've caught in the courtyard.

Shad raised his bow and fired at the guards rushing towards them. Two of the mounted guards fell from their saddles while another clutched at his arm. The others slowed as Shad nocked yet another arrow.

Leith faced forward again as Blizzard surged over the hill and down the other side. Jamie and the four trainees raced toward the northeast ahead of him. Shad's rearguard would halt their pursuers, or at least slow them down.

Brandi stilled, staring over his shoulder. As Nalgar's towers faded from sight, Brandi wilted against him. He relaxed his grip and tucked her against him as comfortably as he could while they charged across the prairie.

He glanced over his shoulder one last time. His heart throbbed in time with his bruised cheek and bitten shoulder. Perhaps he should've let Martyn rip his heart out and give it to Respen on a platter. It would've hurt less than leaving Renna behind.

48

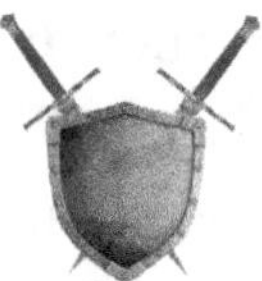

Renna leaned against the wall, now back in the cell. The sound of shouting and tromping boots rang through the cobblestone courtyard and down the narrow windowshaft. Was all that noise a good thing? Did it mean Brandi and Leith had gotten away safely?

She shivered and rubbed her upper arms. Had the cell wall always been this cold? Perhaps she'd never noticed it with Brandi tucked against her side.

But Brandi was gone. Leith was gone. She was alone.

No, not alone. God was with her. She'd have to cling to that extra hard now.

The door creaked open. Martyn held up a torch, his face shadowed, his hair straggling against his forehead. For a minute he stared at her, his head cocked.

Renna clenched her fists against the soft buckskin of her divided skirt. "What do you want?"

"I don't get it. Why would Leith throw away everything

for you? You're nothing special." Martyn ran his hand through his hair, standing the curls into spikes.

A month ago, she would've cowered against the wall at his words. She'd known too well how ordinary and weak she was. Now, she was still the same weak person she'd always been, but she'd learned how strong God could be.

She tilted her head and smiled. "I'm not special, but God is. He's the One that gave Leith the strength to stand up to Respen. In Christ, Leith has already gained everything. For what good does it do a person to have the whole world, but lose his soul?"

Martyn grabbed her arm and yanked her to her feet. He dragged her from the cell and toward the stairs. "Perhaps you believe you've gained something by your faith, but you and Leith are surely going to lose your lives if Respen has anything to do with it."

Renna struggled to hop along as best she could. As they crossed the courtyard, she glanced around at the space and spotted the bustle as guards tried to calm the last few restless horses wandering the courtyard.

"They escaped the castle but don't get your hopes up. They'll be hunted."

Her stomach knotted. All those Blades hunting her sister. She drew in a breath. Leith knew what he was doing. He'd been the First Blade. If anyone could evade the Blades, he could.

She forced herself to smile. "Still, they'll have a head start. That's why Leith waited until this afternoon for the escape. He waited until most of the Blades had already left for their new missions."

Martyn scowled at her. "I didn't say Leith would make it

easy. Yes, he gained a lead by waiting until most of the Blades had left. He delayed the rest by letting lose all the horses. But the Blades pursuing him will catch up."

As she tottered up the stairs to Respen's chambers, she shook his words from her head. Leith had defeated the former First Blade and outwitted Respen for months. Surely he'd be able to escape again.

Martyn knocked on King Respen's door. A growl beckoned them in. Respen paced from his desk to the window and back again in staccato steps. He whirled to face them. His eyes blazed.

Respen grabbed her face and yanked her chin upward. She gasped, the toes of her good leg stretched to touch the carpet. His breath heated her face. "What sorcery do you possess? You have bewitched two of my Blades from me."

She gripped his arm as he lifted her into the air. Her throat closed with the pressure of his hand. Black dots danced across her vision.

Tell Respen the truth. Leith's words drummed in time with the pounding in her head. "Not two. One Blade."

Respen released his grip. She landed on her side on the carpet and coughed. Respen glared down at her, his fingers flexing.

The time for secrets had passed. She met Respen's gaze. "It all started this past winter when Third Blade Leith Torren stumbled into my kitchen wounded from an arrow."

Respen's eyes sparked and grew darker as she told how Leith had joined the Resistance and defeated Vane. She left out anything that might be a secret the Resistance still wanted to keep.

As she finished, she glanced toward the doorway. Martyn

leaned against the wall, one hand pounding the wood. His head hung. His shoulders sagged as if her words pressed against his back.

He straightened, and his eyes met hers. For a moment, pain shone. Then, his face hardened. Whatever loyalty he'd had toward Leith had died.

Respen's fingers rapped the windowsill. When he turned, his expression lacked the rage she'd expected. A smile played along his mouth. "He cares for you."

"What? Leith?" Renna blinked.

A smirk twisted his face. "He may have escaped for now, but he will return. As long as I have you, he will walk into whatever trap I set."

Renna closed her eyes. That's why Leith had asked her to tell Respen the truth. He'd wanted Respen to realize that she was more valuable as a pawn than dead.

He'd saved her life yet again. As long as Leith lived and escaped the Blades hunting him, Respen wouldn't kill her.

A cold feeling itched along her skin. Respen would spare Renna for now because it suited him to play along with the game Leith had started. Leith might've escaped, but as long as Respen had Renna, he commanded the game. He could set the timing.

When the time was right, he'd play his hand. Renna's breath caught. He'd spoken truly. Leith would walk into Respen's trap, and then both of them would die.

DEFY

A traitor to the Blades must die.

The war for Acktar has begun. With his betrayal revealed, former Blade Leith Torren flees into the Sheered Rock Hills, pursued by King Respen's vengeful Blades.

Left behind at Nalgar Castle, Renna Faythe tries to find her purpose, yet that purpose isn't what she expected.

Brandi Faythe has been torn from her sister, and that isn't all right. If Leith can't rescue Renna, Brandi will take matters into her own hands.

War demands sacrifice. Courage falters. Who will find the strength to defy King Respen?

Acktar rests on one hope:

The Leader is ready.

Buy Now

FREE STORY!

Deal

A Blades of Acktar Short Story

Once there was a nine-year-old boy Leith Torren who only wanted to bring food home to his mother...and was noticed by Lord Respen Felix of Blathe.

Free for newsletter subscribers. Sign up at https://triciamingerink.com/my-newsletter/

ALSO BY TRICIA MINGERINK

DAGGER'S SLEEP

A prince cursed to sleep.
A princess destined to wake him.
A kingdom determined to stop them.

High Prince Alexander has been cursed to a sleep like unto death, a curse that will end the line of the high kings and send the Seven Kingdoms of Tallahatchia into chaos. With his manservant to carry his luggage and his own superior intelligence to aid him, Alex sets off to find one of the Fae and end his curse one way or another.

A hundred years later, Princess Rosanna learns she is the princess destined by the Highest King to wake the legendary sleeping prince. With the help of the mysterious Daemyn Rand, can she find the courage to finish the quest as Tallahatchia wavers on the edge of war?

One curse connects them. A hundred years separate them. From the rushing rivers of Tallahatchia's mountains to the hall of the Highest King himself, their quests will demand greater sacrifice than either of them could imagine.

For readers of adventure, fairy tales, and stirring allegories comes this fresh imagining of the classic Sleeping Beauty tale, the first book in a new YA fantasy series from Tricia Mingerink

Buy Now!

BOOKS BY TRICIA MINGERINK

The Blades of Acktar

Dare

Deny

Defy

Destroy: A novella

Deliver

Decree

Beyond the Tales

Dagger's Sleep

Midnight's Curse

Poison's Dance

ACKNOWLEDGMENTS

Two books in sixth months. Yes, that's as crazy as it sounds. Thanks so much to all the readers who have picked up Dare, loved it, and begged for Deny. You all have been amazing. Seriously. Readers rock.

My mom and dad. You've been so supportive during this journey. I wouldn't be where I am without you.

My friends Briana, Paula, and Jill. Somehow, you still manage to be excited for me even after I don't talk to you for over a month. Hopefully the next book release won't be so crazy.

My twin-in-law Alyssa. I wouldn't survive this crazy writing life without crying on your shoulder about characters (also known as going on the walk and ranting).

To Abby. You're such an awesome addition to our family, and a great street team.

To my brothers Ethan, Josh, and Andy. Thanks for teaching me all about guy talk.

Nadine Brandes, amazing editor, mentor, and friend. Any writing question I have, I always know where I can turn (and get a tight online hug).

Sierra, my amazing critique partner. All your line by line comments were so helpful!

All my author friends. You all deserve hugs!

My awesome street team: Hope, Gabriela, Alyssa V.F., Kim, Jaye, Shantelle, Abby C., Jessica, Clairie, Sierra, Briana, Paula, Alyssa M., and Abby O. You've been beyond amazing!

And, most of all, to my Father in Heaven. His Strength sustained me.

www.ingramcontent.com/pod-product-compliance
Lightning Source LLC
Chambersburg PA
CBHW070431170726
48291CB00002B/456